Refuge and Warm Tea

Elaine Glimme

Cover Photo

The cover photo was taken by Tenley Thompson and made available through iStock. The back cover photo was taken by mecaleka, and available through iStock.

.

CONTENTS

ACKNOWLEDGMENTS

Thank you, Gracias, Merci, Danke,
There's no way I could have written this book without friends.

Life was harder, and you were sweeter.
Thank you, Tom, because you are my favorite man.

Thank you for being so special.
Thank you, Lisa, my doctor daughter, for medical advice.

You are the diamonds in the coal mine of writing.
Thank you, my writers' groups:
   Pinole Writers' Group: Linda, Caroline, Margaret, Terry, Yolanda, and Kate.
   Pinole Library Writers' Group: Sandra, Evie, Louise, Eddie, Jill, Chris, and Denise.

Distance is nothing; friendship is everything.
Thank you, my internet friends: Revu2, Square Peg Guy, Selene, and Susan.

Listening is the sincerest form of respect.
Thank you, Parris from Staples, who understands the computer's devious mind.

Things are not as scary with a friend.
Thank you, Lois, for guiding me through the valley of the shadow of marketing.

It's like finding a four-leaf clover—finding a good friend.
Thank you, Margaret, for proofing my work.

Friends make the world beautiful.
Thank you, Paul, for helping me with my website.

Priceless treasures: friends and prayers.
Thank you, Episcopalians on Facebook, who prayed for me for courage.
And thank you, God, for answering our prayers.

Art washes from the soul, the dust of everyday life. Vincent Van Gogh
Thank you, to Tenley Thompson and mecaleka for the photos on the front and back cover.

You are the happy ending, the goal at the end of the adventure, the vision at the end of the quest.
Thank you, readers.

CHAPTER 1

Gray skies over gray asphalt met Johanna's bus in Vancouver. 'I'm safe here,' she told herself, and she knew it to be true. Everything around her was peaceful, normal. That didn't matter; freakish memories of capture haunted her anyway. She shivered, but not from the cold. 'This is just crazy. No one's watching me. No one's following me.' She said it to herself over and over. 'I'm not a child. I'll survive.' In fact, she was more frightened than a nineteenth-century urchin wandering shadowed streets.

She bought a map. Then, fingers crossed, she boarded a city bus and rode through the streets of Vancouver until she came to the address of an internet friend who logged on as Sandy Pumpkin.

They'd never met in person, but Johanna imagined him as Sandy, an easy-going, twenty-something, freckle-faced farmer with pumpkin-colored hair. Of course, he wasn't expecting her, but she had nowhere else to go. She just hoped he wouldn't be too shocked when she appeared on his doorstep. She held her breath and tentatively knocked on the door.

A puzzled, bronze-skinned, silver-haired man answered her knock, not the freckled farmer she was expecting. Startled, Johanna dropped her gaze to the ground, mumbling, "Hello. You don't know me, but . . ." Suddenly speechless, she stared at her shoes.

"Is there something you need?" the old man asked.

His soft voice gave her courage. "I need help. I'm in terrible trouble. I'm Johanna. I used the name Jody on line . . . and I've been chatting on the internet with someone at this address." She hoped he wouldn't be too shocked.

"Oh, my dear," he said, and tears threatened to overcome him. "I am Sandy Pumpkin!" He wrapped his arms around her and brought her inside. His touch was light and tender, as if carrying a wounded bird in his arms.

<<<<>>>

As the old man guided Johanna inside his house, the word "sanctuary" floated in her head.

Outside, the sun was setting, and the sky glowed pink. Inside, a large room and a fireplace with a blazing fire seemed to welcome her. A faded couch with a hand-woven blanket draped over its back caught Johanna's eye, and she sank onto its pillows gratefully, thinking, 'Here in Canada, I'm finally safe.' She stared at the stone fireplace, mesmerized by the swaying flames, and was grateful. She had one friend, someone who promised shelter. She wouldn't have to beg for food, or steal food, or spend the night outside shivering, afraid to sleep lest someone attack her. The basic comforts she'd taken for granted before—now they seemed like gifts from the heavens.

In Canada, Johanna was out of danger. She waited for the muscles in her back and her neck to relax, but they didn't. Her stomach still quivered. 'As if I'm drowning in rushing water; as if the ground is melting away, and there's nothing below me. Is this what crazy feels like? Am I . . . am I crazy?'

If she was safe, why was she still so shaky?

Or was she safe? Was she doing something foolish? Was it a mistake to trust Sandy Pumpkin, someone whom she'd only met online? She knew nothing about him. Was she walking into something dangerous? Perhaps, but it wasn't as if Johanna had choices. She was in Vancouver now, in a strange land, and she was, in every way, a stranger here. The only Canadian she knew was Sandy Pumpkin, and of course, that wasn't even his real name. So, maybe this safety was only an illusion, because, after all, she hadn't resolved anything. She had merely run away from her troubles.

Johanna sat with her head bent forward, rocking back and forth. Her dark hair fell thick in front of her face. The questions were just too big. 'What's going to happen to me? Will I survive as

. . .' She thumbed her fake ID. 'As Sonja Jordanson?' It had gotten her into Canada, but would it get her a place to live? Maybe. Could it get her a job? Not likely. 'What can I do with no identity?' A sense of darkness closed in all around her with a final, chilling realization. 'Legally I don't exist.'

Suddenly it all seemed so daunting—starting her life all over again with a bare slate and all of ninety-seven U.S. dollars in her backpack. It had taken Johanna's thoughts about ten minutes to jump from comfort and safety to fright, loss, and more than a little embarrassment about sitting in a stranger's house asking for shelter. Thank goodness he'd welcomed her in. A door slammed in her face would have utterly defeated her.

She looked up at the old man. She had to trust him. She had no other option.

His face was gentle, with a wide, flat nose, dark eyes, and a smile that peeped out from behind his eyes, then spread across his lips. His hair was mostly silver and pulled back into a tail that came halfway down his back. Johanna guessed his age at about sixty, then figured that he was probably older than he looked. He was dressed simply—in blue jeans that had been washed many times, a red flannel shirt, and on his feet, gray Nikes with worn spots—the nineteen sixties casual look.

Was it too casual? He reminded her of an old hippie, someone who grew weed in his backyard. Maybe the police were on their way to arrest both of them. No, that was too ridiculous. People don't just get carted off for no good reason—except that it had happened to her.

"I'll fix some food," the man said. He was tall and thin. So thin! Johanna guessed that he walked a lot. Or maybe, he was thin because he used meth and raped strangers. Again, that unfounded fear swept through her like raging winds. 'Just nerves,' she figured. But what if it wasn't just nerves? What if she was experiencing some sixth sense that was warning her to get out fast? No. Ridiculous! Still . . . 'Am I too trusting, or too paranoid, or stark, raving crazy?'

The Sandy Pumpkin on the internet seemed to be a kind man. Surly, he was the same in person. If only she hadn't experienced how cruel the world could be!

Meanwhile, the man walked unobtrusively into a spartan kitchen. He filled a dented aluminum kettle with water and put it on the stove to boil. Then he loaded a plate with cheddar and Triscuits.

Returning, he handed the plate with the cheese and crackers to Johanna, along with a napkin and knife. He threw a log onto the fire, took two crackers for himself, and sat down next to her.

They crunched the crackers and cheese without speaking, and as they ate, he watched Johanna. She reminded him of a dark-eyed pixie carrying an oversized backpack. She wore a blue-checked shirt and a pair of jeans that almost fit. Mainly, he watched her movements: the jerky fits and starts when she leaned forward to reach for another cracker, the way her face always looked away from him, and the way she rocked back and forth and didn't even seem conscious of the rocking. All these signs pointed to someone disturbed and struggling not to scream or cry out, someone trying not to let her emotions show.

The kettle squawked, and the elder got up to make tea. He used Lipton tea bags, but added a spoonful of sugar and some herbs from tiny canisters to one of two cups. Johanna took her tea without reservation and drank it in great, greedy gulps. It had a peculiar tangy quality but was very tasty nevertheless. She drank the tea, ate, and began to feel drowsy.

Johanna forced herself out of the sluggishness that was fast taking over. The tea! Was it drugged? She looked into the old man's eyes. "The tea? Did you . . .?" Johanna couldn't find the words. Hadn't the strength to fight. To argue. She put the cup down and stared into his face.

"Yes," he said. "There are herbs in the tea to calm you." His voice was sonorous, deep, and the words came slowly, as if he had all the time in the world for them. "I'll make more tonight, and you'll be able to sleep. Tomorrow, we'll talk." He smiled reassuringly. "The tea won't harm you. See." He took her cup and drank it down to the dregs, then poured another cup for her.

'Tomorrow, we'll talk,' Johanna thought. So much to figure out! Where would she go from here? What would she do with the rest of her life? Tomorrow would be a good day for that. Scarlett O'Hara was right. Tomorrow is, after all, another day. 'Yes, tomorrow, we'll talk,' she thought. As the herbs worked their magic, Johanna lazily traced the rim of her cup with her fingers, ate cheese and crackers, and was grateful. 'Tomorrow, we'll talk.' Tomorrow was a long way away. Tomorrow, they'd sort out her life, her future, where she'd go from here. Today, there was tea, friendship, and a warm place to sleep. For today, that was enough. For today, that was a fortune.

Johanna was content not to say anything more, and the old man didn't push her. Instead, he turned the knobs on an old-fashioned radio until he found a classical station, and music filled in the awkward hole that silence had created.

"What should I call you?" Johanna finally asked. Her voice seemed loud and out of place.

"Close friends and family call me Sandy," he said. "My tribal name is an awkward, multisyllabic mouthful that many have trouble with. Alexander and Mr. Joseph seem too formal." He waited for her to say something, but she stayed silent. "And should I call you Jody?"

"My real name is Johanna, but, yes, I like Jody, at least for now." She looked down at her hands, and Sandy knew she was finished talking.

'Jody,' she thought to herself. It was the name she'd used on her website. It fit. It felt comfortable. Yes, from now on she was Jody.

The day grew to a close. Outside, shadows melted into the night. Sandy threw another log onto the fire. In the kitchen, he set a pot of water on his stove to simmer, and he hummed to himself as he added spices, grains, chunks of meat, and several cups of vegetables to it.

'Tomorrow, I'll help,' thought Jody, for she found she lacked the strength to get up from the couch. It was as if she'd just emerged from a well or just hatched from an egg, still squinting into the sunlight and slightly wobbly. 'Tomorrow, I'll work it all out.'

They ate the soup with a brownish, rustic bread, and as they ate, Sandy watched her. Her thick, brown hair had a few gray streaks, and wrinkles had begun to appear around her eyes. She had to be in her forties, yet her speech and actions were those of someone much younger.

Sandy had been to university, studying premed and psychology, among other subjects. He'd lectured at universities, usually advocating for his people. More importantly, he'd walked the road of a Tutchone man. He'd become a healer, a paramedic, and a therapist, all rolled into one man. With chanting, smudging, and willow bark, as well as with stitches, splints, bandages, vitamins, and common sense, he'd healed his people. So many wounds, so many hurts, so many losses had come his way during his lifetime! He'd healed everything from frostbite to bear maulings, and he'd splinted broken ribs from bar fights and ladder accidents. He'd listened to stories of dying children and jilted lovers. He'd dried tears and held sobbing infants in his arms. Funny how physical pain and emotional loss seemed to go together. But as a healer, he'd mostly served First Nations, descendants of the tribes that had lived in Canada before the first white settlers came. He understood them, understood their struggles to find their way in a world of technology while remaining true to who they were—true to their heritage, to the earth, and to their Creator.

With her olive skin and thick, dark hair, Jody looked as if she might be First Nations, he thought, at least in part, but she was probably Caucasian, and her troubles were more likely ones he'd never dealt with before.

Sandy had walked the Tutchone road and the white man's road, comfortable in both, at home in neither. A Tutchone man stuck into a place where he did not completely belong. This battle he understood. He'd talked about it, both with those who had paid him and with those whom he'd helped for free. And often his fee had been six eggs and a bunch of turnips, so, in truth, what was the difference between client and someone healed for friendship? But how to help Jody? He could tell she was troubled. He could see it by her stooped posture, the way she crossed her arms in front of her as if protecting her chest, and the way she rocked back and forth—a soothing motion. Children did this sometimes when they felt out of control.

He hoped he was up to it. Anyway, he'd never felt as if he'd actually performed healing. Instead, he felt like a channel, like a wire through which electricity flowed and gave life. Like a hollow eagle bone, his people would have said, a conduit for divine energy.

When the meal was over, Sandy gathered the dishes. As he

began soaping and rinsing the bowls and silverware, Jody reached for a dishtowel. They worked without speaking, and Sandy grunted and pointed to the cupboard where the dishes went.

He made a bed for her on the couch using a folded, plaid jacket for a pillow and a hand-sewn quilt of forest colors—browns, greens, and oranges—for a cover. He gave her a final cup of tea before leaving her to settle down for the night, and she drank it gratefully.

The tea left her drowsy and contented, almost happy. 'Like in the Garden of Eden,' Jody thought as she drifted off to sleep.

She hoped there would be no more nightmares.

Jody's Dream

A young man stands beside a sparkling creek. "I'm Adam," he says and blushes. He takes Jody's hand, and they cross the creek, jumping from stone to stone. Cool water splashes their bare feet. His face is a child's face, almost a man's, but still missing that something which responsibility imposes. They splash and giggle, watching tadpoles swimming beneath them.

Beyond the creek, wild pear trees grow in a ring. The pears are ripe, and she picks one with a beautiful pink glow. She bites into it; sweet juices cool her mouth and dance on her tongue. Adam laughs and wriggles his toes in the grass.

Farther on, an apple tree on a hillock seems to call to them—an imposing tree with fiery, red fruit. They stare at it. Slowly, their feet lead them to the base of the tree, and, compelled by something that she does not understand, Jody reaches out her hand for the biggest apple. She bites it and passes it to Adam, who also eats. He tickles her nose with one of the leaves.

No alarms ring; no warnings sound. The apple is ripe, and the crunch is sweet, but something is wrong.

A small crease appears on Adam's forehead. Chilly gusts blow down from the north.

As they admit to an unseen God what they have done, the sky darkens and thunders. Freezing rain splashes across their shoulders. Hail stings their skin like pistol shots. And they know;

they know it isn't good.

Now she is alone. Banished. Scowling angels with fiery swords bar the way back to the garden, forcing her onward, farther and farther into the wilderness. Just a kid. A kid reaching for an apple. A kid who can never go home again. Cold, lost, and hungry, she makes her way into an alien land.

Jody woke crying as the dream's message soaked in. She could never go home again. An image of her mother's face flashed in front of her eyes. She'd never see that face again!

After college, her visits home had been rare, but now all Jody wanted was to go home and to see her mother one more time. So many times, she'd rolled her eyes hearing her mother's high-pitched, fake laugh, and she'd shaken her head, silently passing judgement, at her mother's shocked voice bemoaning, "The neighbors will think we're trailer trash!"

Now, she smiled through tears, remembering her mother's quirks and the worries reflected in the wrinkles around her mother's eyes. Jody spoke to the ceiling, imagining that her mother could hear her. "It was how you took care of me. How you loved me. Why didn't I see that before? Why didn't I understand? Oh, Mom, why was I so quick to criticize and so slow to love you? You hardly ever understood me, but you stood beside me and defended me anyway."

Now, all Jody wanted was to snuggle with her mother's arms around her shoulders and to feel her mother's hand smoothing the hair back from her face.

Exile. Was this to be her punishment? Did warrior angels really bar the way home?

CHAPTER 2

The next morning found Jody sitting bolt upright, reliving the dream of her banishment.

"Bad dream?" Sandy asked.

She nodded.

"Tell me about it." He put his hand on her shoulder. "And tell me about what's happened to you. What are you running away from?"

She shivered and hugged her arms across her chest. "I can't."

Sandy stood over her and frowned. "Tell me."

She shook her head. "Not yet. I can't. Just give me one more day. Right now, I can't talk about it."

Outside, a cricket chirped twice, and somewhere, a motor hummed in the distance.

Sandy gazed at her intently. He knew that one more day would make no difference. "No," he said.

Wide-eyed, Jody hugged her arms tighter around her chest.

"No." He met her gaze. "This is too important." He spoke slowly, and his words gained power with each breath. "No. Your spirit is imprisoned in a lonely hollow where there is no beauty, and no love. Laughter does not touch you. Music is only noise. You cannot see rainbows, waterfalls, mountains, or sunsets. Those things that nourish our souls are hidden from you. You are the hunted, the prey, the food of every boogeyman, goblin, and evil spirit that haunts human minds. With each day, the hollow deepens, and the boogeyman's grip grows stronger around your heart. Each day, your spirit dies a little."

Jody could only stare in shock. How could he know this? He spoke truths that she wouldn't admit, even to herself.

"No," he continued. "Your spirit is precious, too important. Too much is at stake!" He laid his other hand on her shoulder, his touch strong and gentle at the same time. "Don't worry. You are tough, tougher than you know. Your spirit will triumph, and you'll laugh and love again. Your work on the earth isn't done yet. Joy will come back." He removed his hands, and Jody immediately missed their warmth. "It will take me about five minutes to gather some things together. While I do that, you can prepare your thoughts. Then we will begin."

Jody stared at Sandy's retreating figure, amazed by the strength and the passion of his words. His voice was soothing like a lullaby, yet it demanded unquestioned obedience. But the idea of talking about her memory's demons terrified her. 'Prepare my thoughts! Catch wolves barehanded. No difference.'

Unconsciously, she rocked back and forth. How could she ever tell Sandy about what she'd been through or about that dream she'd had? And what did it even mean? Was it really a sign that she could never go home again?

<<<<>>>>

Sandy returned carrying a small drum and a pouch tucked under his left arm. With his right hand firmly gripping her shoulder, he guided Jody into a wooded area a short walk from the house. He picked up rocks, which he treated as living things, and he arranged them in a circle around a clearing. When the circle was complete, Sandy made a small fire in the center of it. Then he took a braid made of herbs out of his pouch and touched the end of it to the fire. "We call this smudging," he said, as he deeply inhaled the smoke and, with cupped hands, lifted the smoke to his face and hair as if washing himself with it. With similar gestures, he smudged Jody.

'Superstition!' Jody thought the word but didn't dare to say it out loud. Tentatively, she inhaled the smoke, wondering if she would be condemned to hell for worshipping false gods. The smoldering herb smelled sweet. A bit like vanilla.

After the smudging, Sandy guided Jody inside the circle, where they sat down cross-legged. Sandy began drumming; a haunting rhythm, calming and mesmerizing. It seemed to reach inside her body.

"Within this circle, you are safe," said Sandy. "Begin speaking. Begin with comfortable, easy words. First Nations wisdom says the drum symbolizes the circle of life and the heartbeat of the earth. Its rhythm opens your eyes, The smudging purifies your intentions. You may say that you are humoring an old man."

Jody looked into his face, gathering courage from the kindness in his eyes.

"I can't go home," she blurted out. "I took it for granted, and now it's gone." After that, the words all came: the dream about the garden with the creek, the apple, the storm, and the scowling angels; and Jody couldn't have held back any of it, even if she'd wanted to.

"When I left Mississippi for college, I thought, 'good riddance.' I hated everything about Pascagoula; that's the city where I grew up. I detested the refinery and the ever-present oily smell. And I hated the gossiping, self-righteous biddies with their disapproving scowls. Always judging. Always finding fault. As if they were the manners-and-proper-dress committee. But after my father died, they took turns coming by to check on my mother and me, and they prayed with us and baked pies." Jody tried to blink back tears. It didn't work. "I remember once, when Mom was exhausted from crying, Mrs. Montgomery washed all our dishes, mopped the floor, and did three loads of laundry. Mrs. Smith tried to make me smile, but I was just a little kid, not even four years old back then, and I wouldn't give her the satisfaction. Still, she held me in her arms and sang to me.

Jody stared into the fire. "See, they weren't perfect, just human, and they probably did think my mother and I were trailer-trash, even though we lived in a two-story house." Tears fell as she remembered the worst loss in her life. "They helped as best they could.

"And they used to bake brownies and chaperone field trips. One time we went boating up the Pascagoula River. Funny I'd remember that now." Jody stopped. The creek in her dream reminded her of the Pascagoula River.

"It's a protected river. It flows undammed through miles of wild forest. Mississippi got a lot of things wrong, but the Pascagoula River—they got that so right. Why couldn't I see it?"

Jody stopped to wipe her eyes. "So much beauty! And love and kindness, and I missed it. I saw myself as this passionate idealist. I wrote about my country's flaws and prejudices. All I saw was cruelty, money-worshipping, power-hungry liars, and the earth getting trashed. But as for kind, well-meaning people just raising their kids and making a living, well, I ignored them."

Jody wiped her eyes again. "That was my garden of Eden, and now I can never go home again. That's why angels with flaming swords bar my way back."

Sandy sat silently watching her cry until the tears subsided. Finally, he spoke. "Tell me what happened to you, and why you can't go home? Why are you here?"

Jody sat bolt upright as if lightning had struck her. Eyes wide with terror, she hugged her arms around her chest and trembled. "I can't tell you." She covered her face with her hands. "I can't." But it was too late to hold back. The words had already started as if a dam had broken, or a pack of caged hounds were let loose. "Why? Why am I scared to talk about it? It's all over. I'm safe now. It's time to start a new life." She started giggling. "A new life!" The giggles turned to uncontrolled laughter. She couldn't stop. "A new life!" She kept laughing, laughing wildly, her laughter high-pitched, almost shrieking. "How many people get a chance to do that?" The laughter took over her whole body. She was hysterical now. "Who wouldn't be happy? Be excited? A new life!" And she began to cry again as she reached for Sandy's arms.

He put his fingers on the back of her neck, rubbing hard until the sobbing and gulping subsided.

After a time, Sandy spoke, and his voice was tender like flute music. "Your internet friends, Brat, Shadow, and I, we have been concerned about you." She could hear the worry in his words. "When you stopped posting, we feared you were in danger. Tell me what happened after your last post. When you agreed to meet the one who called himself Spiderman."

"He was exactly as he sounded on the internet. We talked," she sighed. "We talked and he really got to me. And I got the feeling that he liked me too. Okay, it was a crush, a crush like teenagers get. But I think, in time, it could have turned into something real."

'Some crush,' thought Sandy. The look in Jody's eyes spoke volumes. She was still smitten.

"He's this goofy, funny guy, and yet he really cares about peace, and about truth, and about all the things I care about too. Only I'm a wimp, and he's not. We talked, and he said he'd hang protest signs over the freeway. And I said I'd hang some too."

"Did you say anything about leaving the country?" Sandy tried to say this casually.

"Of course not."

"Go on."

"I wrote the signs on bedsheets. Protesting the Iraq war. Ever since 911, people were jittery and . . . and . . . and . . ." Suddenly, her teeth chattered so hard that she couldn't talk. "And the wind . . . the wind. It was blowing hard." Her voice pierced the air, shrill, crackling. "And these men appeared out of nowhere. And the wind kept blowing. They had uniforms. They hit me, and one of them stuck a needle in my leg. Everything went black after that." She looked at Sandy, and wiped tears from her eyes.

"Go on."

"I woke up." She shuddered. "In . . . I thought it was a hospital. But looking back, it couldn't have been a real hospital. And they kept me." She stared down at the ground. "For a long time. And then, they . . . they . . . beat me and . . ."

"Keep going. You are stronger than you think."

"They left me. It was in a box . . . like in a coffin . . . for dead." She blurted out the last words, her head dropped, and she sank to the ground like a deflated balloon.

"Well done," said Sandy. He drummed a calming rhythm, giving Jody time to recover. Then he held his hand out to Jody, helping her rise to her feet, and guided her back inside the house.

"May I tell your friends that you are alive? That you are safe?" Sandy asked.

Jody all but jumped out of her skin. "Tell about me?"

"They worry about you, Brat and Shadow. We still chat online, you know."

"Don't . . . don't tell them anything." Her body twitched awkwardly as she spoke. "Don't say anything about me. Don't let them know where I am. It's . . . too dangerous."

Then she stared at Sandy, wishing she could shove the words back into her mouth. If only she hadn't said, "dangerous." Now Sandy knew. And he'd figure out that he was in danger as long as she was with him. He wouldn't want her around. He'd send her packing.

And she had nowhere else to go.

She cowered and shivered. She saw herself a cornered mouse waiting for the cobra to strike.

"You think I don't know?" He almost smiled as he spoke. "Brat, Shadow, and I have been worried about you ever since you disappeared."

With a shrug and a rush of breath, she blurted the words out. "For that matter, as long as I'm here, you may be in danger also." So, now he knew! He knew, and she was about to face banishment again, just like in the dream. A safe place to live, a chance to start over—apparently, that was just too much to hope for. She turned away hiding her face and whatever was written across it.

"I am an old man. Death holds no terror. What I have done, I have done. My only remaining task is to help heal the wounds inside you. If you'll let me. After that, I think my time on the earth will be over, and a new adventure will begin."

Jody couldn't say anything. So, Sandy was dying while she was perfectly healthy and looking to him for comfort. Why? She hadn't always been so, so weak, so useless. Jody closed her eyes and tried to think back to a simpler time. God had been her best friend, so close that she had felt she could almost touch the hem of Jesus's robe. And He'd fed her with courage as she'd typed her stories, pouring her dreams and her fears into them. Where had all that faith gone? Where was God now?

She was losing everyone: Brat, Spiderman, Shadow, and Sandy. Even God. She'd never met Brat and Shadow, except on the internet, but they felt as dear to her as her own mother. It seemed as though a lifetime had passed—although, realistically, it couldn't have been more than a few months—since she'd had lunch with Spiderman and later that day, had been attacked and dropped into a nightmare of drugs and pain.

"What about Spiderman?" she asked. He'd been part of the chat room too, and she'd had that embarrassing crush on him. "You didn't mention Spiderman."

Sandy paused with a long "hmmm." Jody was fragile now.

How best to tell her? And he had to tell her the truth. If he didn't, it could later prove dangerous. Best to just say it. Get it over with. That was the way of the First Nations people. "We think Spiderman may have played a part in what happened to you. His last post in the chat room didn't make sense. First, he said that you had flown to Iran, but according to him, you were also crying on his shoulder when the plane was supposed to be taking off. That's how we guessed, Brat, Shadow, and I, that you were the victim of foul play. We could be wrong about Spiderman, but I don't think so."

That's why you asked me about flying to Iran."

"I'm sorry to have to tell you this. Spiderman is not your friend."

Jody listened stunned. It couldn't be true. She refused to believe it. Spiderman's logon fit him perfectly. She remembered the innocence in those mesmerizing, blue eyes and the intoxicating warmth of his breath against her cheek. He was gentleness itself, except when he talked about the war, when his eyes blazed with passion. No, Spiderman was exactly who he said he was—a superhero fighting for all that was right and good in the world. He had to be. And Sandy was hateful for suggesting otherwise.

Suddenly, Jody had a thought and latched onto it the way a shark bites meat. "You're lying! You made up the story about flying to Iran. What else did you make up?"

Her eyes flashed, betraying a sudden fit of rage alive behind all that fear. Weird questions and scenarios bounced about in her mind. Was it Sandy? Was he the one who had set up the kidnapping? And what about the others, Brat and Shadow? Were they in on it, too?

She pointed at Sandy. "It wasn't Spiderman. It was you!" Her face twisted into a scowl that made Sandy think of evil spirits. A younger man would have reacted with fury. Sandy merely looked into her eyes and was silent.

Abruptly, she stopped talking. Jody couldn't accuse Sandy no matter how much she wanted to, because here in Canada, her survival depended on him. She didn't have the luxury of anger; she said nothing more out loud, but inside her mind, furies shrieked. 'How dare you, you lying son of a bitch!'

At last, she calmed down a bit. Sandy was as unlikely a kidnapper as Spiderman. He just made a mistake. He'd somehow gotten the notion that she'd flown to Iran and jumped to a weird conclusion about Spiderman. That had to be it. Besides, if he'd wanted to kill her, she'd be dead by now. No, he wasn't a kidnapper—just an internet friend.

Only an internet friend! The thought made her realize how alone she was. He was only an internet friend. He didn't care. Not really. No one cared.

Jody shrugged her shoulders. She should apologize; she knew that. Instead, she turned away. She was done talking. The darkness settled around her once more, and like a shroud over her face, it stifled her, suppressed her, and would not leave.

"What are you thinking about?" Sandy asked.

Jody shrugged again stubbornly. No one cared. Why should she be civil? He put an arm about her shoulder.

"What are you thinking?" Sandy asked again.

"Spiderman," she whispered finally, and her long sigh and bowed head said it all.

Sandy turned his attention to stoking the fire.

Minutes passed while Sandy stared into the flames. Of all the men to fall in love with, Jody had to pick that one!

Sandy touched her shoulder and indicated a computer. "This may help," he said. He pulled up the United Religions Initiative website and clicked on a prayer chain. He scrolled down looking for the entries from Jody's friends. "Look here," he said.

"Dear God, comfort and protect our friend, Jody, and all the others living in danger."

"Allah, Your name be praised. Have mercy on your child, Jody, and be with her in her peril."

"Lord, we pray, end this war, and bring our children safely home. And I especially ask your blessing and protection for Jody."

"These are the first prayers we entered, Brat, Shadow, and I. There are thousands of prayers from people like us. We like to think that Brat was responsible for the chain. She contacted United Religions, called them religious geeks, and asked why they weren't doing anything."

"The great religious leaders of our time, and Brat called them geeks! Oh my gosh, she's living up to her name!" Jody laughed, and then she cried. For that moment, she was her old self, laughing, remembering friends and happy times. She cried, and laughed, and cried.

"And I'm sorry for what I said before."

And then it was over, and the smile was gone.

CHAPTER 3

Two days passed and with them the last brisk autumn weather. Chill winds blasted their way south from the Yukon, bringing rain and the occasional early-bird snowflake. Soft breezes turned into hard blows, and Jody never failed to jump at the sound of loose tree branches hitting the side of the house. To her, violent winds had always been the precursors of disaster. She sat by the hearth and stared into its fire, trying to ignore the wind howling outside.

Meanwhile, Sandy had gone out for wood, and returned with a grim expression on his face. "Soon, I will have to leave for my cabin in the north," he said.

Jody flinched. "It's winter, and you're going north? How far north?"

Turning his head away, he began stacking the wood. "Far enough. Into the Yukon. About two days' drive from here. It's time for me to go back. I was born in the Yukon. It's my home."

He threw two logs on the smoldering fire, and poked the embers into life. "And I have to leave soon—within the next two weeks at the most. If I wait too long, I'll risk getting stranded in a snowstorm.

Jody's face turned pale. He was going to leave her.

"My car is old. You may come with me, but the weather will be fierce, and I've seen you jump in fright when the winds blow loudly. It will not be easy for you up north, but I'll help you as much as I can." He stared into the fire. "Or I'll take you wherever you decide you want to go. It's up to you."

No one would look for her up in the Yukon. No one would find her there. She'd be safe. "I want to go with you," she said, her voice pleading, almost crying.

<<<<>>>>

They spent the next few days packing and planning. "You will need clothes for the cold weather," Sandy said. "Boots, gloves, a parka, and a set of overalls. But I have only enough money for one of each." He dug into his pocket and pulled out a short stack of bills tied up in a string. "And buy three sets of socks and three sets of long underwear."

He frowned again as he looked directly into Jody's eyes. "And you must learn to talk to strangers."

<<<<>>>>

It felt uncomfortable speaking to complete strangers, some of whom gave her puzzled looks in exchange for her friendship. She chose older folks to talk to because they often liked the opportunity to show photos of grandchildren and to discuss the weather. "It'll be a bad one, but not like '95, or was it '97, or was it '87? My mind's not as sharp as she used to be."

Along with shopping and greeting people, Sandy made a point of walking outside with Jody. They walked farther each day until, on the final day, their outing looped through five miles of Vancouver's streets.

<<<<>>>

The next day, they left the city well before dawn. Sandy's car was a rattletrap. An old jeep something, colored the dull gray of undercoat paint, it truly rattled as Sandy drove it.

The air was wet with the promise of more rain. Jody could smell the approaching storm—a pungent, earthy smell. And after the sun rose, she could see signs of foul weather in the mist shrouding the roads and in the black underbellies of brooding clouds.

As they drove north, freeways and houses gave way to thinner patches of human existence. Pines and shrubs replaced the neighborhoods and malls. Maples, standing tall, portended the days ahead; most of their leaves had already turned to bright yellow-orange, red, and brown preparing to fall to the ground below. While Sandy drove, Jody pretended not to be afraid as she watched the sky grow darker.

By late morning, the rain, which had been threatening, started coming down, first in large plops, and then, abandoning kindness, in blurry sheets of water with occasional drops hardening into bullet-like hailstones.

"Should we pull over until the rain dies down a bit?" Jody asked hopefully. The storm was unnerving. She wondered if Sandy had enough money for a cozy motel room to wait it out. Even a damp, moldy motel room would do. Just something that wasn't so, well, so vulnerable in the rain and wind.

Sandy drove on. "Long way ahead of us. We must make good time. We'll rest when we can go no farther."

A streak of lightning shot from the sky, followed several seconds later by thunder, a soft rumble indicating that the heart of the storm was still miles away. Predictably, the second streak was brighter and the rumble louder.

Jody rocked back and forth, back and forth, harder and faster in an unconscious reaction to the storm. Pretending not to notice, Sandy began a hypnotic chant, and soon Jody was drawn in, humming and tapping the rhythm on her leg. As they drew closer to the center of the storm where the thunder and lightning were born, the car seemed to shake with the crashing sounds; and Jody shook and shivered along with the car as she tried to hum with Sandy and to keep time to his rhythm with her tapping.

They stopped in Prince George for gasoline, a box of granola bars, two half-pint cartons of milk, and a chance to use a public restroom. Sandy pulled out bills from a frayed, hand-tooled, leather wallet, and handed them to a young man with a green earring who stood behind the counter.

Still shaking from the storm, Jody crouched behind Sandy, trying to make herself invisible. But that only made the man with the earring take notice. He winked at her and licked his lips. "You look like a tasty meal for Wendigo." He rubbed his hands together suggesting trouble. "Better watch out, little miss. He'll be wandering about in a storm like this." He leaned over the counter with a threatening stare. "He's hungry for human flesh, you know." Chuckling, he knocked an iron pot over, and it fell to the floor with a crash that made Jody scream and jump.

Embarrassed, she looked up at Sandy.

"Hmph, superstition," said Sandy and quickly steered Jody out of the store.

"Who's Wendigo?" she asked.

"Superstition. No one believes in Wendigo anymore, and, anyway, he's supposed to haunt the eastern parts of Canada. I'd smudge you now, but we don't have the time to stop."

North of Prince George, the towns became scarcer. Sandy and Jody drove on through forests lush with trees covered by dripping moss. The rain eased up a bit. Ahead of her, Jody saw more forest going on and on into the distance, and mountains capped with snow.

As they made their way farther and farther north, patches of snow began to show up on the roadside. At first, they were small and far between, but soon they became a common sight, eventually lining the side of the highway in an unending white blanket.

Sandy pressed onward, and Jody, stiff from sitting for hours, longed to stop and stretch her legs but didn't dare say anything.

The winter sun sets early in the north, earlier than Jody was accustomed to. Shadows lengthened and disappeared with the darkening sky. The forest grew wild, and Jody began rocking nervously. Travelling in the dark, Wendigo seemed believable. 'Just superstition.' She said it to herself over and over, trying to make herself believe it.

By the time Sandy pulled up to a red and white restaurant called The Maple Leaf Café, Jody's stomach had gone beyond empty to ravenous. Gratefully, she got out of the car, stretched, and followed Sandy inside where they ordered hamburgers and fries.

'Weird fries,' Jody thought but didn't dare say anything. Gravy and bits of batter-fried cheese covered the potatoes.

"Poutine," Sandy said, grabbing a handful and shoveling it into his mouth as if he were starving. "Canadian French fries."

Jody wished she could nibble slowly, allowing the sensations to linger on her tongue, but Sandy took huge bites and made gestures encouraging her to do the same. "We need to hurry if we want to reach Fort Nelson before everyone locks up for the night." he said.

Jody nodded and wolfed down her food. All too soon, they were back in the car and driving.

By the time they reached Fort Nelson, it was almost eleven o'clock. Sandy pulled up to what looked like a bar but was, in fact, the main entrance of the Last Chance Motel. "We can sleep here," he said.

Their room looked out onto snow-covered forest, but Jody only cared about sleeping. She flopped onto one of the beds like someone who'd spent the day chopping trees and was soon fast asleep.

The next day they woke to snow piled up in white hills around their motel, and more snow was falling as they left the town. Sandy and Jody stopped for a quick meal in Whitehorse, Yukon's capital, and then pressed on.

Three hours later, as Jody was settling into a semi-conscious lull, Sandy gasped and braked hard. A moose appeared suddenly from behind the trees lining the side of the highway. It darted halfway into the road and stopped, startled, right in front of Sandy's hood. Sandy turned the wheel sharply and managed to avoid the moose, by inches it seemed. Predictably, the jeep began to skid.

Feeling the car slipping sideways, Jody screamed, closed her eyes, and threw her hands in front of her face. When she opened her eyes again, Sandy had turned the car toward the skid, and it was plowing through piles of newly-fallen snow. Jody kept screaming as the jeep headed toward a giant maple. Without thinking, she grabbed Sandy's shoulder.

"Stop it!" Sandy's voice barked the order, as he shrugged his shoulder free of Jody's grip. Regaining control, he eased the car to a stop before it hit the tree. Jody was trembling at the near miss. Unperturbed, Sandy got out of the car to examine the jeep's wheels, the snowbank, and the road on which they'd been travelling. "Snow tires aren't enough." With Jody still shuddering, he got back behind the wheel, started the engine, and eased the car out of the snowbank and back onto the road.

"Black ice," Sandy mumbled. "Very dangerous." He inched the car forward until he came to a spot where he could safely pull off the road. "Come out and help," he said. Without a backward glance at her, he opened the trunk and rummaged through the contents searching for chains.

Reluctantly, Jody joined Sandy outside in the cold. Kneeling on ice, they spread out the chains. Sandy drove over the treads, and together they looped the catches that secured the chains around the tires. Jody shivered, in part from the cold but mostly from their near misses of the moose and the tree, along with the occasional coyote calls.

It was well after dark when Sandy pulled off the main road and onto a path so narrow that a bear would have found it challenging. He pushed forward for about a hundred feet while branches scraped along the outside of his jeep, and the chains gripped hard into the powdery snow.

Finally, he stopped in front of the tiniest, most humble of cabins. "We are here," he said. Jody looked around. There was no visible sign of civilization surrounding the house.

"Wow," was all she could think to say.

Sandy grunted, pulling a suitcase from the trunk while Jody stared dumbly at the darkness surrounding her. He shook his head, nudged Jody's arm and handed her the suitcase. Then he lifted two of the heavier boxes out of the trunk and led the way to the front door of the cabin. It was bigger than a hut, but smaller than any house Jody had ever seen. With gloved hands, she felt the outside of the cabin, and, yes, it was built of logs. She blinked, imagining herself going back a few centuries to pioneer times.

They went inside.

In the main room, six chairs surrounded a table, all made by hand from split pine branches. A green plaid couch appeared to be the only store-bought item. A gigantic, handcrafted, river-rock fireplace dominated the far wall, and a caribou hide lay in front of it. Charming or primitive? Jody wasn't sure. 'Please let there be electricity—and a real stove.' She crossed her fingers. To Jody's right, a door led into a kitchen equipped with a sink, a relatively modern stove, a mini-refrigerator, a standing lamp—which didn't turn on, and, miracle of miracles, an old-fashioned, rotary phone. A door on the other side led into a tiny bedroom with a quilt-covered bed, a cedarwood chest, and a door which opened into an indoor bathroom. "Thank you, thank you, thank you," she said to no one in particular.

Wind blowing through the open doorway increased the chill inside the cabin. Jody shut the door, then looked about for some way to warm the place up. She found a small space heater in the bedroom, but, when she tried to set it up in the main part of the cabin, she couldn't get it to turn on. 'Of course. The power's not on.' The fireplace appeared to be the only possible source of warmth. She found logs, kindling, and yellowed newspaper next to the fireplace, and, kneeling, she began stacking them while Sandy left for another load of provisions from the car.

Jody poked and prodded until a flickering promise grew into a warming blaze. There was something satisfying, something earthy, about making fire. She looked for Sandy, but he wasn't inside the cabin. Reluctantly, she left the beginnings of warmth to help with the last of the boxes.

Jody didn't see Sandy at first. Puzzled, she called his name, but no one answered. Finally, she found Sandy sitting in the snow on the other side of the jeep, his face pasty gray and twisted into a grimace. "Sandy," she shrieked. Then she knelt by his side. He groaned and rubbed his chest. "Are you okay? Say something." Sandy opened his mouth, but no words came out.

Jody ran inside, hoping Canada's emergency number was 911, but when she picked up the receiver, there was no dial tone. Familiar terror cloaked her, and she couldn't move or speak. Thoughts came in jumbles. She was alone. No one could hear her scream. She'd never survive. They'd throw her in jail for killing Sandy. She saw herself helpless. Attacked by strangers, or dying from hunger, or freezing to death. In her fright, there was no room to think of Sandy except as someone who could no longer take care of her.

Not knowing what else to do, Jody dragged him inside by his parka. She pulled him across the floor next to the fire, where he lay making gasping noises. She shouted her fear in echoes of, "Are you hurt? Are you sick? Say something. Speak to me."

"Nitroglycerine," he finally managed between gasps, and pointed at a cardboard box where Jody discovered a bottle of tiny pills—nitroglycerine, according to the label. She removed one, put it under his tongue, and waited.

The thought of Sandy dying was too much for Jody to bear. 'What am I supposed to do now?' she wondered, but no answer came to her. She wanted to hide, to cover her eyes, to run. Instead, she sat next to him, listening to his breathing, and humming the tune he had chanted in the car.

It seemed as if hours passed, although it was only minutes. Eventually, some color returned to Sandy's face, his breathing became less labored, and he was able to sit up on the floor. "How do I get you to a hospital?" Jody asked, afraid he'd suggest that Jody drive.

"Not necessary."

"You never said . . ."

"I told you before—I'm dying."

Jody shook her head. "You're not really dying, are you? I mean, you drove all the way from Vancouver. And you carried boxes, and put on the snow chains, and we walked for miles, and . . . everything." Jody watched Sandy. More color was returning to his face. "Okay, that was scary, but you're okay now. Aren't you?" She tried to sound cheerful. She had to tell him he was okay. For Pete's sakes, that's what you're supposed to do when someone says he's dying. Jody forced a smile. "You can't be dying," she said, ashamed because all she could think of was how she'd survive without him.

Sandy managed a smile. "Not today. Not next week. But I will die. I see visions: my body lying still beyond sleep and my spirit riding the wind. I think, before I die, you will stand strong and laugh. I don't know this, but I think it is true."

"Why?"

"Because you are here. And because you need me."

Jody sobbed. She wrapped her arms around Sandy and wept like a small child, concern for Sandy making its way through her fear. "Then I don't ever want to stand strong and laugh," she said, "not if it means that you'll die."

"While you cry, unpack these boxes," said Sandy. "There is much work to be done before we sleep."

"Is that why we had to go north? Because you're dying?"

Sandy gave a faint nod. He pointed to the stack of boxes again.

<<<<>>>>

The next day dawned clear with a bright blue sky, and the snow lay like clouds on the hills. Jody worked hard, unpacking boxes. Sandy moved slower than before and stopped to rest more frequently, but, other than that, showed no signs of illness. As they worked, Jody kept thinking that many people had died in hard winters, and these were people more used to cold weather than she was. She looked about her.

A shed next to the cabin housed a generator with space left over for the jeep and a few tools or supplies. Just inside the door of the shed, Sandy had stacked several boxes. Beside them, lay a pair of cross-country skis and a pair of snowshoes. So, if things got rough, one of them could leave the cabin to get food. Clearly that was going to be Sandy—Sandy with his weak heart. Jody had no idea how to ski or snowshoe. Totally useless! That's what she was.

She pawed through the boxes. Some of the items in them made sense—jumper cables, hand warmers, blankets, flashlights, batteries, a battery-run radio, a snow brush, shovel, scrapers, deicer spray, kitty litter. Why the kitty litter? For traction on slippery roads?

Sandy had mentioned a root cellar. There might be more food stored somewhere. They certainly hadn't brought up enough to last through winter, however long that would be. Three months? Four months? Longer?

About thirty feet behind the cabin, a pallet was piled high with wood—logs and kindling. Enough for a few weeks? Not enough to last until spring.

Sandy, by himself, could live up here through the winter. Jody couldn't do it. There was no way she'd survive. But Sandy couldn't take her back to Vancouver. No, she was stuck. She tried to talk to God, to ask for help. And she searched for the comforting feeling that God was there beside her, but all she got was static and fear. Apparently, God had figured out that she was useless too.

CHAPTER 4

The following day shortly after the sun had reached its highest point, a white SUV with a panel of lights across its top drove up to Sandy's cabin. Jody cringed as soon as she saw the logo on the doors—a crown above a wreath of leaves which surrounded a buffalo head, and below it, the words, "Royal Canadian Mounted Police." Had they somehow found her? And sent the Mounties out to get her and bring her back?

The man who got out of the car was clean shaven and moved with a tiger's grace. He wore a dark-blue policeman's uniform. Jody looked at the holstered gun hanging at his side and wanted to run away into the forest. Unperturbed, Sandy walked out of the house to welcome him, and Jody felt compelled to trail behind.

"Dänch'ea," the Mountie said in greeting. He was tall and muscular. Jody got the impression of a tree as he towered over Sandy who was not a small man by any means.

Sandy hugged the man as if greeting a brother, then nodded toward Jody. "Will, this is Jody," he said.

The Mountie gave Sandy a questioning look.

"She needs a place to stay."

Will shrugged. "Any friend of Sandy's."

'Stray cat, stray dog, stray woman.' That's what his shrug seemed to say.

"Jody, meet Will Campbell." Sandy wasn't much for detailed introductions.

"H . . . hello," Jody stuttered. 'Don't look guilty,' she told herself and turned to Sandy. "Did we do something wrong?"

Sandy shook his head. "Will is my son-in-law."

"Everything okay?" Will asked.

"Everything is fine," said Sandy. "Stay for lunch, please."

"Not today."

"A cup of coffee, then?"

Will nodded. "I have a few things for you," he said and brought in two boxes of provisions from his car: tins of meats, salmon, and tuna, dried jerky, some canned vegetables, sauerkraut, crackers, and flat breads. "That'll keep you for a while," he said, "in case we get a hard blow. Wish I'd known you had company."

Meanwhile, Jody busied herself stacking logs next to the fireplace and trying to make herself invisible.

"This country is harsh," Will said to Jody. "I keep an eye on the folks here, especially the elders. I'll come by from time to time. To make sure you're both okay."

Sandy set the kettle on the stove and spooned coffee grounds into a filter. Soon everyone was drinking fresh-brewed coffee.

Will looked at Jody and grinned. "What brings you to the Yukon just before the worst of the winter storms? Insanity? A death wish?" He laughed. "An inexplicable need to prove something? The heart of a warrior beating inside an unassuming maiden?"

Jody laughed back almost hysterically, frantically trying to think of a good answer. 'I need a place to hide. I'm in terrible trouble, and I may be wanted by the police. I'll go quietly. I didn't do anything, honest!' She laughed some more, stalling for time. "All of the above, I guess," she finally squeaked. Then, changing the subject, she pointed at the window which looked out onto piles of snow. "So, this is the good weather?"

Will and Sandy exchanged looks. "Wait till you experience a real blizzard," Will said. "I take it you're not used to snow."

"No," she answered. And there was uncomfortable silence. Jody squirmed. "There's not much of it in Mississippi where I grew up. Or in Berkeley, for that matter. I never lived anywhere else."

Will drained the last of his coffee and stood up to leave.

"Go in peace," said Sandy.

"Stay in peace," said Will.

Jody gave a half-hearted good-bye wave, then covered her face with her hands and collapsed with her head on the wooden table.

"He's a good man," Sandy said to her.

"The uniform scares me," she answered." It's silly, I know, but . . ."

"You must build up your courage and your strength. You will need both for the days ahead."

"I can't help it. I'm terrified."

"Then you must face what frightens you. That is the First Nations way."

<<<<>>>>

Will drove away conflicted. Obviously, that woman was hiding something, and, if she were hiding from the law, it was his sworn duty to bring her to justice. And he wasn't about to let any harm come to Sandy. What wasn't she saying? What was she covering up?

Sandy trusted her. He was an honest man with good instincts about people—not the type to harbor a fugitive, at least not without a reason. But Sandy also held the First Nations belief that he was spiritually connected to every living being on the earth, good and bad. And of course, the ways of the Northern Tutchone required extending hospitality to strangers.

And Jody's body language! Will was used to people being nervous around a uniform, but this woman wasn't just nervous. She was terrified. That wasn't normal.

Will shook his head and resolved to learn more about Sandy's guest.

<<<<>>>>

"Where are we going?" Jody asked. They were on the road in the jeep heading west. Two weeks had passed since she and Sandy had made their trek to the Yukon. The sky was clear, and the temperature, at eight in the morning, was barely above freezing.

"I want you to get to know someone." Sandy wasn't much for details. "Besides, we both need a rest from chopping wood."

After a fifteen-minute stretch of driving, they arrived in a town straight out of the 1890s, except that the buildings had better paint jobs. They came in all colors—white, red, yellow—and they were topped by turrets and steep, gabled roofs trimmed with Victorian filigree.

"Brown's Harness Shop, General Store, Sourdough Joe's Restaurant." Jody read the names out loud. "Where the heck are we?"

Sandy grunted. "Dawson City. Heart of the Yukon."

They drove along streets resembling sets from a cowboy movie until they came to an avenue with modest, twentieth-century houses. Sandy stopped his jeep in front of a gray house with a steeply-pitched roof and honked. Jody hoped she wouldn't have to get out of the car. It was still cold outside, at least by her reckoning.

Minutes later, a man, followed by three children, stepped outside of the house, closing and locking the door behind them. With a shock, Jody recognized the man. He was that Mountie, Will Campbell, the one who had come to check on Sandy two weeks ago. What was happening? Was this a set up to arrest her?

'That's just plain dumb,' she decided, hoping that nothing awful was about to happen.

The oldest child, a teenage boy with spiked hair, frowned and slouched. He followed behind his father, dragging worn-out sneakers along the ground as he walked. Next came a girl of about eight wearing a pink "Hello, Kitty" parka and carrying a bundled-up baby on her hip. She was talking to the baby, making smiling faces, and kissing the baby's head.

Jody did a double take. Were these Will's kids? They all had dark skin, dark eyes, and black hair— First Nations features— whereas Will was light-skinned with blue eyes and reddish-brown hair.

Then Jody remembered that Will's wife was Sandy's daughter.

Will waved at Sandy. Then he and the children piled into a dark-green truck, and Will started the engine.

'Face your fears.' That's what Sandy was always telling Jody. So, this was another of Sandy's "face your fears" lessons. 'Rats!'

They drove in tandem for a bit, Will's truck behind Sandy's jeep, until they came to Diamond Tooth Gertie's Saloon. Sandy parked and got out. "You go with Will and his children," he said, and waved at the group before disappearing into Gertie's. Reluctantly, Jody got into Will's truck.

"This is Jody, Sandy's friend," Will told his children. "Jody, this is Liam, my oldest, Emberlee, and our baby, Chioke."

Jody mumbled an awkward greeting, smiled at the children, and tried to appear normal.

The boy, Liam, mumbled back and turned away with a shrug. Apparently, he had better things to do than to ride around with a geeky woman.

"Hi," Emberlee said and looked away quickly. Her hair was pulled back into two thick, black braids, and she stuck the end of one of them into her mouth.

Will was the only unperturbed person in the group. "Sandy asked me to show you around. This is wild country, Jody, and loners don't do well here," he said, "particularly loners who aren't used to living this far north."

He started the truck, turned on the radio, and ten minutes later, they were in Dawson City's Historical Complex. "Boring," Liam said, but Jody was taking it all in. Most of the buildings were one-room, log cabins with honest-to-God sod roofs. Some larger buildings—general stores, saloons, and such—leaned drunkenly. Their paint had worn off decades ago, exposing weathered timbers.

"This is it," said Will. "Yukon history, the real thing. It was a boomtown in the late 1890s. That's Robert Service's cabin on the left. You know—the poet who wrote 'The Cremation of Sam McGee.' During the heart of the Klondike Gold Rush, a hundred-thousand prospectors came from all over hoping to strike it rich."

"Is there any gold left?" Jody asked quietly. For just a moment, she forgot to be afraid of the Mountie. Maybe she could somehow find enough gold to live on. Enough so she wouldn't be sponging off of Sandy.

"The gold is mostly mined commercially now," Will said, "although some independent prospectors have claims and find enough gold to make the effort worthwhile."

"Really?" Jody looked down. Suddenly, she had a terrible urge to check the dirt under her feet for gold nuggets.

"Gold fever is a nasty disease." Will gave Jody a hard stare and a raised eyebrow. There's just something about the idea of picking up a fist-sized nugget; it messes with people's heads."

"Boring," Liam whispered. He poked Emberlee with his elbow.

"Ow! Knock it off." Emberlee tried to kick her brother, but he jumped out of the way, then swatted her bottom. Emberlee was still carrying Chioke and couldn't defend herself.

Hastily, Jody took the baby from Emberlee. Chioke put her hand on Jody's nose and smiled, oblivious to the squabble.

Emberlee tried to sock Liam. He dodged her then swatted her again. "Dad, he's hitting me. Make him stop."

"It's gold fever. It's messing with my head." Liam's voiced cracked as he spoke. "I can't help it."

"Dad!"

There's a tone police officers use—deep, loud, commanding. It demands obedience. "Liam, knock it off now."

"Yes, sir."

"And apologize."

"Sorry, Emberlee."

"And to our guest."

"Sorry, Ms.—Jody."

Will's voice knocked the stuffing out of Jody. She nodded at Liam because she didn't trust herself to say anything.

"What's your last name, Jody? My kids should be more respectful."

"That's okay," Jody squeaked.

"No, they've been raised better than that."

"It's Jacobson," Jody's voice was still squeaky. "Johanna Jacobson."

Will held back a smile. Teenage rebellion had its uses. Now that he knew Jody's last name, he could look her up in the police files. "Liam, apologize to Ms. Jacobson."

"Sorry, Ms. Jacobson," he mumbled, and his voice cracked again.

"That's okay. And you can call me Jody."

Liam bit a fingernail. "Dad, Steve's working at the general store. Can I go see him?"

"No." Again, the voice that could crack cement! "We're going to visit the museum and then have lunch."

"Shit. I've seen the stupid museum a hundred times," Liam muttered.

Will grabbed his son's shoulder. "What did you just say?"

"Nothing."

Silence.

"Sorry . . . sir."

Jody stepped back three steps. As if she'd been chastised too.

<<<<>>>>

Most of the museum's South Gallery depicted the Klondike Gold Rush. A life-size display featured dance-hall girls entertaining sex-starved prospectors by dancing the cancan. They'd pulled their skirts and petticoats up high above their waists revealing legs, garters, and panties. Another exhibit depicted a saloon with whiskered patrons downing shots of whiskey. Old-time photos covered the walls. There were pictures of husky sled teams mushing through waist-high snow, the dogs, apparently, oblivious to the cold. And next to the sienna photographs, hung a modern-day, color photo of a shiny pile of gold nuggets which seemed to shout, "Come, follow me. Be mine, and I will reward you with women, liquor, and a life too fine to be imagined."

Next, Jody was drawn to an image of prospectors, a line of sorry-looking souls trudging up the Chilkoot Trail with the snow melted to mud by thousands of weary feet. Her knowledge of Canadian history was woefully lacking, so she read the narrative posted next to the photo.

The prospectors started their quest for gold in Skagway, Alaska. From Skagway, they took either the Chilkoot Trail or the White Pass Trail to Lake Bennett and, from there, sailed, paddled, or rowed down the Yukon River to the Klondike. Only about a third of them made it to the gold fields.

Most of these prospectors were city slickers, unprepared for life in the Yukon. To prevent them all from starving to death, the Mounties required each man (All but a handful of the prospectors were men.) to bring with them a year's supply of food—close to a ton—which they had to carry over the passes in stages. Most carried their supplies on their backs.

Jody kept staring at the photo of miners climbing the Chilkoot trail. Finally, Will and his kids moved on, and she, reluctantly, followed.

In the north gallery, Jody found an exhibit of the Hwëch'in, the First Nations tribe that had inhabited the Klondike area before the white settlers came. These were the Han, the people of the river, a tribe of nomads who followed the salmon runs and lived on caribou, bear, moose, and smaller game when ice covered the rivers.

Liam spoke, breaking the silence. "You don't like Steve, do you, Dad?"

"I do like him." Will's voice was abrupt.

"Then why can't I go see him?"

"Because I said so."

Liam's voice was loud. On purpose. "Why not? At least tell me that. Is it because he's Han?"

Will looked at Jody and at the few other people around him. "We're not discussing this now." He lowered his voice. "This is not the time nor the place. Understand?"

"Yes, sir."

Jody looked away. So, Will was a bigot? But his father-in-law was First Nations. So were his kids—at least in part. Puzzled, she furrowed her brow but said nothing.

That's when Chioke began to cry. Jody had been carrying her, and she switched the baby to her other side and patted her back. Chioke kept crying. "She's hungry," said Emberlee. "So am I."

Jody wanted to chime in but decided not to.

Will checked his watch. "Right. We'll stop at Klondike Kate's for lunch."

Jody blinked. In two seconds, Will had changed from terrifying to, well, normal. Jody shrugged. She followed the others into the truck, and minutes later, they walked into Klondike Kate's Restaurant.

They ordered hamburgers and poutine. Jody was acquiring a taste for poutine. 'I'll never eat regular French fries again,' she thought, and then realized how true that was. She'd probably never be able to get back into the United States.

"It'll be about twenty minutes," the waitress said. "Is that okay? We're shorthanded in the kitchen today." Will nodded. The waitress looked at Chioke, who was about to cry, and she put two packs of oyster crackers on the table. "For the little one," she said and left. The group fell silent. For Jody, it was an uncomfortable silence, the kind that makes you want to squirm and say stupid things. That kind of silence.

Emberlee tugged on Will's sleeve. "Tell us a story," she said.

Will hunched over the table. He glanced to his left and to his right. "Shh," he whispered, holding an index finger to his lips.

Emberlee smiled. Liam turned away. Jody just watched and listened, hardly believing that this was the same man who had terrified her earlier—the man whose voice could stop traffic, whose voice left her quaking and shivering.

Will's eyes grew big. "This is the story of . . . Soapy Smith . . . the meanest, baddest hustler to ever darken the doorways of Skagway, Alaska." He drummed his fingers on the table, playing an imaginary piano as he hummed melodrama music.

Emberlee joined him, singing, "La, la, la-la-la."

"This story happened a long time ago, when Alaska had more outlaws than grizzlies, if you can believe it." He paused, savoring the silence.

"Wake up!" Will pounded the table, making Jody jump. He twirled an imaginary mustache.

"Smell your armpits." He raised a burly arm and demonstrated.

Jody smiled and Emberlee laughed.

"What would you pay for . . . a bar of soap?"

He pointed to Emberlee. "You, young fella', will you buy a bar? Only five dollars." Emberlee giggled. "You're funny, Papa."

"But this ain't your average bar of soap. No, sirree. Inside the wrapper, some lucky patrons will find a hundred-dollar bill."

Will chuckled. Now he was talking in his regular voice. "Well, no kidding. The young fella' found a hundred-dollar bill inside. After that, the rest of Soapy's onlookers clambered to buy the overpriced soap. Trouble was . . . the young fella' was Soapy's shill, and the soap with the money was marked. Everyone else found . . . just soap."

Will shook his head. "For a while Soapy Smith owned Skagway. He owned the law; he owned the politicians; he owned Skagway's only telegraph office. When the miners struck it rich, Soapy agreed to telegraph money to their families in exchange for gold. Only trouble was—the telegraph wires from the rest of the U.S. didn't reach Alaska until several years after Soapy's death. The wires in Soapy's office . . . went nowhere."

Will pounded the table. "That man was a scoundrel. He swindled those poor miners every time he turned around, and that's the gosh-darned truth."

Emberlee listened with her mouth open. Liam picked at his nails with a penknife. Jody fed oyster crackers to Chioke and took it all in.

"What happened to Soapy?" asked Emberlee.

"A vigilante shot him," said Will. "They were desperate times . . . and there weren't any Canadian Mounties in Alaska." Will drummed on the table. "That was the end of Soapy Smith, and, with his death, law and order returned to Skagway, Alaska."

<<<<>>>>

After they'd finished lunch, Will dropped Jody off at Diamond Tooth Gerties, where she met up with Sandy for the ride home. Jody climbed into Sandy's jeep and slammed the door. "You know that Mountie gives me the shivers. You left me with him anyway."

Sandy started the engine. "Fear is a luxury you cannot have. Here in the Yukon, we rely on each other, especially in winter."

Jody folded her arms. "Did you know he's prejudiced?"

"Will?" Sandy laughed. "Where did you get that idea?"

"You should have heard him talk about Liam's friend, Steve. Liam said Steve is Han, and that's why Will doesn't like him."

"Just what did Will say?"

"He didn't deny it. He didn't defend himself. He just told Liam they weren't discussing it. Period." When Jody thought about it, Will's voice was what had bothered her. That 'Don't you dare question me' voice. "He doesn't like Steve, and he wouldn't explain why he doesn't like him," Jody finally said. "Probably because he has no good reason."

Sandy sighed. "Liam has had a chip on his shoulder ever since his mother died. He blames his father for her death. He never got over it."

"Why?"

"I don't know. I was in Vancouver when it happened; I flew up here just long enough to attend the funeral and then flew back. Will doesn't speak of it." Sandy frowned. "Will hasn't gotten over Emma's death, either. She died delivering Chioke. That's all I know."

"Emma was Will's wife?"

Sandy nodded.

"And your daughter?"

Again, Sandy nodded.

"So, what's Will's problem with Liam's friend?"

Sandy grunted. "Steve always seemed like a good kid to me. He's older than Liam, and Liam looks up to Steve."

Suddenly, a caribou appeared in front of the car. Sandy hit the brakes hard, mumbled something unintelligible, then drove on as if nothing had happened.

Jody turned to watch the caribou's retreating figure and shrugged. If Sandy wasn't worried about the caribou, Jody figured she should be either. "So, what's Will's problem?" she asked.

"I don't know, but he probably has good reasons for distrusting Steve. And Liam has been acting out a lot lately."

"So, you're saying it's all Liam's fault?'

Sandy shook his head. "Liam is a good boy—in spite of the way he's been acting. Don't be put off by the hair, the clothing, and the teenage insolence. Only thirteen years old, but he watches the younger children when Will is working, so Will can arrange his shift accordingly."

"Somehow, he seems older."

Sandy nodded. "Liam used to be such a happy child. And respectful to his parents. But all that changed after Emma died. Such a shame!"

"Can't you do anything, Sandy?"

"Not unless Will asks for my help." Sandy's face was grim. He turned on the radio, and they didn't speak for the rest of the way home.

<<<<>>>>

Later that afternoon, Will requested permission to search the United States' FBI criminal records. Thankfully, Jody's name didn't appear anywhere. He glanced at his watch. No time to search state and local records. He had many more questions, but they'd have to wait for another time. The Yukon had more pressing problems.

CHAPTER 5

It was about eight in the evening. Even with a fire blazing in the fireplace, the air in Sandy's cottage was chilly. Jody shivered and wrapped a blanket around herself. Snow had stopped falling, but the winds were still whipping tree branches about in a frenzied dance, and a curtain of blue-green light rippled across the sky. It was Jody's first aurora borealis. She watched the show through the window of Sandy's cabin, trying to get used to the surreal ribbon of light and the moaning sounds of the wind.

Close to the ground, light jumped and flickered in bright red, orange, and yellow spurts resembling fire. Jody kept watching. And then a blast sounded, accompanying a blaze of light. "Sandy," she called, "I don't think that was the aurora." Instead of answering, Sandy dialed 911.

A half-hour later, Sandy answered the knock at the door, and a Mountie stood before him. Jody wrapped her blanket tighter around herself because she was shivering. In halting words, she described what she'd seen. She stuttered when he asked for her name, and she gave it as Sonja Jordanson—just in case he'd ask for ID. Thankfully, the Mountie wasn't Will. "My friends call me Jody," she added. "I was watching the northern lights. I'd never seen them before. So, at first, I figured that the orange was just part of the aurora. And then I heard this really loud booming, like an explosion, and that's all I know." She pointed in the general direction of what she'd seen, but she was too frightened, both by the explosion and by the uniformed Mountie asking the questions, to give more than a general idea of where the fire was.

<<<<◇>>>

The next day, Will appeared at Sandy's door. "May I drop the kids off at your cabin if I need to? I'll be taking on extra shifts, and I don't feel comfortable leaving the kids with Liam for so much of the time."

Sandy nodded. "Is something wrong?"

"The explosion you heard, that was an accident caused by someone cooking methamphetamine in the forest. We didn't catch anyone. The crime lab is dusting for prints. We spent the night looking for evidence, but there wasn't much." Will fingered his badge. "The problem is that two overdose cases came into Dawson City Hospital this morning. A total of five this week and eleven this month. No big deal for a city like Whitehorse, but for Dawson City, that's an epidemic. Most of the victims—and yes, they're victims, not criminals—most of them are kids. What we do know is this: whoever is cooking the meth . . . they don't know what they're doing. They're not just selling meth; they're selling bad meth. One of the kids died. That's why I'm pulling extra shifts. We want to get a handle on this thing before it gets out of control."

<<<<<>>>>

A few days later, Will turned up at Sandy's house with the kids in tow. "Do you know when you'll be back?" Sandy asked. Apparently, he'd been expecting them.

"About eight. In time to get them to bed. Thanks so much for doing this." With that, Will handed Chioke to Jody, kissed Emberlee on the head, gave Liam a quick hug, and with the parting words, "You kids be good," he was gone.

"Come," Sandy said. He motioned for Liam and Emberlee to follow him. "I have something to show you," and the three disappeared behind the cabin leaving Jody holding the baby. Curious, Jody wrapped Chioke in a blanket and followed them.

Sandy produced a basketball. "Now help me make a hoop for this," he said. Soon, Liam and Emberlee had bent pine branches into a circle and Liam was trying to figure out how to attach their hoop to a tree.

Alone in the house, Jody played peekaboo with the baby. When that got old, she set Chioke down on the floor of the cabin and desperately searched for something with which to amuse her.

An hour later, Sandy, Liam, and Emberlee came back inside. "I have to go into town," Sandy said. Jody began to protest. "Face your fears, little one," he told her and was gone.

Minutes later, Liam was walking out the door as well. "Where are you going?" Jody asked. She tried to sound calm, in control, but her voice squeaked.

"Just out back to shoot hoops." And he was gone.

Jody looked at Emberlee, who stared back and didn't say anything.

"What do you want to do?" Jody finally asked.

Emberlee shrugged her shoulders.

"I suppose we could bake cookies if I can find what we need in the kitchen."

Emberlee pulled a rattle and a pacifier out of her pocket and handed them to Chioke. Then together, she and Jody searched through Sandy's cupboards. They found flour, salt, shortening, sugar, eggs, and baking powder. Jody figured she'd eyeball the quantities of each ingredient and hope that the cookies would come out edible.

"Do you have chocolate chips?" Emberlee asked hopefully.

Jody looked and looked. "Sorry. Cinnamon is the best I can do. We can make Snickerdoodles."

<<<<>>>>

It became a common occurrence for Jody and Sandy to watch Will's kids. Often, Sandy disappeared for hours at a time, leaving

Jody to take care of the children. It was a chance for him to visit old friends, perform healings, and deliver medicine—both modern and traditional. It was also an opportunity for Jody to have to face her fear of people.

She got good at entertaining Emberlee. They made paper airplanes and played thumb wars. They baked cookies, cakes, and muffins. And they made jewelry out of rolled-up strips of paper torn from pages of old magazines. Jody felt comfortable with Emberlee and Chioke. Emberlee was a mellow creature. She giggled a lot. And as for Chioke, she was an easygoing baby. She'd crawl around on the floor playing with anything Jody gave her. If she started fussing, a sippy cup of juice or a couple of crackers were usually enough to cheer her up.

Liam was another matter. Always sullen, he answered Jody in monosyllables. His conversations usually consisted of grumbling about the lack of a television. Thankfully, he spent much of his time bouncing a basketball against the back of the cabin or playing games on his Game Boy, and Jody was relieved that she could just ignore him.

<<<<>>>>

The first heavy storm of winter blew down out of the northeast, trapping Jody and Sandy inside the cabin. Temperatures plunged. The sky outside was black or dark, dark gray for the better part of the day and night.

Sandy and Jody spent their time huddled in blankets, sitting around the fireplace. It was their sole source of heat and light, since Sandy only ran the generator for a couple of hours each day. It was a lonely, quiet time. Jody cast about for some activity with which to occupy herself, but there was precious little to do. They prepared food, cooking it in the fireplace, and they cleaned up after the meal. They stoked the fire. There was nothing else to do. 'So, this is what a harsh winter in the Yukon feels like,' Jody thought. And, in that seemingly endless, empty time, frightening memories filled Jody's head, and she couldn't sit still.

Sandy smiled to himself watching Jody trying not to squirm like a six-year-old. "You are welcome to read any of my books," he said. "Look inside the chest in the bedroom."

Gratefully, Jody raised the chest's cover, eager for any distraction. Most of the chest was filled with books: history books, advanced mathematics, a book on the religions of the world.

"There are medical texts in here," Jody said. "And books on astrophysics and medieval times. These are university textbooks. Did you go to college?"

"University of Toronto," Sandy answered.

Digging deeper into the chest, Jody found an assortment of fiction: Margaret Atwood, Amy Tan, Thomas Clancy—as well as Shakespeare and Dickens. Apparently, Sandy was an eclectic reader. With a shudder, she sidestepped George Orwell's *1984*. (Much too heavy; it might bring back more unwanted memories.)

Instead, she picked up *First Nations Legends and Lore,* and turned to the introduction:

In early days, these legends were not written anywhere. Instead, storytellers passed them down from generation to generation. In recording these tales, I have tried to reproduce for you that sense of wonder I felt as a child, listening to my father telling stories on moonlit nights sitting next to our campfire.

Jody closed her eyes and imagined Sandy dressed in caribou skin clothing. She could almost hear him drumming, chanting, and telling tales in his clear, mellow voice. She flipped the page to the first legend: *How Raven Stole the Light:*

Way back in time, in the beginning of everything, there was Raven. It was a time when the land was covered by darkness—so much darkness that you could not walk without tripping and stumbling. Imagine you are standing inside the belly of a giant bear or in a tunnel deep in the earth. That is how dark it was.

In those days, an old man lived in a house by a great river, and he was the one who caused the darkness. You see, he had, hidden away in his house on top of a tall shelf, a box carved from the wood of a giant maple. The box was the size of a man's fist, maybe. I do not know. An amazing box it was—and in this box was all the light of the universe.

Why did the old man keep the light hidden and not share it with the rest of the world? Perhaps, he was stingy. But perhaps, there was another reason.

The old man had a daughter. "What if she is ugly?" the old man asked himself. "What if her skin is like a frog's skin – covered with blisters? Maybe her hair is dry like dead grass." The old man did not want to find out, so he hid the light in his marvelous box.

Now Raven was flying home, but he could not see where he was going, and he flew into a tall maple tree. Bam! He rubbed his beak which was very sore from bumping into the tree. "This is not right!" he said. "I will steal the light and take it for myself."

Now Raven was a trickster, and he could change his shape into anything he wanted.

One day, Raven saw the old man's daughter by the river filling a bucket with water, and he got an idea. (How he could see the girl, I do not know. Please do not ask.) Raven turned himself into a pine needle and he floated down into the girl's bucket. When she drank from the bucket, she swallowed Raven.

Inside the girl's body, Raven found a comfortable place where he went to sleep, and he slept for nine months. After that time, the girl bore a little boy. The old man immediately loved the boy and gave him everything he wanted.

"I want that box," the boy said, but the old man shook his head.

"I cannot give you that box," he said. "It is mine and you may not have it."

So, the boy began to cry, and scream, and shriek. "I want that box. Give me the box. Give it to me right now." So much noise! He kept screaming and crying and did not stop.

Finally, the old man could not stand the noise any longer. "I will let you hold the box, but just for a minute," he said, and he held the box out to Raven.

Quickly, Raven snatched the box out of the old man's hand and took the light out of it. He turned himself into a giant bird and flew out of the old man's house through an open window carrying the light in his beak.

Raven flew through the sky, and the world become beautiful from the light that he carried. He marveled at all the colors in the rivers, trees, and mountains below him, but while he flew, cawing in delight at all he saw, he failed to notice Eagle chasing him.

"I want the light for myself," said Eagle, and he swooped down on Raven, sinking his talons into Raven's back. Raven dropped pieces of light which fell to the ground, then bounced back up to become stars. The biggest one became the moon.

Eagle chased Raven across the sky to the edge of the earth and beyond. At last Raven was too tired to fly anymore. He dropped the last piece of light which became the sun. The sun lit up the sky, and it lit up the entire world with its forests, mountains, and rivers. And it lit up the old man's house. That was when the man saw his daughter for the first time. She was not ugly at all, but beautiful, with hair dark as midnight and soft as a rabbit's fur. Her skin was unblemished like new-fallen snow.

"I was selfish to keep the light all to myself," said the man, and from that day on, he shared all he had with his people.

And so, the old man was happy, the people were happy, and there was light in all the world.

Jody read on. Some tales were frankly terrifying, or at least they would be to a four-year-old. Jody imagined Sandy as a kid sitting by a campfire hearing stories about killer owls and bushmen who ate families—probably a warning to kids not to stray far from their parents. The stories reflected a time when death lurked everywhere, a time when loyalty to friends and family ensured the tribe's survival.

Different tribes told different tales, but one theme ran through most of the stories: respect for all of creation; those people relied on the land with its plants and animals for their very existence.

In a land where death was always close, they prayed for short winters and heavy salmon runs. Warmth and a full belly. Simple requests.

<<<<>>>>

The book kept Jody's interest for a few hours, but, after she'd finished it, an uncomfortable energy took over, and she began to pace. "How can you be so, so mellow?" she asked Sandy. "Don't you ever just—I don't know—don't you ever just want to move, or stretch, or go outside and run?"

"I have spent a lifetime learning patience. Like an animal in the wild. I am like a moose in the middle of the day. The moose, he must be still and patient. You see, if he is angry, if he makes himself known, he will be shot."

"But you're not a moose."

"No, but I have had to tread softly."

"Why?"

Sandy stared up at the ceiling as if pulling long-ago memories out of the air. "I was luckier than most. When I was a child, it was the time of residential schools. The aim of the schools was to teach First Nations children the ways of the white man's world, to prepare us children for life in the twentieth century. They were boarding schools, mainly run by priests and nuns. But some cruel things happened there. And I do not understand how these things could have been done in God's name. In the long run, I suppose humans do the best they can. And some humans are very good, and some are not."

Jody examined Sandy's face for some trace of fear or anger, but there wasn't any.

"I was supposed to go to the residential school when I turned seven," he said, "but when they came to get me, my mother was heartsick. She couldn't stop crying. You see, my younger brother and I were sick with tuberculosis. He had died three days before I was to go to the school. So, when the police came to get me, my mother, in a fit of hysterics, told the police that I was the one who had died. 'And my youngest, Alexander, he lies in the corner by the fire,' she said. 'He coughs and coughs all through the night. I pray and pray.' She didn't tell the police whom she prayed to. She didn't tell them of the healer's visits, of the herbs and poultices he used to heal us. But my brother died anyway. That's how I became Alexander, or Sandy. My name used to be Jacob."

Sandy sighed, his only hint of emotion, remembering his younger brother and the fear on his mother's face. "In any case, the police were reluctant to bother our family further, probably not out of respect for our suffering or concern for my health, but, more likely, out of fear of catching our illness. Tuberculosis was quite contagious and carried a stigma. At any rate, they didn't come back, and I stayed in my home for a few more years. The elders took the fact that I was passed over as a sign. They said I was meant to teach the ways of the Tutchone to the next generations, and they crammed as much learning into my head as they could."

Jody tried to imagine Sandy as a young boy, one of the kids in the museum's First Nations photos. Nope, she couldn't see it.

"I worked hard alongside my father. We trapped salmon and hunted elk. We smoked the fish and dried the meat that fed us through the cold, winter months. And he taught me . . ." Sandy stopped and stared into the fire, remembering his father and a time long ago. "He taught me to be grateful for the animals who sacrificed themselves so that we could eat. You see, we Tutchone believe that we are a part of the land and are united with all the creatures, and the plants, and even the stones. If you harm another, you harm yourself."

"That's a heck of a lot for a kid to take in," Jody said. "Are you sure you were only seven?"

Sandy's eyes took on a faraway look. "Meanwhile, my mother taught me the skills she knew. And my favorite lessons of all—our tribe's medicine person taught me how to heal with herbs, songs, chanting, and drumming."

Jody wrinkled her nose. "Did you ever have fun? Did you get to play? Did you—I don't know—did you ever get into trouble?"

Sandy shook his head. "Not much," he said. "The elders had placed a responsibility on my shoulders, and a Tutchone boy does not displease his elders. And remember—all my friends had been taken to the residential schools. Fortunately, I was a somber sort of child, so I didn't mind as much as you'd expect. The work was hard. The studying was hard. Living this far north is not comfortable, but for me this was paradise. I was free, and most important, I learned who I was: First Nation, Na-cho N'yak Dun, Tutchone."

The two of them stared into the fire without speaking.

<<<<>>>>

It was a beautiful Saturday morning—what Yukoners would call warm. The outside temperature was above zero centigrade, and a bright sun shone down from the sky. As often happened, Jody was watching Will's kids, and Sandy had made himself scarce.

Jody and Emberlee had baked a batch of muffins, and Emberlee was reading a book, waiting for the muffins to cool. Chioke sat on the floor happily banging on pots with a wooden spoon. Liam was practicing basketball with the makeshift hoop behind the cabin. And Jody was almost happy. 'I can do this. I'm watching the kids. Emberlee and Chioke like me. Liam and I are getting. . . are starting to . . . get along. I'm not useless.'

Meanwhile, the logs in the fireplace had burned down to embers, and the room became chilled. Jody poked at the embers. There was only one skinny log left in the hopper next to the fireplace.

"We need more wood for the fire," Jody called out to Liam.

"Get it yourself. I'm busy," he yelled.

Jody wasn't sure how to handle his sassing. "Then come inside and watch the kids for a minute," she finally said.

"They'll be fine," he yelled back. "They don't need a zookeeper. God, I'm so fucking tired of watching babies."

'Now what?' Jody couldn't let Liam get away with that. She knew it. But how she hated confrontation! She squared her shoulders, tried to sound as if she was in charge. "Liam, get in the house, watch your sisters, and watch your mouth. Your father would be furious if he heard you talking like that."

'Stupid, stupid,' she thought.

Liam mumbled something that sounded like "fuck" under his breath, but Jody wasn't sure she'd heard him right, so she chose to ignore it. "Thanks," she said instead, relieved that Liam had come inside.

Jody threw on a parka as she walked out the door. She stretched, looked up at the bright yellow sun and a blue cloudless sky, and smiled. She was coping with winter in the Yukon. And she was coping the kids. Her life was okay.

In the woodpile outside, there weren't any logs small enough to fit in the fireplace. She had to chop and split the larger ones—hard work, but she was getting better at handling the saw and axe. She sang as she worked and ended up with an armful of firewood which she carried back to the house.

Inside, she unloaded the logs into a hopper by the fireplace. She stacked rumpled papers and a pile of kindling on top of the dying embers, then poked at them until they sprang to life with dancing flames. 'I'm getting good at this,' she thought, as she carefully set three logs on top of the kindling. The house was quiet.

The kids were entertaining themselves, probably in the kitchen. Life was very good. Soon, the logs had caught fire creating a cheerful blaze, and the room was filling with warmth.

Jody got up and went into the kitchen to check on the kids. To her chagrin, Chioke was asleep on the floor, and Liam and Emberlee were nowhere in sight. "Liam, Emberlee," she called out, but there was no answer. Her voice woke Chioke, who began to cry.

"Hush, shh. It's okay. Don't cry." Jody picked up the baby and held her against her chest. She swayed in what she hoped was a soothing motion, trying to still the crying. But Jody was nervous, her movements were jerky, and the baby picked up on Jody's anxiety and kept on crying. "It's okay. Don't cry. Please don't cry." She found a pacifier and worked it into Chioke's mouth. Eventually, Chioke began sucking, and the cries turned into sobs, and finally into sighs and sucks. With Chioke on her hip, Jody called softly, "Emberlee, Liam, where the heck are you? If you're playing a game, it's not funny." She looked inside the one closet, under the bed, and everywhere else she could think of, calling the children's names all the while, but there was no answer and no sign of Liam or Emberlee.

Hastily, Jody shrugged on a parka, wrapped a blanket around Chioke, and stepped out of the cabin, still calling Liam's and Emberlee's names. She walked a few steps in all directions, but there was no sight of the kids. Even though the weather was warm by Yukon-in-winter standards, it was still too cold to be wandering the streets with a baby wearing indoor clothing and wrapped only in a blanket. Defeated, Jody headed back into the house. "I have to call your father," she said to Chioke. "And now he'll know I can't even be trusted to babysit."

She shouldn't have left the kids alone. But Liam was old enough to watch the younger children. Heck, he'd been in charge of Chioke and Emberlee before.

'I'm the world's worst babysitter,' she figured. 'The kids hate me. It had to be Liam's idea to pull this stunt and make me look like an idiot, but I thought Emberlee liked me.'

Suddenly, she realized how much worse it could be and almost threw up. What if . . . what if something truly horrible had happened?

What if someone kidnapped them? Maybe, the drug pushers that Will was after . . . in retaliation for something he did. No. If there'd been a struggle, she would have heard it. But snow tends to muffle sounds. How much time had she spent chopping the wood, anyway? It couldn't have been that long. No. Probably, they just ran away. Either way, she had to call Will. Reluctantly, she reached for the phone.

But before Jody could dial Will's number, the cabin door slammed, and Jody looked up to see Liam and Emberlee jostling each other aside to get the best place in front of the fire. Their shoes were soaked, and their parkas were streaked with mud.

"What happened? Where did you go? You had me worried to all get out." Then Jody hugged the both of them, even though she knew yelling was more appropriate.

"Chill, Jody," Liam spoke slowly as if talking to a three-year-old. "We just went out for a walk. We were hardly gone at all. It's no big deal."

"You weren't in the house. I was scared something awful had happened."

"We're sorry, Jody," Emberlee said. "We didn't mean to scare you."

"You left Chioke lying on the floor. You didn't tell me you were going. You didn't even leave a note. Nothing."

Liam tsked in disgust. "We're fine. And the brat was sleeping."

"You know, I'll have to tell your dad about this," Jody said.

That's when Liam's whole body tensed up. "Don't do that. He'll just go apeshit. You know how he gets. It's because he's a cop. God, I wish he was a trucker or a plumber or something. Maybe then he'd get off my case, give me a chance to breathe without—without me having to explain myself." He rolled his eyes. "We just went for a walk outside. That's all. Okay? Chioke was sleeping. If I'd picked her up, she'd have probably started crying. Anyway, you were right there. You'd have heard her if she woke up."

"Just out for a walk?" Jody asked.

Liam all but exploded. He banged his fist against the wall. He began to pace, and his voice was so loud it made Emberlee jump. "What is it with everyone? I take my sister out for a simple walk, and suddenly I'm a serial killer? Christ! It's like living in prison!"

Jody looked at Emberlee, who was staring at her shoes.

"Emberlee?"

Emberlee gulped. "It's like Liam says. We didn't do anything. I just got tired of being cooped up. It was my idea. Don't get mad at Liam."

Jody thought a minute. Emberlee was trustworthy. So, it was probably nothing. Besides, she was none too pleased at the idea of telling Will that she'd lost his kids. And—she hated to admit this—she was afraid of Liam's anger. "Okay," she said finally, "but next time, tell me you're going or leave a note." She smiled at Emberlee to take the edge off the conversation. "Now get those wet shoes and jackets off before you both catch pneumonia."

Liam scowled. "So, you trust little miss perfect, but I'm a liar?" He scuffed his shoe on the floor. "Figures!"

"Sorry." Jody sighed. Would she ever make any headway with Liam? She wished Sandy would hurry up and come home, but he was gone for another hour.

<<<<>>>>

The sun had already set by the time Will came to pick up the kids. Sandy was in the kitchen preparing a simple soup for supper, and

Jody and Emberlee were putting away the pens, scissors, and scraps of paper from Emberlee's art project. Will slumped into the cabin. He must have had a rough day. "Everything okay?" he asked.

"Just fine." Jody choked on the words, feeling guilty for lying to Will and even more guilty for letting Liam manipulate her.

As the kids got ready to leave, Will noticed their clothes. "Your jackets! Your shoes are soaked!" He looked at Jody. Then at Liam. "What did you do to your clothes?"

Liam rolled his eyes. His voice dripped of condescension. "Just chill, Dad. We were playing in the snow, and there was this puddle with slush and mud that we didn't see at first."

"Don't you ever talk to me in that tone of voice." Will stared at Liam. "And be more careful, for Christ's sake. You're not stupid."

Will shouldn't have snapped. He knew it, but he couldn't seem to stop himself. Earlier that day, he had dealt with one OD and two drunk kids who'd gotten belligerent. A quarrel ensued, and the two had pulled out their knives. It was a party gone out of control. Suddenly, a fourteen-year-old girl was in the hospital with stab wounds, thankfully minor, and two kids, who'd never been in trouble before, had arrest records. Will couldn't shake the fear that someday one of those kids, either the one in the hospital or the ones with arrest records, could be Liam. "Are you drunk? Is that what happened?" He leaned into Liam's face to smell his breath. The cop mentality had taken over.

"What's with you? I'm not a screw up. Why are you always accusing me of stuff I didn't even do? We had an accident in the snow. Okay? God!"

And now Will was furious. He was a peace officer, and his own son was talking back to him. 'I shouldn't even be trying to raise these kids,' he thought. Liam had been out of control ever since Emma had died. If only she were still here! Emma would know what to do. She'd always known what to do.

Will grabbed the shoulder of Liam's shirt. "First, you'll apologize. To everyone. Second, you're grounded. When we get home you're to march into your room and stay there until I tell you otherwise."

Liam pulled free. "This is Canada, not jail. I didn't do anything, and you've been acting like Cujo ever since . . ." He took a big, angry breath. "Ever since Mom died."

Will gasped out loud.

Jody picked up Chioke with one arm, and put her other arm around Emberlee who was shaking.

"You're a Mountie. You're supposed to be this good guy, this superhero, and because of you . . ." Liam poked his finger into Will's chest. "Because of you, my mother is dead. You're just a common murderer."

Now, Liam was shouting; he was out of control, a volcano of anger spewing words instead of lava. His hands were fists; his face had turned red; and his eyes had a glint of madness in them. "You're worse than any of the gangsters you arrested because,

because people look up to you, and you're really just, just this . . . this tyrant. They should lock you up."

Will grabbed Liam by the shoulder. "Don't you ever speak to me like that."

Liam wiped his nose with his sleeve. "Bully!" With all his strength, Liam slammed his fist into Will's stomach.

Will's face went white.

Then he slapped his son.

Before anything worse could happen, Sandy stepped between father and son, the two of them locked into some kind of macho battle. "We need to dry the children's clothing," Sandy said. "Emberlee, get the wet shoes and parkas and put them on the hearth to dry. Jody, we need another log on the fire. In the meanwhile, I'll make tea."

Sandy stopped and looked at Will and Liam. Will's face was still pale, and Liam appeared out of control and itching to fight. "On reflection, you had better stay for supper," Sandy said. He set the kettle on the stove, and when he spooned out the tea, Jody noticed that he opened two small canisters and added two scoopfuls of their contents into the teapot. Then he added a third scoopful.

<<<<>>>>

The next day, Will knocked on Sandy's door. "I'm sorry," he said. He fingered the hat he held in his hand as he spoke. Apologizing didn't come easily to Will. "I don't know what got into us. For the life of me, I can't seem to handle that boy lately."

"Can I make you a cup of tea?" Sandy asked.

Will nodded. Sandy put the kettle on the stove. Then two men settled themselves at the table, and Sandy waited for Will to speak.

"Those wet clothes—did you believe Liam's story about falling in the snow?"

"I question it," Sandy said.

"They were either playing in the creek or, more likely . . . they were exploring an abandoned mine."

"Oh."

"Sandy, I hate to ask this, but would you and Jody be willing to watch the children more often? I don't want to leave Liam in charge by himself any more than I have to."

"Of course. They bring sunshine to an old cabin and an old man." Sandy debated whether or not to say anything about Liam's outcry. Then the healer in him took over and he asked, "Why did Liam say what he did? Why did he say you killed Emma?" Sandy's voice was soft but commanding. No one refused an elder, especially if the elder was a medicine person.

Will's voice dropped low, and it was hard for him to get the words out.

"Because I did.

"Emma died the day that Chioke was born. I . . . I didn't get her to hospital soon enough. The weather was bad that night. Not a blizzard, but close.

"Dawson's hospital was overflowing with patients—far above capacity. I knew because, earlier, I'd worked on some of the car accidents that had sent patients there. And I knew that the power at the hospital had gone out, but not if it had come back on.

"Anyway . . . I was the one who made the decision. I decided we could deliver the baby at home. Our first two births went easily enough. We knew what to expect. I was so sure we could do it.

"If it were anyone else, I would have told them to get their act together and drive to hospital. If something goes wrong and you need to get help in a hurry, you don't want to deal with weather like what we had that night. But when you're a Mountie, when you're a responder, you figure that the precautions you take with everyone else don't apply to you. It's sort of a macho thing, I guess. Anyway, whatever it was . . ." He whispered the words. "It cost Emma her life."

He stopped, and his hands were shaking.

"The birth wasn't going well, but I was too thick to know it. Or maybe I didn't want to know it. I kept encouraging her. I made inane comments like, 'You can do it; it'll be okay; just a little bit more.' That sort of thing. Finally, I saw the blood, and that's when I packed her into my truck, and we headed for Dawson Emergency. But it was too late."

Will stopped. He turned away so Sandy wouldn't see him crying and wiped his eyes with the sleeve of his jacket. "She groaned a lot in the truck on the way down, and when we got close to the hospital, she began screaming. 'What?' I remember asking. I was concentrating on driving and not plowing into anything. 'I have to push. It's coming now,' she gasped, then screamed. So, I pulled over. And I delivered Chioke in . . . in my truck. I cut the cord with a Swiss army knife and clamped it with a hairclip. And I thought everything was okay. She was still bleeding, but we were almost there.

"And . . . and when I pulled up to the emergency entrance . . . She was so pale! Oh, Sandy, her face was almost white. And I remember her eyes; they had this funny, glassy look. And that's when I noticed just how much more blood she'd lost. I kept saying things like, 'Hang on, honey.' Stupid stuff like that."

Will tried to keep his voice steady, but it didn't work. "She was the most loving wife and mom, and just the best all-around mate, friend, and lover I could ever have hoped for."

And there was silence.

"Emma died soon after that. She'd lost too much blood. The doctors checked Chioke out and pronounced her amazingly healthy and beautiful. So, I left Dawson's hospital the next day with a brand-new baby and no wife.

"Chioke's the sunny spot in the middle of all that darkness. She never knew Emma, so she doesn't miss her.

"But the other kids . . ."

Again, Will turned away. Sandy slipped into the kitchen, then returned with two cups of tea.

"Emberlee is the peacekeeper, and she's made it her mission to make me happy and to smooth things out between Liam and me. She's only eight. Too young to take on the cares of a broken family. And she's always sunny. Always chirpy. But I can't help wondering if it's all a charade, an act that she's putting on for my benefit. I'm not sure if she's ever grieved Emma's death."

Sandy sipped his tea. "And Liam?"

"I don't think I've seen him smile more than a handful of times since Emma died. And he used to smile all the time. That grin was like summer in the mountains. And now he's this sullen, miserable . . . And he's so angry! All the time. You heard him. He blames me. Heck, I blame myself. One stupid decision."

Will sipped his tea. "And, yes, teenagers are supposed to rebel. But Liam? I don't know how to talk to the boy. I try to watch him, try to show up at the house when he doesn't expect me. Make him feel like my eyes are always on him. But sometimes . . . my job. People rely on me. I can't let them down, either.

"And now, just when I thought things couldn't get any worse, Steven Graywolf shows up at our house, and apparently, he and Liam have become fast friends."

"What about Steve? You seem to have some objection to him. He's always seemed like a fine boy to me."

"In the last few years, Steve's been in and out of trouble. Only minor mischief at first. Some drinking, ditching school, graffiti. That sort of thing. Then he 'borrowed' Jim Ogee's truck, took it into the back woods for a spin, and plowed it into a tree."

Will traced the rim of his teacup with his finger. "Steve ended up with a broken arm and a police record. He's three years older than Liam. Liam worships him. And now . . . well, it looks like Steve might be using meth. I have no proof—just the way he acts, the way he fidgets sometimes, and the way he turns his head away, as if he's hiding his eyes. But there's more meth around here these days. As a Mountie, I see so much of it that it's the first thing I suspect when anyone acts up. And I'd hate like hell to learn that Steve is using it, but it would flat-out kill me if he took Liam down that road with him."

Then the two men sat in silence, finishing their tea.

CHAPTER 6

A frigid wind ushered in the second hard storm of the season, again trapping Sandy and Jody inside the cabin. It cried with that horrible keening sound that made Jody want to stuff her fingers into her ears and run for cover.

On the third day of the storm, the wind died down, and the falling snow let up a bit; Jody decided to go out for more logs. She tugged at the door until it opened. The snowpack at her feet stood three feet deep. Outside, small trees and bushes appeared as white mounds with occasional twigs poking out from one side. She could barely make out the shapes of the mountains standing like tall giants watching from afar.

Breathing through cupped hands, Jody squared her shoulders and tromped to the woodpile. At least it was something to do. She came back, frozen through and through, with an armful of wood which she dropped into the hopper next to the fireplace. Then, shivering, she got as close to the burning logs as she could.

But as soon as Jody had warmed up, boredom set in. She looked at Sandy, who seemed content just to stare into the fire.

"Now what do we do?" she asked.

Sandy smiled. You've never been snowed in before, have you?"

"There's hardly ever snow in Pascagoula. Nor in Berkeley, for that matter."

Sandy chuckled. "In the Yukon, most babies are made during blizzards."

Jody wanted to laugh but she couldn't. "I didn't think I was all that spoiled, but we have a whole winter of this to get through."

"You are a writer. You should write."

"But when I worked for the paper, I had things to write about. I could read the newspapers, listen to the news on TV. We don't even have a TV here. And I don't really know very much about Canada. You can't just write about nothing."

"There is you. There is me. There is snow. There are your thoughts. There are the memories that you run from and the memories that would bless you if you could find them. That's hardly nothing."

Jody began pacing. "Don't you ever get frustrated?" she asked. Her voice was whiny. She couldn't help it. "Or angry, or . . . or anything?"

"Whenever I feel that life is unfair, I remember the residential school, and then I know my life is fine just the way it is."

"You said that you escaped getting sent to that residential school because they thought you were dead. What happened?"

"I did escape—for a while. And then, one day—I was ten years old, I think—they came for my brother. Instead, they found me, and I was taken to the school in place of my brother. They didn't question my age. Thankfully, I was not very tall back then. They believed that I was Alexander, and I've been Alexander, or Sandy, to this day."

He got that far-off look in his eyes. "You see, Jody, nothing lasts forever. Not the good times, not the bad times."

"Was it really that awful?"

"The priests taught us to read, to write, and to do basic sums. Things like that. But mostly, they taught us how to be white. We spoke only English. It was forbidden to speak our native languages or to practice our religions and customs, and we were severely punished for doing so. And, of course, we learned to be Christians."

Sandy's face grew serious. "I was luckier than most of the children in the school. Oh, life was hard—for all of us. But since I had entered the school at an older age, I was not so easily intimidated. Of course, I was whipped whenever I got too cocky, and, again, the few extra years helped me endure the beatings and . . . the other."

"What did they do?"

Sandy whispered the words. "There was sexual abuse as well." He sighed. "I learned then that sometimes it is right to question authority."

"Did they ever? You know. Did they ever do that to you?" 'What a horrible question to ask!' She blushed as soon as she realized what she'd said.

Sandy turned away.

"I'm so sorry." Jody wanted to put her arms around him but didn't think he'd welcome the touch.

He nodded ever so slightly. "Thankfully, it only happened to me three times. And . . ." Here he let out a long sigh. "And, the third time, after the pain, I received a great blessing."

"I don't understand. How could anything make up for . . . that?"

"Ah. You see . . . that day, I was in the basement. Father Thomas had beaten me, and . . . I was humiliated and angry. Because of the shame, I stared at the ground, unwilling to lift my head. And that's how I noticed it—a book lying under a rotting, wooden bench. Father Thomas was not looking. Curious, I picked the book up and stuffed it into my pants as I was pulling them up. That night, the moon was almost full, and I was able to make out the words on the page. It was *Treasure Island.* Excitedly, I turned page after page. After I had read the whole book from cover to cover, I started at the beginning and reread the whole thing."

Jody shook her head. "But a book seems like such a small thing compared to, you know, compared to . . . that."

Sandy did his patient, half-smile. "There's more, little one. One night, I reached under my pillow, and the book was gone. In its place, I found Jack London's *The Call of the Wild*. And next to it, precious as water, a flashlight. I never found out who my mysterious benefactor was. But every so often, there were other gifts waiting for me: history books, mathematics, Tolkien, chemistry, *The Little Prince,* astronomy, *A Midsummer Night's Dream.* I never knew what treasure lay under my pillow. It didn't matter. I read everything. Even if I couldn't understand it, I read it. And that's when I fell in love with the white man's learning."

He turned to stare into the fire. "The books saved me, and not just for the information they contained. I learned that all people are not the same; I found that, amid the stern priests and brothers who ran the school, there was someone who was willing to give a boy the gift of a book. That was a true miracle. It's how I came to know, without question, that there is a God. Perhaps He is the First Nations' Creator, perhaps the Christians' God, perhaps someone else's God. Probably a God greater than every God that human beings ever dreamed of—all put together. And the greater miracle was that they never caught me reading."

Sandy smiled. "We said the Lord's Prayer each morning in chapel. And sometimes I would pray, 'Our Father, Who art in Heaven,' and sometimes I would pray, so quietly that the brothers could see my lips moving, but could not hear the words I was reciting: 'Oh, Great Creator, whose voice I hear in the wind, whose breath gives life to all the world.'

Then Sandy and Jody stared into the fire, and for a long time, neither spoke. Finally, Sandy broke the silence with a long sigh. "We are one—I, the brothers and priests, you, your tormentors—we are entwined in some way that we do not understand. And my work is not to destroy but to heal and to teach. This is what the Tutchone elders expected of me after I left the residential school."

By this time, Jody had a lump in her throat. "But you were just a boy. And you were hurting. How could anyone expect you to do anything more than survive?"

"I could not have done it then. As you said, all I could do was survive. And for a long time, I was fearful and angry. But now, I can forgive, and I can teach Tutchone children the wisdom of our people. And God, or Great Creator, willing, I can help you."

"That's why you took me in?"

"We have to take in the wanderer. It is the way of our people—really the way of anyone who lives where the land is unforgiving. I had to take you in. Otherwise, you would have perished, and a piece of me would have perished as well."

CHAPTER 7

Jody tried to hide her fear of storms. She really did. But her startled jumps and the way she rocked back and forth as she sat before the fire—these motions betrayed her.

Sandy tried to help, but neither his herbs and chanting nor what he knew of western medicine and modern psychology seemed to make any lasting difference for Jody.

Now, Will's kids, they were good medicine for Jody. Sandy was sure of it. She was braver, stronger, happier entertaining Chioke and Emberlee.

Liam was another matter. He mostly kept to himself while he was at Sandy's cabin. He observed Jody from afar, and he made his own judgements about her.

<<<<>>>>

It all began with a broken pine branch. Winter was on its way out, snow was turning to slush, and green buds were beginning to peek up out of the snow. A final snowstorm blew down out of the north.

It wasn't that bad as storms go, but it was unexpected. That's what got to Jody.

Sandy was away when it happened, and Jody was minding Will's kids. The wind was fierce that day; it picked up debris and threw it around with the force of a bat against a baseball. It smashed a pine branch into the side of Sandy's cabin, and the sharp thud as the branch hit the wall made Jody scream.

Liam grinned. "You have a problem?" It was a sarcastic question.

"I can't help it. Storms make me nervous."

Liam gave a quick snort and sighed as if talking to someone retarded. "It's just a little old wind. We're safe in the house. That nasty old storm isn't going to hurt you."

"I know. I wish storms didn't bother me, but they do."

<<<<>>>>

A week later, the kids were back at Sandy's house. Sandy had left earlier, and Jody was alone when they got there.

"Morning, Jody. Are you feeling any better?" Liam asked as the kids walked through the doorway.

"What do you mean?"

"You were nervous last time we were here. Remember? Because of the storm. But the weather looks great today. So, you shouldn't be scared or anything." He smiled, and the smile was charming.

"Thanks for thinking of me," Jody answered. Maybe being open with him about her fear of storms had bridged some sort of chasm. She hoped this was the beginning of friendship with Liam.

"No problem," Liam said. "And I'm sorry if I was, well, you know. From now on, if you need anything, you can count on me. Promise."

On impulse, Jody hugged him—a quick peck of a hug. Teenage boys aren't usually keen on demonstrations of affections, but Liam didn't seem to mind.

After the parkas, mittens, and snow boots had been neatly stowed by the front door, Liam put his arm on Jody's shoulder. "I'm going outside to shoot some hoops. Okay, Jody?"

"Of course. Do you want to take your parka?"

"Naw. Just the boots. I'll be fine."

The weather was indeed kind. The snow had stopped falling during the night, and the wind had died down to a whisper of a breeze. More buds were beginning to show themselves in the trees and bushes.

Emberlee plopped herself down on the couch and was soon reading a book she'd brought. Chioke had a stacking game which kept her busy.

Jody had—wonder of wonders—nothing that she had to do. Sandy had given her a notebook earlier, and she decided it was time to try writing again: *There's a place in your imagination where mountains are made of cotton candy. Rivers really laugh,* and the air is so full of love you feel you could explode with a deep breath."

Jody used to write fairy tales with adult themes. This was the first time since her abduction that she'd let herself leave real life behind and step into fantasy. She looked up at the ceiling and realized that she was happy. Emberlee, Chioke, Sandy, they were her cotton-candy mountains and laughing rivers. She had a niche where she fit in, and people who loved—well liked—her. Even Liam was showing kindness. And Will—Will was becoming less of a wolf and more of a Great Dane in her eyes.

'Yukon weather may be harsh, but the people make up for it.' She turned back to her laughing rivers and wrote, "You live there, and you are a princess. Or a prince, or a movie star, or an astronaut. And you dream of the day you'll ride your white horse—or Harley Davidson—out of your Smurfy village to fulfill your destiny." Time passed in a dreamy blur as Jody's imagination wandered, and her pen recorded.

Until an explosion shook the cabin. It sounded like a thunderclap striking a foot away.

Jody froze. 'A bomb!'

Emberlee yelped, and Chioke started screaming.

A second shot blasted through the cabin. Jody picked up Chioke. She had to appear calm for the baby's sake, but Chioke could feel Jody's tense arms and pounding heart; The little one screamed louder. Was the cabin safer than outside? Jody couldn't think clearly.

A third blast sounded behind her.

Jody looked around for the source of the explosion. It was so loud, it seemed as if it were coming from inside the house, and she could smell that sharp, sulphury odor that accompanies gunpowder. With Chioke striding her hip, Jody reached her free hand towards Emberlee. "Let's get under the table," she said. It was all she could think of. She tried to take the girl's hand.

Emberlee shook her head, and her black braids bounced back and forth. "It's my dumb brother." She turned away from Jody and yelled at the air, "You're stupid, and I'm not scared of you." She had to yell over Chioke's crying.

"It's only my stupid brother," she told Jody. "He's probably shooting off cherry bombs."

Liam walked into the room grinning. Then he looked into Jody's face, and his eyes narrowed. "Don't try to tell me what to do," he said. He was breathing hard. "You can't boss me around." His hands clenched into fists. "You're not my mother; you're . . . you're a bloody bitch." His voice boomed, threatening as the fireworks. "Just stay out of my face or you'll be very sorry."

Jody stared. "Liam, I'm not . . ."

"Just watch your back. Because when you're not watching . . ." He bared his teeth. His face took on the expression of a savage animal. "That's when I'll get you. And I'll get you good." He pounded his fist against the wall. Abruptly, he smiled. Then he turned to Emberlee. "Just remember, no one likes a snitch." And he stormed out of the house.

Jody's face went white; she felt faint. She clutched Chioke to her breast, and the baby cried as if the world were about to end.

Emberlee patted Jody's shoulder. "Don't be scared. He didn't mean it. He's just a stupid boy. Stupid boys do dumb things like that." But Emberlee's rosy cheeks were not as rosy as they usually were. She took Chioke from Jody's shaking arms. "It's okay, small stuff," she said to the baby. "My brother's a poo-poo-head. Don't cry." She found a pacifier, worked it into Chioke's mouth, and rocked the baby until, finally, Chioke stopped crying.

"He didn't mean it," Emberlee said to Jody. "Can we make hot chocolate?" She patted Jody's arm. "You know—to calm our nerves."

"You sound like a grown-up," Jody told her, and the two went into the kitchen to find milk and cocoa.

The rest of the morning was tense. Emberlee tried to cheer Jody up, but it didn't work.

Sandy came in at lunchtime, and Jody asked for a cup of his magic tea. "Liam set off some firecrackers," she told Sandy. "And I'm still shaky." Sandy put his hands on Jody's shoulders, felt the tightness in her neck and back, and nodded.

<<<<>>>>

That night, when Will came to collect the children, he found Liam outside playing basketball by himself, and everyone else huddled around the fireplace. The mood was somber. Too quiet.

Will looked exhausted. Sandy considered not saying anything about the fireworks incident, but Jody was just too fragile. In short sentences, he told Will what Liam had done. "I've already talked to the boy, but it would help if you had a word with him as well. I can't allow this sort of prank to happen again."

With a sigh, Will called Liam inside the house. "Apologize," he said.

"Sorry, Jody and Emberlee. I was just having fun. I didn't know you'd get that scared." He turned to his father. "You should have seen her, Dad. She looked like she was watching the end of the world. It was only a few cherry bombs, not that big a deal. It was just a joke. Honest."

Will shook his head. "Not funny."

Liam sighed. "I didn't mean to scare you. I'm sorry."

"That's okay," Jody managed.

"Stay for dinner," Sandy said. Will didn't look like he was up to fixing food for the brood.

Will nodded, and he took Jody aside into Sandy's bedroom. "What is it? I've seen you grow terrified when the wind howls. You all but jump out of your skin at loud noises. Plenty of people are jumpy, but they get over it. You don't. Liam shouldn't have pulled that stunt with the firecrackers, but it was a kid's prank.

That's all. I hate to tell you this, Jody, but teenage boys do this sort of thing. In fact, they do a lot worse."

"It's silly, I know."

"Tell me." Will was wearing jeans and a Pendleton shirt, not his Mountie uniform. His voice was soft. He smiled with his eyes. He put his hand on Jody's cheek, and his touch felt warm against her skin.

"I can't help it. I hear wind, and I just know. Something's coming. I don't know what, but it'll be something bad."

"You've been hurt." Will wasn't asking. He was saying it.

"It's . . . I hear thunder, and . . . I can't explain it. Wind and thunder always mean . . . that . . . something . . ."

Will stayed silent.

"I can't explain. Please don't ask me."

Will's arm was around Jody's shoulder, and it felt strong, protective. "Nothing is going to happen to you. You're safe here."

"I didn't do anything wrong."

'Where did that come from?' Will wondered. "I know you didn't," he said. "You can tell me anything. You know that, don't you?"

Jody's mouth opened, but no words came out. She stared into Will's blue eyes and felt almost safe with his arm still around her. Almost. 'Face your fears,' she thought. 'That's what Sandy would have told me.' Jody took a breath. She searched for words, while images of flying tree branches and sheets of rain falling sideways swirled around in her head. "Every time I hear a loud noise . . ." She searched her mind for words to describe the churning sensations inside of her. Instead, her eyes filled with tears. She put her arms around Will and cried into his shoulder. "Someday," she said.

"Someday," Will echoed. "I'll be here when you're ready to talk."

As he held her, Will wondered about what Jody wasn't telling him and was puzzled. She had an air of innocence that seemed incongruous with someone clearly carrying serious secrets in her mind. Something was off, but he couldn't put his finger on it. She'd said, "I didn't do anything wrong." What was she denying? So many criminals had used that very phrase. But Jody didn't act like a criminal. Will's cop sense wasn't always on target, but he was right more often than not. For now, he held her as she cried, and he let his arms comfort her.

Because Will hadn't bothered to close the bedroom door, Liam had witnessed most of the conversation through the doorway. He couldn't make out all the words, but it didn't sound as if Jody were tattling on him. Mostly, she was whimpering and saying stuff like, "I can't explain." It was pathetic, actually. He saw Will put his arm around Jody's shoulder. Then he saw Jody wrap her arms around Will and cry, and the sight of the two of them touching set him off. He made a fist of his right hand. 'Oh, she'll pay,' he thought. 'Somehow, someway, she's gonna pay. She's not my mother. No matter what Dad thinks, she's not my mother.'

<<<<>>>>

After they'd eaten, Will and the children left. Sandy and Jody cleaned up the dishes, then sat before the fire watching the flames' hypnotic dances.

'I can't be this person any longer,' Jody thought. She looked at Sandy with questioning eyes. "Please, I need to know," she said. "After you left the residential school, you were hurting and angry. And you got over it. You went to college, and you were living in Vancouver when I first met you—in Vancouver among white people. How? How did you do it? How did you get over what they did to you at the school?"

"They were not all bad. But some were. And the system— taking children away from their parents, their homes, their friends—taking them away from everything they knew . . . That was very cruel. And some children died there." For a long time, Sandy just stared into the fire. His eyes took on a faraway look as if he were pulling memories from a long-forgotten pocket of his mind. "It was the Tutchone elders," he finally said. "They told me my anger served no purpose. And they said our people needed me."

"But how? What made the anger go away?"

Sandy smiled. "Anger doesn't just go away. Neither does fear. It can lie in your stomach for a long time. Sometimes for the rest of your life."

"But how? How did you do it?"

"The elders told me to go on a vision quest. As I said before, a Tutchone boy does not question his elders."

"So, you went into the forest and came back cured?"

"It wasn't quite that simple. I prepared for months before my quest, with prayers and acts of reverence to the Creator. Then the elders took me up to the top of a mountain. They left me no food and only a little water, and they told me to stay there for three days and then to come back to the village. I made a circle of rocks for protection, and I sat beseeching the Creator for guidance and for a vision. I can remember it even to this day. By the third day, my mind blurred, and I heard many voices. My white man's teachings tell me that I was hallucinating. My Tutchone training tells me that the world of spirits had opened to me. I think both are correct. 'Oh, Great Creator,' I said. I believe I said it out loud. 'I lay my anger and my fear before you. I beseech you. Take them.'

"Then I saw anger—black, wingless wasps the size of walnuts crawling on the ground around me, their stingers like small knives dripping venom. And I saw fear—yellow beetles with festering wounds. In this way, my anger and my fear were all around me.

"And then a herd of moose—the largest herd of moose I'd ever seen—they came towards me, and they began to eat the wasps and the beetles, until, one by one, all the insects had disappeared. Then the moose, all together, began to howl. One moose braying makes a deafening, roaring sound much like a wounded, dying bear, or more like a bear about to kill. Imagine a field of moose, too many to count, each making such a sound. I wanted to run. It all seemed real, and, in one sense, it was real. I almost did run. But the elders had told me to stay. So, I stayed. And when the moose had finished their braying, they vomited. The insects emerged dead, and from them appeared green sprouts. And I knew that I was to turn my anger and fear into healing."

"And after that?"

"After that, I returned to our village. Our tribe was poor back then, much poorer than it is today, and some of our people looked to the past and closed their eyes to the future. Others, however, thought someone needed to look forward, to learn what was happening outside our tiny village, and I was chosen. They gave me textbooks to read, textbooks on every subject you can imagine—everything the elders could get their hands on. I managed to obtain a scholarship, and our tribe provided money and everything else that I needed. And so, you see, that's how I was able to attend university, the University of Toronto. But after my first year, I was the one sending money, clothes, and medicine back to my people."

<<<<><>>>

That night, Jody dreamt.

Jody's Dream

Jody sits inside a circle of chattering stones. Laughing voices float in the air, and the stones are laughing too. 'They're laughing at me,' she thinks, mortified by the mocking voices. An angry wind picks up. It howls, throwing tree branches about with startling thumps. The wind's keening increases. Branches hurl themselves at Jody as if someone were playing a terrifying game of dodgeball.

And as she sits, a churning black cloud appears on the horizon, drawing closer and closer until she can see that the cloud is made up of wasps. Closer and closer. Finally, the cloud envelops her. Thousands of wasps buzz furiously. Jody flings her arms in front of her face, but it does no good. The bugs become tangled in her hair; they buzz in her ears, and they fly into her nose.

Jody tries to call out to an unseen God. And she knows He is there—just beyond reach. She tries to call to Him, but something flies into her mouth. She feels a crunching between her teeth. She reaches out to God.

But He is not there.

Jody woke screaming. A minute later Sandy was by her side. "I can't do this anymore, Sandy," she said. "You can't keep coming to me every time I have a nightmare, and I can't keep running from invisible boogeymen for the rest of my life. I don't think I have any great purpose like you do, but, somehow, I have to get over this. I'm not Tutchone, but if it takes sitting alone in the woods for three days, then I want to do it. I want to do what you did. It's not just First Nations. Gurus, hermits, as well as ordinary Christians, go into the wilderness to fast and pray. Christ and Buddha did it. In Spain, pilgrims walk the El Camino. In England, they trek to Canterbury. Muslims journey to Mecca, and Hebrews visit Jerusalem. When I was a student at Berkeley, I used to sit in this grove of oak trees and talk to God. Sandy, God used to be my best friend. I'll do whatever it takes." She bit her lip.

Sandy nodded. "You're ready. But, Jody, be aware. This isn't a reality television show. It's not a game you are undertaking. You're asking to meet God. And you do not know what He will say to you."

Jody shivered but did not lower her gaze.

After a while, Sandy told her. "Before you embark on this quest, prepare yourself. Begin with prayer. And remember, you are tougher than you think."

CHAPTER 8

Even in the Yukon, winter doesn't last forever. The day came when young crocuses and narcissuses peeked up out of the ground. Meadows bloomed and creeks sprang to life as chunks of ice cracked, groaned, and broke away to float downstream and melt under the warming sun. Flocks of birds chattered and sang, flitting from one tree to the next. Eggs hatched. Pups of all species climbed out of their mothers' darkness to squint into the light. Spring had finally come to northern Canada.

And Jody was ready for her quest. Half afraid, half excited, she hummed the theme from *Star Wars* as she loaded her backpack: water, flashlight, tarp, pen, and notebook. ("You're a writer. You must write," Sandy had said.)

Sandy watched Jody, and the white man's voice inside him wondered, 'Was this foolish?' The woods did contain wild animals. Sometimes people died in the forest. Not often, but it did happen. In the end, he lent her his knife. Then he told Will where

Jody would spend the three days of her quest and extracted a promise from him to check on her each day.

The quest began an hour before sunrise. Sandy took Jody to the spot he'd chosen. The trip involved a ten-mile car ride followed by a one-mile trek along a path made by wildlife through virgin forest. They didn't speak.

As they walked, Sandy's thoughts were prayers of thanks for the wonder surrounding him. He savored the scent of pine resin floating in the morning mist and the stillness, occasionally broken by the chatter of a waking woodland creature. This was Sandy's home, and he was at peace.

But as for Jody, she was struck by the wildness of the forest, and how small she was, how insignificant and vulnerable. She was truly facing her fears—three days alone, surrounded by unseen dangers. The air was warm, but Jody shivered, chilled with fright, as possibility became reality. She wanted to go back. She would face her fears another day.

Jody turned to Sandy, summoning the courage to ask him to take her home. She'd make the quest later on—after she'd said more prayers. She wasn't ready for this. She tapped Sandy's shoulders, and as he turned to look at her, she saw spiritual wonder, God's grace, reflected in his eyes. Sandy, the woods, this quest—they were all part of something beyond her understanding. She was not in control.

Sandy had told her, "A Tutchone boy does not displease his elders."

She understood and was quiet.

The trek ended deep in the forest. Aspen trees grew in a stand close enough together that the branches high overhead created a green ceiling with patches of blue sky and pink-tinged clouds peeking through their leaves. Dawn was breaking. A sunbeam shone through the leaves like a sacred light from the heavens. "Like my oak grove in Berkeley," Jody whispered, feeling a bit as if God were welcoming her. Sandy merely nodded. He hoped this spot would be sacred to Jody, but there were no guarantees. Not all quests were successful, at least not by mortal reconning. You couldn't demand that God give you a vision. Sandy said a prayer of protection and made a circle of stones (to humor an old man), and then he left.

Now alone, Jody prayed, "Our Father." Then, staring at the sky, she said, "This is my intention. To face my fears, and not let them control me any longer. Help me to be strong and brave and to do the work You give me to do. I ask this in the name of Jesus. Amen." After that, she recited some of the prayers she'd learned as a child and then talked to God as she would to a friend who understood everything inside her.

Time passed, and Jody's sense of fear and reverence subsided. Back in Berkeley, she used to talk to God as if He were her best friend, but she'd never sat with God for more than an hour or two. Now, she talked and felt a bit stupid. She sat still watching, listening, and letting her mind wander. Through the green canopy, she watched clouds drift by. She watched the ants, spiders, and other critters scutter around the trunks of the trees. Birds called, and crickets chirped. The odor of pine resin hung in the air like incense. All around her, the forest was alive with the beginning of spring. She justified her departures from the divine path by telling herself that all this beauty was God's doing.

And after several hours, Jody admitted to herself that she was bored.

Nothing was happening, and she was bored.

<<<<>>>>

Sandy hadn't been back to his cabin for more than a half-hour before the phone rang. "A couple of kids are missing," Will told him. "Jim Hanson's two boys, Kyle and Bobby. I'm part of the search team. What I need is for you to watch my kids. Can I bring them by later today?"

"Of course."

Will fed the children their lunch, then drove them over to Sandy's cabin. He kissed the girls "good-bye" and ruffled Liam's hair. "Be good," he told them. He turned to leave, then paused at the doorway. "Sandy?"

"Yes?"

He hated to ask the question, but it had to be asked. "How well do you know Jody?"

"We became friends on the internet." Sandy walked over to the doorway and lowered his voice. "Then she disappeared, and several months later, she reappeared in Vancouver. I know she's in some kind of trouble. Why do you ask?"

Will lowered his voice as well. "It's just that the drug problems in Dawson somehow increased at about the same time that she showed up."

'Interesting,' thought Liam. He pulled his Game Boy out of his pocket and leaned against the cabin wall, pretending to play while straining to hear what his dad and Sandy were talking about.

Sandy gave Will a patient smile. "Jody has spent most of her time here with me. She hasn't been away from the cabin long enough to make drugs or cause trouble. Besides, she's terrified of loud noises and almost everything else. She's not likely to run off to the woods to cook up a batch of methamphetamine."

"Except that she's out in the woods alone right now."

Sandy patted Will's arm. "Relax," he said. "She's harmless. I promise you. She's a victim, not a perpetrator."

Will left, and Sandy shook his head. Thank goodness Will didn't know about Jody having been drugged. Sometimes, having a Mountie in the family was more than a little inconvenient.

Sandy turned his attention to the children. Chioke was sitting on a blanket, while Emberlee dragged her around the cabin singing, *The Wheels on the Bus*. Liam was pulling a history book out of his backpack.

All was well.

<<<<>>>>

Later that evening, Sandy got a phone call from Will. "Can the kids stay the night?" Will asked. "We might be searching the woods until morning."

"Of course," said Sandy.

<<<<>>>>

Ten o'clock. The kids were camped in the front room of the cabin, with Liam on the couch and Emberlee and Chioke sharing Sandy's old sleeping bag. They hadn't brought pajamas, but that didn't seem to be a problem. Sandy took a last look at the sleeping children and went into the bedroom to read until he fell asleep.

As soon as Sandy had left the room, Liam's eyes popped open. He waited until he heard snoring coming from the bedroom, then tiptoed over to the corner of the room where Jody's spare clothes lay neatly folded on the floor.

'Not much to look at,' Liam thought to himself. He pulled out the clothes and, piece by piece, examined them, then threw them into a heap on the floor. But stuck inside one of Jody's socks, he felt something hard—money perhaps? He reached into the sock and pulled out a wallet-size ID card. Could he get her deported if he stole the card? Possibly. Liam tiptoe to the window to examine it by moonlight.

Jackpot! His eyebrows shot up. The name next to Jody's picture read Sonja Jordanson. 'Curiouser and curiouser,' Liam thought. 'I can use this.' He put the ID into the pocket of his jeans and looked around the room at the mess he'd made. 'Best leave the crime scene without evidence,' he figured and carefully folded the clothes into a neat pile just as he'd found them.

<<<<>>>>

Meanwhile, Jody was ready to give up on the whole idea of the quest and return to Sandy's cabin. Unfortunately, she didn't know the way back; she'd have to stick it out for the three days until Sandy came to get her.

In her notebook, Jody had written poems about ants and aspen trees. She'd started to write about being kidnapped and then decided to save that for another time. She wasn't up to thinking about it. The woods were spooky enough.

The forest grew cold after the sun set. 'I wish I'd brought more clothes,' Jody thought as she curled up under the tarp, pulling her jacket tightly around her. The vision quest was disappointing. A dumb idea. So far, she was cold, hungry, bored, and not any braver or more spiritual than when she had left Sandy's cabin. In fact, the woods scared her. Unseen eyes, claws, and fangs lurked behind trees and bushes. She was sure of it. She'd jumped and screamed countless times after hearing unidentified forest sounds. Were there poisonous snakes in Canada? And what about poisonous insects? For sure, Canada had bears. Bottom line, Jody wasn't brave. She wasn't Tutchone.

In spite of the cold and in spite of her empty stomach, Jody fell asleep, still hoping against hope for a dream of some sort— something significant or spiritual, just something to make the effort worthwhile. But when she finally fell asleep, all Jody dreamed about was a huge platter of poutine, a hamburger, and a hot fudge sundae.

<<<<>>>>

Will showed up at Sandy's house early the next day, looking exhausted but happy. "We found them," he told Sandy. "The kids heard a rumor about an old lady from Mayo finding three gold nuggets in the old Millstine's Mine, and they wanted some gold too. They said they needed the gold to buy a Game Boy because everyone else in their class had one." Will shook his head in disgust. "Anyway, they walked in far enough to get lost. Then, their flashlight went out, and they were stuck. Luckily, we found footprints at the adit where they had entered, and we were able to get to them before too much time had passed. They were cold, hungry, and frightened, but otherwise just fine."

Sandy sighed. "Emma and her friends went off searching for gold once when she was ten. Scared me to death."

Emberlee tugged on Will's sleeve. "Is there really gold in the Millstine's Mine, Papa?"

"If you ever even think about pulling a dumb stunt like that, you'll be grounded until your hair turns white. Those mines are dangerous."

"I was just asking."

"Anyway," Liam added, "you'd have to be pretty dumb to go into a mine without extra batteries."

Will considered delivering a lecture right then on the dangers of snooping in abandoned mines—getting lost, tunnels collapsing—but the kids had to get to school. "You two know enough not to try anything like that. I taught you better." And with that, the Campbells trooped out to Will's truck.

<<<◇>>>

"Day two of my quest," Jody wrote. "I'm supposed to face my fears. Well, here they are. I was hanging a protest sign on a freeway overpass. All I remember was their uniforms – dark blue and puffed out where a bullet-proof vest might go. They beat me, and grabbed me, and took me to some weird place that resembled a hospital. Sort of. Everything was fuzzy after that. The drugs made me crazy. Sometimes I'd want to chew my arms off; other times I just wanted to escape reality, go to sleep, and never wake up. At the end, I was tired to the point of death, and lying face up in a box the size of a coffin.

Maria saved me. She was a caregiver at the place; to me she was a pair of warm, soft hands in a frigid world. She took me to her home. For a while, she took care of me, but we both knew it wasn't safe for me to stay with her. So, I left my country and everything that meant anything to me, rode a bus to Canada, and ended up in Sandy's house." She paused and her mind simply turned away from the memory. Jody didn't fight it.

"Writing this is supposed to be cathartic, but—surprise, surprise—it's not. It's like swallowing bad tasting medicine that leaves a worse taste in your mouth and makes you feel sicker. Nothing is happening."

She took a couple of sips of water and stared at the sky and the clouds. 'They're puffy like marshmallows drifting through the tree branches. Marshmallows and hot chocolate. I could go for a cup of hot chocolate.' She picked up her notebook and wrote, "If Sandy and Emberlee showed up right now with a cup of hot chocolate . . . well, if they did, this whole quest thing would be almost okay. I don't see how Sandy could have spent three whole days praying and beseeching."

Jody waited for more inspiration to hit her. It didn't. She continued writing, following her train of thought. "Oh, shi . . . Oops! You're probably not supposed to curse when you're on a quest. Then, phooey! I wonder what the kids are doing now." A rustling sound somewhere nearby startled her, and she screamed—about nothing, as it turned out. And so it went until the sun turned crimson and dropped below the horizon.

Jody's Dream

Jody is a toddler wearing a thick, furry, pink pajama, complete with pink, fuzzy feet. She runs from Mommy to Daddy and back again, back and forth, over and over. Mommy is soft and whispery, and Daddy is so big and so strong that he can pick her up with just one arm. The house is cozy, dry, and smells of vanilla. Bright yellow light fills every space; it fills Jody with happy giggles.

Outside, the wind howls, and rain begins to fall. The storm grows louder and shakes the walls of the little house.

Then Daddy goes out into the storm.

"We have to be with Daddy," she whimpers, as the walls shake harder and louder. She puts two fingers into her mouth and sucks and sucks. "I'm scared. I want my daddy." She grabs Mommy's hand and pulls. "We have to go. I want Daddy." But Mommy won't listen. "Where are you, Daddy? I'm coming, Daddy. Wait for me." She yanks on Mommy's hand, then pulls Mommy's leg, trying to make her move. "We have to go find Daddy. He needs us." But Mommy won't budge. Jody tugs the door open and toddles out into the rainy night.

The house sits on the point of a peninsula jutting out into a turbulent ocean. A skinny, dirt path, only inches above sea level, leads to the mainland. As the storm grows ever fiercer, Jody walks along the path with waves breaking on either side of her—higher and higher until they splash her legs, then her stomach, and then reach up as high as her chest. Finally, the waves are taller than she is. They crash over her head, and she is walking under the water. She passes the lowest point of the path, still walking underwater. Now, the path begins to rise, and slowly she comes out of the ocean. Soaked by the water, all alone, walking the path to dry land, Jody feels nothing—no exultation for having beaten the storm, no fear, no pain, no sadness.

Jody feels nothing as she trudges on, alone.

Raindrops splashing on the tarp woke Jody from her sleep. She reached for her notebook and wrote down the dream before it slipped away from her, and then she kept on writing—about a time when she was almost four years old:

"Daddy had to fly to London for four days. I remember the storm that night. Winds howled like the goblins in my fairy tales, and I remember branches hitting the side of the house. I was scared. I told Daddy that he shouldn't go, but he said everything would be okay; only I knew it wouldn't be. He stroked my cheek and promised me he'd come back with a surprise. Then he left, even though I told him not to. No one ever listens to children.

"Four days later—and I knew it was four days because we'd made marks on the calendar, one mark for each day that Daddy was gone—four days later, he was supposed to come home. But he didn't. He promised he'd come back, and he didn't. Mommy was crying, and she told me he had died. I know that I screamed. A lot. And I remember Mommy telling me that God had taken him up to Heaven. And I just screamed. It was like all the good times were over, and the love in my life was gone. Like all my goodness was falling out of my heart, and I was going to dry up until I was nothing but hurting. I'd told him he shouldn't go, not even to be with God in Heaven. And I told God that He was a meanie for taking my daddy.

"And then everything was sad and awful. There were dreams, tangles of nightmares, about searching for Daddy. And in the end of it all, I dreamed that Daddy was up in Heaven watching over me.

"I remember His arms. Not Daddy's arms, but God's. It wasn't really God holding me, just the feeling of arms stretched out to hug me. And He told me everything would be okay. It wasn't really a voice. More like a feeling. That's when I knew that God would always be with me."

Jody looked at what she had written. Then she added, "Any halfway decent psychiatrist would say that, in my mind, I had replaced my father with God. But Sandy would say that God was there when I needed Him. And I would say that both are correct."

She'd finally done it. She'd faced her fear and triumphed. Jody felt light, almost giddy. The rain had stopped, and she was warm, even though the sky was still gray and somber with clouds that threatened more rain. She put away her notebook and lay on her stomach, content to watch a beetle climbing over tiny pebbles which were like boulders to it. Jody had completed her quest. Now she could lie, surrounded by aspens, until Sandy came to take her home.

<<<<>>>>

The clouds were full of unshed rain, and the sky darkened until it looked like dusk in the middle of the day. Jody looked up to see the first drops fall. They quickly turned into heavy rain and then a downpour. The dark sky was eerie. A flash of lightning and a clap of thunder made her jump and scream. Another lightning strike and thunderclap followed seconds later. Rain fell in sheets. Sharp cracks of thunder blasted all around her as more menacing flashes lit up the sky. Nearer and nearer. The strikes seemed to converge on Jody. Every so often, a lightning bolt hit the ground way too close for comfort—as if God were telling her, "So you think you'll never be afraid again? You're insignificant and powerless, and I can strike you down dead at any moment."

Jody knew that lightning tends to strike tall objects such as the aspens which surrounded her. She considered running, but there was nowhere to run to, and trees were everywhere. Anyway, Sandy had told her to stay in the circle, so that's what she did.

And then a bolt hit just a few meters away from her. The thunder was so loud that the aspens surrounding her shook, and she could smell the sharp odor of electricity. Panicked, she screeched at the top of her lungs, and her voice echoed through the menacing forest along with the thunderclaps.

"It's too hard!" she yelled at the sky, and her terrified heartbeat pounded in her ears. "Why me? I did what I was supposed to do." Suddenly, she found herself yelling, not in fear but in anger. "Find someone else to throw lightning at. I thought You were my friend," she screamed at God. "Some friend! So, kill me. I dare You. Love your enemies. Forget it! Forgive your enemies. When hell freezes over! I don't, and I won't. I hate the bullies who held me. And . . ." Such anger poured out! Anger she didn't know she was capable of. "And I hate You for letting them, and for siccing the lightning on me. And I hate You for taking Daddy."

As the storm continued to threaten, Jody continued to hate everyone, including herself and God.

Then her body trembled as she cried.

And then she slept.

<<<<>>>>

Meanwhile, Will watched the storm worsen and phoned Sandy. "I'll get Jody. You shouldn't be out in weather like this."

Sandy didn't argue. The rain was pouring down by buckets, and Sandy's arthritis was reminding him how old he was. "Leave the kids with me," he said, "and I'll have dinner ready when you get back. We need a celebration now that Jody has completed her quest."

So, Will set out into the forest. He found Jody writing in her notebook, with the tarp protecting the pages from becoming soaked.

"Ready to head back?" he asked. Jody nodded and packed up her things. Then the two of them began the walk back to Will's truck as the wind whipped the trees into frenzied swaying, and the rain poured down on them.

They walked, not speaking until they reached Will's truck, and Jody sank into her seat, grateful to be out of the cold and wet.

"What's your story?" Will asked. "Why did you feel compelled to make this vision quest?"

"Because I'm tired of being scared all the time," she said simply.

"What are you afraid of?" he asked.

"Nothing."

"And are you still afraid?"

Jody looked out her window watching the rain and the swaying trees. "Yes, but it's different. Just now, I walked through the forest during a storm. The sky was almost dark, and the wind was blowing like invisible monsters loose in the woods. And even though those monsters were loose inside my head all the while, and they're still loose inside me now, I'm okay."

Will lowered his voice. "You faced your fear."

"And there's something else."

"Something else?"

"I . . .I need to do something besides mooching off Sandy. He doesn't complain, but it feels wrong. He's . . ." She wanted to say that Sandy was dying, but she wasn't sure if Sandy had shared that information. "Well, he's old, while I'm perfectly strong and healthy, and I should be doing something."

"So, what do you want to do?"

"Back in the States, I used to write for the *Upstart Gazette*. Sometimes, it was frustrating when I had a deadline and couldn't think of anything. But most of the time, something would pop into my head, and I'd worry and fuss over it until I came up with a crazy twist. Then I'd read over what I'd created, and when it worked, that was heaven. And the best part was knowing that someone read my story and liked it. Or maybe they hated it. Either way, my readers knew I existed. Most people are starving for that."

"True."

"Sandy told me to write during my quest. So, I wrote. At first, my writing was all garbage, but on the third day, I wrote about a dream I had, and reading it made me cry. I'd forgotten how satisfying it is to come up with stories that mean something, and to find words that paint pictures, and to make up phrases that sing.

"Well, I want to write something, send it to the *Whitehorse Star,* and see if they'll print it. I guess I'll have to submit it under Sandy's name. I don't think he'll mind."

Will's cop's ears perked up. So, Jody didn't want to use her own name. He remained quiet.

"Anyway, the storm terrified me. I wanted to run away, but there was nowhere to run to. I stuck it out. Not because I was brave, but because I had to. And then I got angry, and then . . . At first, I was angry at the lightning, and then I was the lightning. I mean not really, but . . . but it was as if a power within me was a reflection of the lightning's power. And then it was just beautiful. It was raw, powerful, and majestic. To me, that was a miracle."

"I hate storms," Will said. "They always spell trouble. For Mounties, severe weather means looking for lost hikers, pulling stranded motorists out of ditches or snow piles, and helicoptering heart-attack victims to hospitals when it's dangerous for the copters to fly."

And then the words just shot out of his mouth. "My wife died during a killer storm." Will hadn't meant to say it. It was too raw, too personal. He turned his head away. "So, no, I don't see beauty in lightning; I see devastation, heartache, and long, cold, lonely, wet nights which I should be spending with my kids."

Will stopped. He'd meant for Jody to talk about herself, but somehow, the conversation had gone off track. He steered it back to Jody. "Why did storms scare you so much?" he asked. "Did bad weather have anything to do with you leaving the States?"

"In a way."

"Tell me about it."

"It was raining, and the wind was blowing . . ." Jody stopped talking, wide-eyed. She looked at Will, like a startled moose staring into a set of headlights. "Nothing," she finally said.

"What are you scared of?" Will asked softly.

"Nothing."

"You're scared of something. It's written all over your face. What are you running away from?" Will's voice turned hard. "Is it the law? Are you running away from the law? Tell me about it now, and I can help you. But whatever you're hiding, the Mounties will figure it out eventually, and when they do, it'll be too late to ask for leniency. It's a cliché, but it's true: the Mounties always, always get their man. And they get their woman too."

Jody froze. The people who'd captured her had worn uniforms. And Will was a Mountie. Did he have to side with the uniforms? Would he have to turn her in? "I don't want to talk about it," she finally mumbled. Then she stared into Will's eyes. "I didn't do anything wrong. I promise."

"Because if you cause Sandy any trouble—any trouble at all—so help me . . ."

"I'd never hurt Sandy. Right now, he's my best friend." She stared straight into his eyes. "I didn't do anything wrong. I promise. And I'm no threat to Sandy. But I can't tell you about it. I'll probably never be able to talk about it. You'll have to trust me."

Will was used to interviewing criminals and spotting liars. His cop's sense was usually right on. Usually. He believed Jody. His voice softened. "You have to trust me too," he said. "The law is here to protect you, not to hurt you." Will smiled, but he knew it was too late. He'd already said the wrong thing. He'd pushed too hard; he'd come on too strong. "Okay, let's leave it alone. You said you wrote for . . . a newspaper, was it?"

Jody nodded. "The *Upstart Gazette*. About environmental issues mostly, but I made them into fairy tales. I made my readers laugh, and I made them think. Then I got political, and that's when the trouble started."

Abruptly, Jody stopped talking. She didn't want to say anything about herself anymore. "Why did you become a Mountie?" she asked.

"I wanted to be the good guy. Make a difference. Help people." He shrugged. "Especially the kids," he said. "Some of them have it rough. If I can say or do something to help one of them, well, that's a good day. Unfortunately, those good days are rare."

"Do you have any good cop stories?"

"There was one kid, Ricky. Not the sharpest nail on the workbench, but he had this heart that wouldn't quit. Only he was always helping the wrong guy, and he was always the one we'd catch. It was just little stuff—shoplifting, graffiti, that sort of thing. So, before he could get into real trouble, I got him a job after school helping out our local vet, Doc Loman, and it kept him out of harm's way. Plus, he got to be with all those animals."

Then Will took her hand and squeezed it. His touch was warm, comforting. And then, in Jody's eyes, Will was no longer the frightening goliath of a Mountie. He was just Will.

<<<<>>>>

Will and Jody approached the cabin laughing. He had his arm on her shoulder, and she was holding her water bottle up to his mouth.

Staring through the window, Liam watched the two of them. He slammed his fist against the wall. He wanted to slam it through the windowpane. He wanted to throw something. Break something. No, he wanted to hurt someone. Hurt his dad. Hurt Jody. Mostly, he wanted to hurt Jody. She wasn't his mom. She wasn't good enough to take his mother's place. No one was good enough, and Jody, especially, wasn't good enough. He'd do it. He'd hurt her. He'd cause her as much pain as she was causing him right now.

'I'm gonna get you so good! Just wait.'

CHAPTER 9

Will was dropping the kids off at Sandy's more and more often. The whole childcare scene—snacks, homework, playtime—it was all becoming familiar to Jody. She knew the kids. She knew how to rock Chioke when she'd start to cry. She knew to put a note under Emberlee's sandwich. And she knew that Liam liked the homemade treats that she and Emberlee made, and that he usually wanted to be left alone. One day, Jody had tried shooting hoops with him, but that was an uncomfortable hour, and Jody never did it again.

Chioke was trying to walk. She'd pull herself up by grabbing a chair leg. Her cheeks would turn red, and she'd get up to a standing position, then plop back down, usually landing on her bottom with a startled expression on her face. Her mouth would make an "O" shape, her eyes would get big, and then she'd let out a short giggle and try again.

One afternoon, Chioke was pulling on the chair leg, determined to get that standing thing right. It was nap time, and she was a tired, grumpy baby. As she pulled on the chair leg, her hands slipped, her face bumped into the chair, and she started howling. Jody swooped Chioke up in her arms and held her tightly to her chest until the sobbing stopped. "It's okay," she said and kissed the rosy cheeks. She moved Chioke to her left hip and poured soymilk into a sippy cup with her free hand. "Here you go," she said. "You're okay. There's nothing that we can't fix with a cup of milk and a cookie." A batch of chocolate chip cookies sat in a jar on the kitchen counter, and Jody replaced the sippy cup in Chioke's hand with a cookie.

"Mama."

Jody was so startled that she almost dropped the baby. Surely, she hadn't heard it right. Had Chioke really called her, "Mama"?

"Mama." She said it again. This time, there was no mistaking the word.

Emberlee ran over to her side. "Did you hear that? She called you Mama!" She kissed the baby on her forehead. "Did you just say Mama? You're so smart. Yes, you are. Wait until Papa hears this!"

Liam grimaced and stared at his Game Boy, working the buttons and pretending that everything was normal. 'She's not your mama,' he thought to himself. 'You don't even know who your real mama was. But I know. And Jody's not getting away with this. Not ever.'

Will came home to a grinning Jody and a bouncing Emberlee.

"Chioke said, 'Mama.' We heard her. She called Jody, 'Mama'." Emberlee hopped around, proud to be the one to report the news to her father.

<<<<>>>>

Only a few nights later, Will walked into the cabin with a bottle of wine in his hand. Sandy and Jody had been babysitting and they planned on the Campbell clan staying for dinner. Jody had already set the table and was about to put Chioke into her highchair; but before Jody could reach her, Chioke pulled on the chair leg until she stood upright, and then she . . . let go. She gave a quick bark of a laugh. 'Look at me,' her eyes seemed to say.

"She's standing!" Jody made "bring it here" gestures to Sandy. "Quick, get a camera. She's standing by herself." Jody clapped. Emberlee clapped. "You're the smartest baby ever!" Jody said. Chioke took a step forward, and another. Then plop, back down on her bottom. And then she smiled, happy for all the attention surrounding her. She must have done something wonderful. Everyone was looking at her. She was brilliant. She didn't know the word, but she knew she was brilliant.

Sandy disappeared and came back with a Polaroid.

It didn't take too much coaxing to convince Chioke to try it again. Emberlee and Jody held Chioke's hands while Sandy stood ready with the camera. Then they let go. The first picture came out a blur, but the second was a perfect candid of Chioke standing all by herself and laughing.

Sandy trimmed the photo to wallet size and handed it to Will. "Here you go, proud Papa," he said.

Will stared at the picture of his youngest. "Soon there'll be no stopping you, little one." He turned to Sandy. "Remember when Liam learned to walk? I swear that kid went from crawling to running in the blink of an eye. Back then, it was all Emma and I could do to keep track of him." He pulled out his wallet and loaded the new photo of Chioke into it.

"Ooh, can we look at your pictures?" Emberlee asked.

"You've seen them before."

"I want to see them again. Please?"

Will handed Emberlee his wallet, and Jody, Sandy, Will, and Liam crowded around her as she slowly flipped through Will's collection.

There was a toddler photo of Liam with birthday cake smeared across his face and another of him about ten years old, standing chest-high to Will with a fishing rod in one hand and a trout in the other. Next came a picture of Will with his arms around a beautiful woman.

"Mama was so beautiful," Emberlee whispered.

Jody bent forward to get a closer look. So that was Emma. She had Sandy's dark eyes and bronze skin. Her thick, black hair fell loosely over her shoulders, and the vest she wore was intricately decorated with beads and fringes.

The next photo was of a baby about Chioke's age asleep in Emma's arms. "That's me and Mama," Emberlee said.

Will ruffled her hair. "That's right, Kit-kat."

'She was made for motherhood,' thought Jody. 'So relaxed. She's in her element.' The hint of a smile on her lips said it all.

A snapshot of Emberlee followed, riding a tricycle, with her mouth wide open and her cheeks the brightest pink Jody had ever seen on anyone.

The last picture in the wallet was of a mountain meadow surrounded by brilliant splashes of autumn's orange and crimson leaves. A stark, black, snowcapped mountain stood behind it with auburn streaks highlighting the folds in its sides. 'Primitive. That's the sense I get,' Jody thought.

But something was missing from Will's wallet. Then Jody realized that, until this evening, there were no new pictures in the wallet. The one they'd just taken of Chioke was the only one Will had of her.

Sandy took the wallet and handed it back to Will. "Now we eat," he said.

After they'd finished dinner, Sandy, Liam, and Emberlee cleared the table, then washed and dried the dishes, giving Jody and Will a chance to drank coffee and talk.

"That picture in your wallet—the one of the mountain— what's special about it?" Jody asked. "I mean, it's not that beautiful, at least not by Canada standards, but there's something about that photo."

"That's Mt. Frank Rae. No big deal really. Just a place I like to go." Will stared at the ceiling. "Sometimes."

"And you keep a picture of it in your wallet?"

"Well, yes."

<<<<>>>>

Liam's worst nightmare was becoming reality. It was obvious that Jody and Will were starting to like each other. True, they had few chances to be alone together. Still, there was a lot of unnecessary handholding and funny looks between the two of them. When they were together, they seemed happier than usual, and they laughed a lot, even when there was nothing funny to laugh about. They just acted . . . wrong. And every time Liam saw them together, it was like getting gut-punched.

When Will was around Jody, he acted the same way that Steve did around Melissa Backman. Steve had admitted that he had it bad for Melissa and couldn't wait to nail her. And Steve knew what he was talking about. At the ripe age of seventeen, he'd already gone steady with four girls, not counting Melissa, and had had enough sex to understand romance.

Liam, on the other hand, at fourteen, was a virgin who still got tongue-tied talking to members of the opposite sex. But there were a couple of girls at school who made it hard for him to think straight, and his stomach turned to mush when he saw them. So, he figured he knew what his father was going through.

Well, he had the goods on Jody. First, he'd give his father a chance. That was only fair. He'd have a talk with his dad, man to man. He wouldn't shout. He wouldn't call his father an idiot or anything. He'd just lay out the facts and explain that Jody was untrustworthy, and the sooner they were rid of her, the better.

The best time for an important talk was after Chioke and Emberlee were in bed. Liam waited for the end of Emberlee's bedtime story and prayers before approaching his father. "Dad, can we talk about something? Man to man?"

"Of course, Son. What's on your mind?"

Liam felt ever so mature as he opened the door to his bedroom, and the two sat down on Liam's bed.

"It's about Jody, Dad. She's bad news. She acts all innocent and sweet, and she bakes cookies and plays with Chioke, but . . . but she's lying. She a fake, and, and . . . and . . . she doesn't really like any of us." He had meant to say his piece calmly and rationally. Instead, his voice cracked and got louder and louder while his brain seemed to fly around the room like a mosquito. He threw his hands up into the air, frustrated. "It just makes me sick!"

"Why do you say that? What did she do?" Will was frustratingly reasonable about it all.

"She's a fake. She's a criminal. And you should lock her up without any possibility of parole." This was Liam's chance. He strolled over to his closet and flung open the closet door with a touch of drama. He rifled through the pockets of his jeans, ready to take out the fake ID. Then it would be bye-bye Jody, and Liam would have his family to himself again. His mother would have been proud.

Five pairs of jeans hung in the closet. The ID wasn't in any one of them. He kept searching through the pockets but couldn't find it. Had it fallen out somehow?

Liam choked. He opened his mouth to speak, but his brain was a tangled mess. 'Think fast,' he said to himself. His mind didn't cooperate. "It's just . . . You don't get it." He threw his arms into the air again and looked around the room, desperately hoping for the ID to magically appear by his pillow or on his desk. 'Say something, anything,' he thought. "You know, Dad, how you're a Mountie and everything. And sometimes, you just know. You can tell by looking at the criminals that they're criminals, and they should be locked up. Well, I'm your son, and I have the same . . . power . . . or whatever you call it." His voice trailed off. 'So lame!'

Will put an arm around Liam, and Liam didn't shrug it off. "It doesn't work that way. I might have suspicions or misgivings about a suspect, but I need hard evidence, proof that the person has done something illegal, before I arrest him or her. And sometimes I'm wrong." Will furrowed his brow as he searched for the right words. "It's why we have a court of law. It's why we have trials. But you know that." Will stood up. "Did Jody do something? You can tell me."

'Make something up. Lie,' Liam thought, but all he could come up with was a mental image of her kissing his dad. He shook his head.

Will squeezed Liam's shoulder. "We can talk more about this later. I need to get some things done before I turn in tonight. Thanks for the talk." And with those parting words, Will walked out the door.

As soon as Will left, Liam tiptoed through the house to a small room that housed their washing machine and clothes dryer. He looked inside the dryer, and sure enough, he found a pair of his jeans there with Jody's ID in one of the pockets. Liam shrugged. Well, he'd just have to move on to Plan B for getting rid of Jody.

As soon as he figured out what Plan B was.

<<<<>>>>

Meanwhile, Will was mulling over his conversation with Liam. Should he be trusting Jody with his kids? Was there actually something wrong with her, some clue that he was missing? She'd been through a lot, and there was a mystery about her. That was for sure. Still, his Mountie's instinct said Jody was basically a good person. And, yes, he was beginning to have feelings for her. Thinking about Jody made him smile. Was he letting his feelings cloud his judgement?

Well, before he let down his guard, before he allowed himself to get any more serious about Jody, Will resolved to try to get her to talk about her past one more time. After all, he had the kids to consider. They'd already lost one mother. He didn't want them getting attached to Jody and then having their hearts broken all over again.

Puzzled, Will stared at the ceiling. Was that what Liam was trying to tell him? That he was afraid of loving Jody and later getting hurt? No, Liam's dislike for Jody was genuine. So, what was that kid trying to say? Was this normal teenage angst or something more? If only Emma were around to interpret! Did Liam equate liking Jody with being disloyal to Emma? Is that what Liam was trying to say? Will should have asked, 'Is this about your mother? Is that what this conversation is all about?' Oh well, it was too late now. He'd ask the question later if the opportunity arose. Damn, but understanding a teenager was hard!

<<<<>>>>

The kids had spent the afternoon at Sandy's. On his way to pick them up, determined to find out what was going on with Jody, Will rehearsed what he'd say to her. He was a Mountie, for heaven's sakes. It was his job to get people to talk, and he was good at it. He entered Sandy's cabin and walked straight over to Jody, shoulders back and a set look on his face. "We have to talk," he said. He took Jody's elbow and steered her out the door while Liam watched anxiously from the window.

"You're entitled to your privacy," Will said, "but I have Liam, Emberlee, and Chioke to think of. I'm trusting you with my kids, for God's sake. Do you have any idea what that means? I'd walk through fire to keep them safe. Tell me what's going on with you. Whatever trouble you're in, I can help. But, if you're in danger or if you broke the law, I have to know. I have to protect my children."

"I didn't break any law." Jody took the slowest of breaths. "Okay. Here goes." She looked up into Will's eyes.

'A good sign,' thought Will. 'Usually, liars don't look you in the eye unless they're really good at it.'

"You have to know," she gulped, "I'm not brave. If I'd known what was going to happen, I wouldn't have done what I did. I never would have said anything, or written anything, or posted anything. But I have this thing about . . . about . . . I can't stand it when people lie. Especially people who are supposed to be our leaders, the good guys. Or maybe I would have done it anyway."

"What exactly did you do?"

"I . . . hung signs."

"And?"

"That's all. I hung signs. Over the freeway."

"What was on the signs?"

"I was protesting the war. And on the internet, I called my president a liar. I said he was torturing prisoners. I said that he was lying about anthrax, and that Osama bin Laden couldn't have been responsible for the poisoned letters."

"And?"

"No 'and.' That's it. Except that no one else was saying those things." She hung her head. "And when I hung the last sign, they grabbed me."

"Who are *they?*"

"They had uniforms. They looked like cops. That's all I know."

"That's why uniforms terrify you?"

She nodded.

"Did they have warrants?"

"I don't know."

"So, they took you down to their station."

"No. They took me somewhere, but it wasn't a station."

"So, they weren't police. They were thugs posing as police?"

"Maybe. I don't know."

"How did they know where you'd be?"

Jody shrugged.

"Who knew you were hanging the signs?"

"Just my internet friends: Sandy, Spiderman, Shadow, and Brat. Except for Sandy, I don't know their real names. Oh, wait. Spiderman's real name is Homer Perlman."

"Homer Perlman?"

"It was his idea to hang the signs."

Her story was hard to believe, but Will hid his skepticism. "Then what happened? What did they do?"

"Mostly, they drugged me and asked me who'd been talking to me. But I hadn't been talking to anyone. And then . . ." Her eyes filled with tears.

"And then what?"

Jody shook her head. "They beat me up. And then they left me for dead. Inside . . . I thought it was a coffin." Jody blurted it out. And then she shivered and began crying in earnest.

That's when Will allowed himself to believe her story, to allow himself to love her without holding back. In his role as Mountie, he'd seen plenty of tears, but they'd never affected him this way.

"They thought I was dead. And . . ." She couldn't finish the sentence.

"Shh. It's okay. I'm here. I'll stand by you, protect you, keep you safe. I promise." Will wrapped his arms around Jody, as she kept on crying. And his arms felt so comforting that she wanted to hold on forever. Finally, she wiped her face on his shoulder. "Sorry," she said. She kept her arms around him and held on tightly.

"Does your family know you're here? There must be people somewhere worrying about you."

"I was thinking of writing to my mother. To let her know I'm okay. I have a few friends back home; no one who's going to worry about me. But I'm scared to contact Mom, even by snail mail. If the wrong people find out I'm alive, they might try to kill me."

She stared at the ground thinking, 'Or, for that matter, they might kill Sandy, or Will or the kids.'

Jody shrugged. "So now you know all of it."

'Not all,' thought Will. 'Something's still missing. Please don't be lying because I'm falling in love with you, and I'm falling hard.'

<<<<>>>>

It was unexpected. Will showed up on a Saturday morning, his time off work, which he normally spent with the kids.

"Can you watch the munchkins for a bit, Sandy? I want to show Jody something."

"Of course." Sandy held his arms out to Chioke. "Come to Grandpa, small one."

Will kissed her cheek and handed her over to Sandy.

"What's this about?" Jody asked.

"Just a bit of an adventure."

Emberlee tugged at Will's sleeve. "Can we come too?"

Will shook his head. "Not this time."

"Please. Poppa." She looked up at him, smiled, and wrinkled her nose. It was endearing, and she knew it.

"Sorry, Kit-kat, this trip is just for Jody and me." He hugged Emberlee and clapped Liam on the shoulder. Then he and Jody left.

"Where are we going?" Jody asked.

"It's a place at the foot of the mountains, somewhere special to me. If I were to make a vision quest, it's where I'd go."

A short drive brought Will and Jody to Tombstone Territorial Park.

"You're up for a short hike, aren't you?" he asked. He'd packed a picnic backpack, and he slung it over his shoulder.

Jody nodded, and Will guided her down the road and onto a path that had probably been made by bears or moose. Soon, she found herself standing in the middle of a meadow. Here and there, pale shoots and grassy spikes poked their way through the slushy ground. And she got the strangest feeling—as if she'd seen the place before. Which was impossible. And then she remembered.

"It's the photo in your wallet." Jody looked up at Will. "This is your place, isn't it?"

Different season, different colors, but Mt. Frank Rae still towered in the background, its ebony slopes capped with snow. In the distance, creaking and groaning sounds of ice boulders breaking away from larger blocks announced the end of winter.

She took a deep breath. "It smells like wet grass and pine trees. If I were Tutchone, I'd say that the Creator lives on top of that mountain."

Will took Jody's hand, and they wandered across the meadow until they came to an almost- dry, grassy spot several yards above a creek. Chirping birds and splashing water filled the air with music.

"This place is special to me," Will said. "I'm not spiritual like Sandy. This meadow is as close as I'll ever get to God."

He unzipped his backpack and removed a hand-stitched quilt. "More comfortable than a blanket," he said. "You've been hurt. This is the best place I know to heal."

Jody sat down on the quilt, while Will unpacked a bottle of white zinfandel, still chilled, and two plastic wine glasses. He poured the wine. "To us," he said, raising his glass. "To good times in our future."

He sipped his wine. "I brought cheese," he said, "brie, cheddar, and Swiss, and bread to go with it." The bread was a crusty French baguette, carefully wrapped in a towel and still warm. It smelled yeasty, as if it had been baked only hours ago.

Jody tasted her wine and smiled. "Heaven, I think," she said as she stared into Will's deep blue eyes. She'd always been a sucker for blue eyes.

Will had also packed a tub of berries and another of whipped cream. "And no picnic is complete without chocolate," he said, holding out two mocha truffles. "I'm a bit out of practice." He was blushing. "At picnics, I mean. I haven't been on one since Emma . . ." He stopped abruptly, then busied himself slicing the bread with a Swiss army knife.

"It's perfect," Jody said. She wanted to add, 'And you're perfect too,' but the words stuck in her throat.

"I've never taken anyone here before," Will said.

They'd finished the bread and cheese, and Jody reached for the berries which, it turned out, were fragrant and sweeter than any she'd ever tasted. She dipped them into the whipped cream and ate slowly, making the picnic last longer.

Will took a breath, gathering courage. "I usually come here when I'm confused or in pain. After Emma died, I came here a lot."

"Did you ever bring Emma here?" Jody felt funny saying her name.

He shook his head. "We had our own place. It didn't have a name. We used to go there when we could; we'd pack a picnic, and, well, we'd make love. It was our special place—mine and Emma's."

Picnics with Emma. His eyes became misty. The memories were so real that it almost seemed as if Emma were there with them in the meadow, as if he had only to reach out a bit farther to touch the hem of her skirt. He remembered feeling the soft skin of Emma's shoulders. He could almost smell the scent of her perfume—some kind of spring flower—and he remembered the musty, animal scent of their passion.

"I said 'goodbye' to that place after I said 'goodbye' to her. Those happy times, it feels like they happened a lifetime ago." He stopped and stared up at the clouds as if he were asking Emma's permission. Permission to move on. Permission to start something with Jody.

No one would ever be Emma.

No, Jody couldn't replace Emma. Still, Emma would have wanted Will to move on. He knew that. Jody was good for the kids. Heck, she was good for him. She made them all happy. To love and to be loved, that's what Emma would have wanted for all of them. Yes, he knew that. But looking at Jody, thinking what he was thinking, and feeling what he was feeling, it seemed intensely disloyal.

Mounties don't cry, but Will did. Silently. Tears rolled down his face, and he left them there. They weren't sad tears, though. They were the kind of tears that cleanse.

He shook his head as if shaking his way through the memories of Emma, and he smiled at Jody. "This meadow has always been mine alone. Like I said, it's curative; it's magic. Somehow, it feels as if God spends His time here. Or maybe He prefers the top of that mountain. Sometimes, I imagine Him somewhere high up, looking down on all of us. During this last year, I've come here a lot to think, usually when I'm stumped about how to raise the kids, or something really hard comes up at work. And sometimes, rarely, I'd just come out here to say, 'Hi,' and 'Thank you,' to God, or the Universe, or Whoever is running the show."

He looked into Jody's eyes. It felt as if he were looking into her heart. "I wanted to give you something special." He shrugged. "So, this is it—my meadow and my mountain."

"And I love it." She handed Will one of the truffles and took a big bite out of the other. Rich chocolate and coffee with a hint of rum exploded in her mouth. "The mountain, the meadow, the chocolate." When they really counted, the right words didn't come. "And getting to be with your kids." She wanted to say much more. "And I get it. Why God touches you here. It's like . . . it's like my oak grove back in Berkeley. When I was in college, I used to sit under those oak trees, and I'd talk to God and feel at peace. That's what this meadow reminds me of. It's all perfect. Thank you."

'And I love you.' That's what she really wanted to say but was afraid to.

Will put his arm around her. "You mean a lot to me. You have to know that. When my wife died, I did too, in a way. The best part of me went numb, froze. I kept going, took care of my kids, whom I love more than my life. I did my job, which I also love. But everything was hollow, empty. As if my soul had died with Emma, and I was only a robot that kept things together. And then you came along. At first you were just Sandy's friend, and then you became my friend, and then, somehow, you became . . . more."

He leaned his head against Jody, and he could smell the shampoo in her hair. She was redemption. She melted the frost that had been crippling his heart ever since Emma's death. He looked up at the sky as if asking Emma—asking for what? For permission? For blessing? Was his touch a betrayal or a sign of healing?

His finger touched Jody's cheek. "I was afraid to care for you, and then . . . It's as if I jumped into a creek of snowmelt. Daunting at first, and now I'm swimming, and the world is full of color where it used to be gray and brown." He'd overdone it.

Things were getting awkward. Will pulled back. Next, he'd be telling her that he loved her. "I don't buy truffles for just anyone."

She poked him, and they both fell over, letting laughter break the tension.

Will and Jody finished their truffles in silence. Then, together, they loaded up the backpack with the remains of the picnic. Will zipped it shut and looked at Jody. She was staring back at him. "What are you thinking?" he asked.

"I think I'm falling in love with you," she blurted out. Finally, she'd said it. "When I first came to Canada, Sandy said I reminded him of someone stuck at the bottom of a black hole. It was as if he could see inside of me. Maybe, he could. I was scared of everything and of nothing. I jumped each time something made a noise. But besides the fear, there was nothing inside me. No laughter. No . . ."

She leaned forward, and he took her in his arms and kissed her. He kissed with the passion of a man who hadn't kissed a woman in almost a year. Right then, without thinking, he gave her his soul. She was "the one." He hadn't thought he'd ever find love after Emma, and now, here he was, completely smitten.

And Jody—she hadn't dared to dream of romance. She'd figured that love was a dream that had been dreamed out a long time ago, that all her juices were sucked out, and that, after everything she'd been through, she was too broken to ever take the risk of loving again. And yet, here she was—vulnerable and handing her heart over to Will. "I'm alive," Jody whispered when the kiss finally ended. She savored the lingering taste of Will's lips on hers. "It's as if I were born only days ago, and everything in the world is fresh and new."

He put down the backpack, took Jody in his arms, and kissed her over and over.

The sun was low in the sky when Jody and Will walked back to Sandy's cabin. She had her head on his shoulder as they approached the house. The thrill of the kisses lingered on her lips and stayed there for days afterwards.

<<<◇>>>

It seemed as if Sandy and Jody were watching the kids more and more often. Jody's heart skipped every time the phone rang, and it turned out to be Will asking to leave the kids with them. She wanted, oh so badly, to please Will, to make him happy, and watching the children was all she had to give him. Well, that and the cookies and muffins which she and Emberlee baked almost every time they were together.

Chioke was a happy baby, easy to please. Everything was new to her, every outing an adventure. If she did start crying, a cookie usually solved her problem. And Jody craved snuggles and kisses as much as Chioke did.

Emberlee was an eight-year-old version of joy and wonder, and Jody loved doing crafts with her and helping her study. They read to each other. Emberlee's homework was fun because Jody seasoned it with math races, and spelling bees.

Science experiments were the best—almost magic lessons. One time, outside the cabin, Emberlee unscrewed the top of a one-liter bottle of diet cola. "I observe that the liquid is fizzing. According to this science book, the bubbles are carbon dioxide." She wrote down her observations in her science notebook. "Next, I am going to add six Mentos candies. I expect the Mentos to act as a cat . . . catalyst and speed up the release of the carbon dioxide." Emberlee put on her safety glasses. "In other words, bombs away!" She dropped the candy into the soda bottle. There was no time for her to duck or get out of the way. A fizzy spray of cola shot twenty feet into the air and drenched her.

"Oh, my goodness!" Emberlee was squealing as she ran.

"That's one heck of a catalyst!" she said, nodding vigorously while soda dripped from her hair.

Jody and Emberlee had serious talks as well, about honor, forgiveness, truth, and gratitude.

"Grandpa calls the fish his brothers."

"It's the Tutchone way," said Jody. "I don't see it quite the way that Sandy does, but, yes, I think that everyone and everything on earth is somehow connected.

Jody even loved Liam in spite of his sulky ways. She admired the spark of fierce loyalty to his mother's memory that burned inside him. And she loved his quirky wit. Liam was such a teenager! He tried hard to be a man, and sometimes the little boy inside of him peeked through. Yes, she could find a lot about him to love, even if he did make it difficult.

The kids made Jody feel connected to the world, and she'd often battled isolation.

Best of all, when Will arrived to pick up the children, she and Sandy usually had dinner ready for the Campbell brood. Liam and Emberlee would set the table, giving Jody and Will precious minutes of holding hands, hugging, and stealing kisses when they thought that no one was watching.

When Jody thought of Will, her heart beat harder and faster, smiles came to her face unbidden, and she felt deliciously warm through and through. The world was a kinder place; people were nicer; every day was easier, happier, brighter because Will was in her life.

<<<<>>>>

One Saturday morning, Will told the kids he was taking Jody out for a picnic—just the grown-ups. Emberlee giggled. "Papa, you and Jody just want to kissy, kissy, smooch; don't you?" She made a kissy-kissy-smooch face with puckered lips, and she hugged herself, running her fingers up and down her back imitating two lovers kissing. "Oh, Jody, I love you," she murmured.

Will grinned and put his finger to his lips.

"Awe, mush," said Emberlee.

<<<<>>>>

The slopes of Mt. Frank Rae were still capped with snow, but in Will's meadow, the frost was gone. Fireweed grew everywhere in pink and purple patches. More hesitant buds of prairie crocus and Kinnikinic peeked up through the grass.

It was too early for lunch. Will spread a waterproof sleeping bag on the ground to lie on, and he and Jody watched a pair of eagles gracefully soaring above them.

Even though spring had turned Will's meadow green, the morning breeze still carried the last of winter's chill, and Jody started to shiver. Will reached into his backpack, brought out a thick quilt, and spread it over the two of them. Sandwiched between the sleeping bag and the quilt, Jody snuggled up against Will for warmth. He turned his head toward Jody to kiss her, and his breath was warm against her neck. Warm and exciting. She turned to him, eager to feel his lips on hers. And then he kissed her.

This wasn't like the wimpy kisses they'd shared in Sandy's cottage where they'd had to be discreet because of the kids. No, this was a full-out, bonfire of a kiss, a tingly, spicy kiss that buzzed on Jody's lips and fluttered in her stomach.

And then without warning, the sparks became fierce. More than a bonfire, Jody became a wildfire out of control. Suddenly, she was breathing hard and fast. Like a chameleon changing colors, timid Jody became the Jody who'd returned from her courage-seeking quest—the Jody of the lightning storm. She'd waited for this all her life. She wasn't about to wait any longer. She wanted more. She wanted Will.

Jody slid her hand under his shirt, touching bare skin. More tingles and flutters bubbled inside her as she breathed in the scent of the soap he'd washed with and the musky scent that was all Will.

That bonfire kiss had taken Will by surprise as well. Then, feeling her hand on his chest, his body swelled and stiffened as long suppressed urges sprang to life, and memories of lovemaking flooded his thoughts. He wanted to brush his hands along her body, his fingers teasing her. He imagined his hands gliding along her neck, her breasts, inside her thighs, lightly at first, then harder and faster. He imagined his tongue on her nipples. He wanted to be Superman, taking her to places of passion she'd never known.

And he wanted her body against his, and her hands and her lips touching him, feeling him—like an explorer, finding places where his desire lay waiting. And he wanted to be inside her. He wanted Jody probing, stroking, kissing. He wanted more. He wanted her driving him crazy, making him mad with pleasure. He wanted to be inside her. More than anything, he wanted to be inside her.

But what did Jody want? She was such a fragile thing, and she'd been through so much! If he took her, would it be passion or rape?

Then, out of the blue, an image of Emma formed in his mind, as clear as the clouds floating above him. He could almost see her. It was as if Emma were hovering over him, as if he only had to reach out an inch more to stroke her face, to touch her body.

He looked up at the sky imagining Emma staring down at

him. Then he looked at Jody. 'Was this betrayal?'

Jody kissed him again with desire on her lips. She stroked his chest, then let her hand wander under his belt.

'For Heaven's sake, she wants you, you fool!' It's what Emma would have said. Will could almost hear her laughing.

He reached under Jody's clothes running his hand along her waist and her hips. He kissed her mouth and her neck. He ducked under the quilt and kissed her belly. He stroked the inside of her thigh, and Jody quivered. "More!" she cried. "Please . . ."

The curve of her waist was different. The sounds she made, the cries, and groans were not Emma's. No, they were the sounds of the woman who loved him now, the sounds of the future, not the past, the sounds of a new adventure. He reached under Jody's blouse and cupped her breasts while Jody cried out. She gasped and panted. Her face was flushed.

Then, they came together with Jody begging for more. Will's lusty grunts quickened, and their delighted cries echoed across the meadow and bounced off the slopes of Mount Frank Rae.

After their lovemaking, Will and Jody lay back on the sleeping bag, with Jody's arm resting on Will's chest and the quilt lying alongside them in a heap. The eagles were gone, but hawks flew above them, swooping and gliding in circles. For a while, they watched the birds, and were at peace.

Will's eyes were on the hawks, but his mind was on Jody. He'd forgotten how glorious sex could be until now. So, he lay on his sleeping bag in a fuzzy stupor, in his special meadow, watching hawks, and remembering how he'd made love to Jody all the while.

Will rolled over and looked into her face. Was she as happy as he was?

He should say something.

"Are you hungry yet?" he finally asked.

"Oh, yeah!"

Will sat up and reached into his backpack to pull out a sandwich.

"But not for bologna," she said.

"I brought ham and cheese."

"I don't want a sandwich." She raised an eyebrow.

And chuckled.

"You want . . .?" he laughed.

"Oh, yeah!" She laughed too.

"Then, forget the sandwiches." He tossed the backpack aside. "I can take care . . ." He couldn't finish the sentence. He was laughing too hard. Then they both laughed. Like children released from school.

"Again, please," she whispered. She whispered it into his ear, and he gasped, feeling the beginning of arousal.

They kissed like teenagers. They kissed as if he were a soldier returned from war.

"Please, Will. More."

With a lusty moan, he kissed her, caressed her, licked her

breasts, and delighted in her groans and uninhibited cries. Then he rolled his body on top of Jody while she panted and cried out. Finally, their passion spent, they came apart and lay back on Will's sleeping bag, in the most wonderful meadow on earth, watching the clouds float by.

CHAPTER 10

Liam's chance came one evening a few days later when Will had to go into the office unexpectedly. "You're in charge until I get back," Will told Liam. He braced himself for an argument, or at least, a nonverbal sign of contempt. Instead, Liam said, "Sure, Dad. Can I use your computer and printer? I have a history project due tomorrow."

Will nodded and clapped Liam on the shoulder. 'The kid's going to come out okay after all.'

As soon as Will left, Liam turned his father's printer on and made a copy of the photo ID Jody had used when she'd entered Canada. Then he replaced the ID in the pocket of his jeans, booted up his father's computer, and began typing.

Dear Sir,

    I have information that a woman named Johanna Jacobson entered Canada posing as Sonja Jordanson. She goes by the name Jody. I also have information that this

Johanna Jacobson is connected with the gang that has been selling drugs in Dawson City. In fact, I think she is the ringleader.

She is armed and dangerous. She is a terrorist and should be arrested.

She is staying with Alexander Joseph, who goes by the name of Sandy.

She is in cahoots with William Campbell, who is a Mountie.

Liam considered the last line and decided against it. If his dad got arrested, Liam could end up in foster care or something. He deleted it and replaced it with:

She is a friend of William Campbell, who doesn't know anything about any of this and is innocent.

And he didn't want to get his grandfather in trouble either.

Alexander Joseph is also innocent. Sandy is just his nickname, not an alias.

'Better,' he decided. Then he added:

But William Campbell is acting really stupid and probably shouldn't be a Mountie anymore.

Even better.

I am enclosing a copy of her fake ID which she hides in her sock.

Sincerely yours,

Anonymous.

Liam addressed the letter to the Royal Canadian Mounted Police office in Whitehorse.

'That'll show her!'

<<<<>>>>

The Mounties forwarded Liam's letter to Sgt. Hendricks in Dawson City.

"Bloody hell," muttered Hendricks. "Campbell? Nothing wrong with Campbell. Nothing wrong with any of my officers." He buried Liam's letter under a stack of other complaints.

When he did, finally, check it out, Hendricks was unpleasantly surprised to find a record of Sonja Jordanson entering Canada, and an interview with Sonja Jordanson concerning a methamphetamine lab explosion, but no record of a Sonja Jordanson ever having lived in the United States. Thankfully, Johanna Jacobson didn't show up in any police file, but a record he found of her flight to Iran was troubling.

Sgt. Hendricks was not pleased. "Send Howard and Pelletier," he said, "and get Campbell down here in my office

ASAP."

<<<<>>>>

Jody was out walking just for the pleasure of it. In spring, the Yukon is a truly magical place. Everywhere she turned, something was budding, or blooming, or hatching. Only a few minutes ago, she'd seen a baby moose stumbling about on spindly legs and making a funny, humming sound. This goofy creature with ears way too big and legs far too long for the rest of its body, had the sweetest, silliest face. Jody had watched from a distance. She didn't want mama moose to get the wrong idea.

What a wonderful country in which to fall in love! Yes, improbable as it seemed, she was in love. This feeling was more than a crush, and it was intoxicating. Being with Will warmed her heart in the same way that the spring morning did. She felt as if she were floating instead of walking along the path leading to Sandy's cabin. For the first time in a long while, Jody belonged. Yes, it was love—life-changing, spirit-renewing, all-consuming love.

The real thing.

<<<<>>>>

"Sonja?"

Jody heard the voice, but the name didn't register. "Sonja Jordanson—police. We need to talk to you."

Jody froze. 'Not now,' she thought as it dawned on her that the voice was talking to her. 'Please not now—not now, just when everything is finally working out.' Slowly, she turned around. Two Mounties in uniform were holding out their badges. Jacques Pelletier was a man in his mid-fifties with a beaky nose and just a bit of a paunch. His partner, Rebecca Howard, stood tall and trim, her hair looped into a neat ponytail below her hat. Neither was smiling.

Jody and the two Mounties entered Sandy's cabin in silence.

"We need to see your ID, Miss Jordanson."

'Face your fears,' Jody thought, and she pulled the fake ID out of her sock.

"Is that your real name?" Officer Howard asked. "The truth, please."

Jody shook her head.

"What is your real name?"

"Johanna Jacobson."

"And you are a citizen of?"

"The United States."

"Are you aware that carrying falsified identification is a felony?"

"I didn't do anything wrong."

"You entered Canada under an assumed name."

Jody didn't know what else to do; she just told the truth. "I was attacked. They thought I was a spy or something."

"Who are *they*?"

"I don't know." She waited through an uncomfortable

silence.

"Why did *they* think you were a spy?"

"I posted some stories in a chatroom, and they figured I'd gotten my information from a snitch. I thought free speech really meant free speech."

"And?"

In a halting, frightened voice, Jody began the story of her abduction. As she talked, she searched the Mounties' faces for a sign that they believed her, but there was none. "Finally, when they'd figured out that I wasn't really a spy, they drugged me and stuffed me into a box. I think it was a coffin. And they left me to die." Jody felt as if she'd just run a marathon.

"And yet, here you are." Pelletier rolled his eyes. 'Biggest pile of bullshit I've heard in a long time,' he thought. "Still alive."

"Yes."

"And? You were left to die, remember?"

Jody hesitated. "Someone rescued me."

"And who was that?"

"She saved my life. I won't reveal her name. I can't."

'Piled higher and deeper,' he thought.

"You'll have to come with us," said Officer Howard. "Forging identity papers, entering Canada under an assumed name—Canada takes these things seriously."

Jody slumped against the wall.

"Go," Sandy said. "I'll call Will." Jody had forgotten that Sandy was in the room.

'Face your fears,' Jody thought, and she burst into tears and kept crying while the officers escorted her to their vehicle.

<<<<>>>>

Will stood at attention while Sgt. Hendricks shouted into his face. "You are a liability, a bloody disgrace." The sergeant's face burned red, and veins stood out in his neck. He slammed his fist on his desk. Will flinched. Hendricks knew how to bring on the thunder. "Campbell, you're a Mountie. You carry the reputation of the Royal Canadian Mounted Police with you. That should mean something. I expect you to hold yourself to a higher standard of conduct."

Then Hendricks was quiet. Somehow, the silence was more unsettling than the slammed fist.

"And yet, you have the stupidity to shack up with a terrorist floozie and end up on the wrong end of . . . this." He threw a copy of the letter at Will. Will looked at the letter and struggled to contain the anger building up inside him. Finally, the sergeant calmed down—just a bit. "I expect more from you. What have you to say for yourself?"

"I was suspicious at first, but I couldn't find any criminal records on her. Since she hadn't done anything wrong, I didn't ask for identification." An exasperated sigh escaped. "I don't normally check the ID of every person I meet."

Hendricks slammed his desk again. "Can the sarcasm."

"Outside of the fake ID, there's no evidence that she did

anything wrong. She's living with my father-in-law, and she's in some kind of trouble. That's all I know."

"Are you involved with her?"

"She's . . . my friend. She and my father-in-law watch my kids sometimes."

Sgt. Hendricks raised an eyebrow. "Are you romantically involved?"

Will was dumbfounded. If any of the accusations were true . . . If he was endangering his kids . . . Will sighed. If it came to a choice between Jody and his children, he knew he'd stand by his children.

"Well, are you?"

"No, I'm not." Will looked down at the ground. 'Not anymore,' he thought, remembering conversations that had touched his soul and the softness of her skin while they had made love.

"Don't be," said the sergeant. "Did she mention that she's been to Iran?"

Will shook his head. "For what it's worth, she doesn't fit the profile of a terrorist."

Sgt. Hendricks laughed. "Too bad they don't wear identification tags!"

"And last I heard, flying to Iran isn't a crime."

"True, we have no hard evidence against her, only an anonymous accusation, but if it's true, our jobs will be a lot easier with her gone. What we do have is a fake ID. And that's all we need to get her deported and out of our hair." He grinned. "Let the U.S. deal with the rest of it. They have the resources. Hell, if you're really her friend, talk her into leaving voluntarily." Hendricks smiled at the thought. "It'll get her out of here faster." Then he scowled. "Try, Campbell, try to keep your nose clean."

"Yes, sir," said Will.

<<<<>>>>

Will walked out of Sgt. Hendricks' office shaken. He needed time to think, time to sort things out. "Here goes," he said to himself and booted up his computer.

First, he checked airline records and, sure enough, Johanna Jacobson's name appeared on the passenger list for Flight 472 to Iran. So, Jody had travelled to the Middle East. Well, that really didn't mean anything. Will sighed.

Next, Will looked for Homer Perlman hoping that Homer could shed some light on Jody's story. He tried every spelling he could think of and came up empty. This Perlman character didn't exist.

Finally, he searched for record of Jody's abduction He hesitated because as long as there was the possibility of her story being true, there was hope that he could have a life with her. He imagined shoving kidnap records into Sgt. Hendricks' hands and laughing in his face. Except that Will wouldn't ever do that. Conduct unbefitting a Mountie. No, he would walk into Hendricks' office and respectfully hand him the records. 'You need to see these, sir.' If Jody had been telling the truth, there would be copious records. Files and more files of interviews, records of her activities prior to the abduction, lists of possible suspects. If they existed, the records would be impossible to miss.

Will found nothing.

That whole abduction story would make a great movie, but things like that didn't happen in real life.

He was hurt, angry, and tired. No, he and the kids had been through enough. They'd have to get over Jody and move on as best they could.

<<<<>>>>

Jody started crying again when Will, still choking on his anger, showed up to bail her out. He was a good Mountie, and his sergeant had chewed him out. All because of Jody. Will had trusted her, and she'd lied to him, betrayed his trust. More than that, he'd allowed himself to love her. Those feelings that he'd guarded carefully—she'd coaxed them out of hiding, and then she had shredded them. He should have known better.

"They want to deport me," Jody said through tears. "Two . . ." She started to say "Mounties" but changed her mind. "Two of them came today and told me that I have to leave the country."

"Then you'd better leave." Will's voice hit Jody like bullets. "I told you—the Mounties always, always get their man and their woman. You could have been honest. You could have confessed what you'd done, and I could have helped you. But no.

Instead, you lied; you kept secrets. Well, good for you. Now enjoy the consequences."

"I'm sorry," she said. She looked down at the floor. "I didn't do anything wrong. I was afraid if I used my real name, they'd find me and kill me. That's why I used a fake ID. And that's why I couldn't tell you. I was afraid you'd have to send me back."

'Oh, Christ! Another sob story.' Will was fed up with lies. No one told the truth anymore. Ever. He'd believed her and paid the price. "Right. The jails are full of innocent people. How stupid do you think I am?"

"You don't believe me, do you?"

"Maybe, if you came from some lesser-known African dictatorship. But the United States doesn't do that."

"They do now." She lifted her shirt exposing the thick scars running across her back.

Will flinched, but he didn't say anything. 'Doesn't prove a thing,' he thought.

She turned away from him. "Don't believe me. I don't care. Only, what happens now?"

"You entered the country illegally with a fake ID. That's serious. The first thing you should do is hire someone familiar with immigration law to represent you. But you'll have a tough time convincing the courts to let you stay. Your story sounds like bullshit. And the fact that you flew to the Middle East and then just disappeared—it's not a crime, but it makes folks nervous."

"I've never been outside of the United States until I came to Canada. Who says I've been to the Middle East?"

"Airline records. You boarded a plane to Iran."

"Well, they're wrong."

Will rolled his eyes.

"So now what do I do?"

"Like I said, get a lawyer." Will made his face and his heart turn to stone. "Or you could leave voluntarily." 'Sometimes, I hate my job,' he thought.

"How am I supposed to pay for a lawyer?" Jody started pacing.

Will knew what he was supposed say, and he said it. "If you leave voluntarily, you'll avoid paying legal fees and having deportation on your record. But if that's what you want to do, then leave right away—before Immigration begins proceedings against you."

"I'll probably need a passport by the time Canada lets me back in." She stopped pacing and looked into Will's eyes. They were the Mountie's eyes—cold and hard. And they said, 'I hate you. Don't bother hoping for help. You have no friends in Canada.'

Jody turned her back to Will. "Maybe I should just stay in the United States. Canada doesn't want me. Liam obviously doesn't want me. You don't want me. Sandy probably doesn't want me either." She managed to stop crying, but her chest ached. 'Ask me to come back. Please, please ask me to come back. Tell me I'm wrong. Isn't there anyone who wants me?' That's what she was thinking, but her lips stayed silent.

And Will stayed silent as well. Losing Emma had been the worst pain he'd ever known. Worse than getting shot. He hadn't believed he'd ever recover. And now, he was finally healing. Emma would always remain a part of him, but thinking about her was slowly turning from an unbearable ache to a mix of pain and sweet memories. And now . . . Will had taken such a risk allowing himself to care about Jody. He'd just started to fall in love. And then Jody turned out to be a criminal and maybe even a terrorist. 'Just goes to show—you can't trust anybody.'

At last, Jody spoke, her voice thin, pathetic. "I'll leave voluntarily. There's nothing for me here. You'll get your bail money back, and it'll save Canada the cost of a trial."

Will made a fist, and his nails dug into his palm. Jody had said, "There's nothing for me here." She didn't care about him and the kids! And now his heart was breaking all over again.

And the kids! Emberlee and Chioke had grown attached to Jody. Liam had been right; Jody was bad news. Now, they'd have to go through pain all over again. It wasn't fair. 'Why did she have to come into our lives?' Will hardened his heart, and he hardened his voice. "Stay in the States, and leave us alone." He felt like a man who'd just eaten rat poison.

Driving home, a small voice was nagging at the back of Will's policeman's brain. He'd overlooked something; he'd made up his mind too early. The scars on her back were bad, but there were many ways that she could have gotten them, especially if she hung out with criminals or terrorists. The scars alone didn't mean anything. There was something else, but he was too angry and hurt to think straight.

That nagging doubt continued to creep into his conscious mind and kept him awake. What if Jody had been telling the truth?

<<<<>>>

Jody's last day in the Yukon was somber. She hugged Emberlee and Chioke. Liam was civil. Will acknowledged her existence. But the hardest goodbye was parting from Sandy. She hugged him fiercely, and her tears and her embrace said more than her words of thanks. Then it was time to leave.

"Go in peace," said Sandy.

"Stay in peace," Jody answered.

And then Officer Howard arrived to escort Jody to the United States border.

CHAPTER 11

For Jody, the flight to Vancouver in an RCMP Cessna was a haze of self-recrimination. Jody was a lowlife, a criminal. She'd been arrested, and Canada was kicking her out because she wasn't good enough to stay in this Eden. Funny, when she'd first knocked on Sandy's door, more than anything else, she had wanted to go home to the States. Now, she longed to stay in the Yukon with its endless forests and to be with Sandy, Emberlee, Chioke, Liam, and Will. She'd miss them so. Even Liam, with his slouching and scowling. Jody realized that, somehow, they'd become her family; the thought of never seeing them again stabbed her heart like pitchforks. She felt as if she were sinking into a pit of despair so deep that she'd never recover. The jostling motion of the plane made her slightly nauseated, and she welcomed the distraction from her blistering thoughts.

From Vancouver International, Officer Howard drove Jody to the United States border. Jody stared at the ground while Officer Howard talked to the guard at the border crossing and signed some papers. Then, with trepidation, Jody signed the papers too.

"Goodbye," she said to no one in particular.

Several miserable hours later, Jody cast a last backward glance at Canada and began the bus ride to Mississippi where her mother lived. 'Welcome back to the United States,' she thought. The seats on the bus were worn. Used napkins and candy wrappers littered the floor, and the air was stale with a faint odor of cigarette smoke.

'If someone shoots me when I get off this bus, will anyone know or care? Is that what it would take to get Will to believe me? Getting shot?' Jody shivered. She wanted to be vindicated, but not by dying.

With a sense of hopelessness, Jody remembered Sandy's words. He had said that she'd stand tall and laugh before he died. Well, so much for his mystical insight! She couldn't see that happening anytime soon. Instead, she imagined herself a butterfly crawling backwards into her cocoon. Although, she did feel like a new version of Johanna Jacobson—a stronger, braver version.

It seemed as if Jody was always leaving somewhere on a bus, but never arriving. Always in some kind of limbo. A moose at midday, as Sandy would say. Never belonging anywhere.

In between her brooding, she'd glance out the window at the fairyland that was the Pacific Northwest. Mist rose from among the ferns and the giant redwoods, the grandfatherly trees that protected the leafy carpet below them. The redwoods were splendid, but they weren't Canadian maples.

The trip wore on, interspersed with jerky bus stops—

sometimes in mega-cities among high-rising towers and sprawling stretches of houses, sometimes in towns five blocks long. Somehow, the bus stations always reeked of asphalt and fuel.

'There's a bright side,' she figured. 'No more nights lasting twenty-two hours. No more endless, boring days staring into the fire, wishing for the snow to stop. No more chopping wood.' She rubbed the rough calluses on her hands. It felt as if she'd chopped half a forest before spring had finally shown up.

But her memories of Canada refused to stop there. No more whispering, giggling, and baking with Emberlee. No more evenings by the fireplace talking with Sandy about everything and nothing. No more hugging and snuggling Chioke. At least, she'd gotten to see the little one take her first steps, but she wouldn't get to see any more of Chioke's firsts. Would Chioke know to miss her? Maybe, if she could have stayed, even Liam would have warmed up to Jody, eventually.

Jody sighed. Liam was beginning his teen years and all the drama that goes with adolescence. His first love, his first kiss— Jody wouldn't be there for any of it. Not that Liam would have shared anything personal with her, but still . . .

And Will—her memories of him were the most painful of all. She probably wouldn't have had any more firsts with him anyway, but . . . no, she couldn't think about him. That was just too raw, too impossible to bear.

<<<<>>>>

Northern forests gave way to deserts and canyons, bright as a Canadian sunset. Prehistoric frosts, rains, and rivers had layered and sculpted the rocky cliffs into surreal orange arches and towers. Crazy, unexpected threads of color—yellows, greens, even pinks and purples—swirled and looped through the blazing orange landscape. Why hadn't Jody travelled more? Back when her life had been normal. "You outdid Yourself, God," she whispered, staring at a boulder balanced precariously at a seemingly-impossible angle.

At the Continental Divide, she took out her notebook and started writing. "It feels like the top of the world."

Suddenly the sky sprang alive with lightning. Bolts shot through the air—every second, it seemed—as thunder rumbled, and rain poured down in buckets. "I'm surrounded by the greatest fireworks show on earth," she wrote and forgot, for that moment, the Canada she was leaving behind.

And she forgot to be frightened.

From the Rocky Mountains, Jody's journey continued through grassland and farmland. "I see a checkerboard of browns, yellows, and greens without a hill in sight," she wrote, "a flat horizon, occasionally interrupted by spikey groves of windmills. Boring, if I'm being truthful."

At last, her bus entered Mississippi, land of tree farms and bayous. Surprisingly, her gloom lifted, replaced by an unexpected love for the country she'd crossed—her homeland, the United

States! With all its flaws, the United States was still a land to love.

And finally, the bus rolled into the station at Biloxi, Pascagoula's neighbor, and the end of Jody's long journey.

She got off the bus, stretched, and gulped. Jody had put off telling her mother that she was coming home, afraid of her reaction. Would her mother welcome her, or—and this was the more likely scenario—would she spew disapproval at Jody for ruining her reputation? Martha's friendships revolved around gossip. To avoid being the object of this gossip, she and Jody had to adhere to certain conventions—unwritten rules of behavior and dress. Almost everything Jody had done in the last year violated these conventions. Jody frowned, looking down at her clothing— torn, faded blue jeans, a Pendleton shirt, and sneakers that the Salvation Army wouldn't accept. To sum it up, she looked like a bag lady, complete with unmanicured nails, no makeup, and hair which hadn't been touched by a professional in over a year.

Of course, Jody's appearance only lent credence to the most hideous social blunder of all—the fact that she'd disappeared for over a year. To put it crudely, that was more than enough time to get pregnant, have the little bastard, and find some clueless family to adopt it. The shame would be too much for her mother to bear.

'After that bus ride, I really need a shower,' she thought, sadly.

Jody found a pay phone; there weren't many around anymore. With halting steps, Jody walked towards it and lifted the receiver. What was she going to say? There are some things you just don't tell your mother; almost everything that had happened to Jody in the past year fit into that category. Jody squared her shoulders. 'Face your fears, and all that,' she decided.

She deposited the coins and made the phone call. "Hello, Mom. I love you. Please don't get upset. It's me, Mom, Jody. I mean Johanna. I'm at the Biloxi bus station. I need a ride home and a place to stay. I'll tell you everything later. Please, just come get me. Okay?"

"Oh, my!" That was all Jody's mother was able to say. What do you say to the daughter who disappeared out of your life for a year? Your hippy, radical daughter who went to school in Berkeley where they had free sex and demonstrations. The daughter who went to work at some dippy newspaper?

A cruel silence hung on the phone line.

"I love you." That's what you say. The rest, you figure out later. So, Martha Jacobson said, "I love you" after she got her breath back. "I love you; I'm coming as fast as I can."

Before she left her house, Martha knelt before her statue of the Virgin Mary. "Thank you, Jesus. Thank you, Mary. Thank you, Joseph." Her hands trembled as she made the sign of the cross. Then she sobbed a bit as she reached for her coat, purse, and car keys and raced out to her car.

<<<<>>>>

While Martha was driving to the bus station, Jody stared at a cigarette carton littering the floor and wondered, 'Who am I? What am I? Fugitive? Criminal? Victim?'

In Canada, she'd been Sandy's protégé and a caregiver for Will's kids. And Will had said he loved her. The *Whitehorse Daily Star* had purchased two articles she'd written, albeit they were published with Sandy's name. And she'd turned fear and anger into energy that was like lightning. In Canada, Jody had started to feel like a normal, basically good person with the right to be happy.

And now? Who was she? A suspected terrorist, forced to leave the country. A grown woman still living with her mother.

'What's my name now?' she wondered. 'Jody or Johanna?'

Well, in Pascagoula, she was Johanna, a victim and a fugitive from some unknown threat. But it wasn't all hopeless. Here, she was also a journalist with a string of well-received newspaper columns written under her own name. Her resume was impressive. Hopefully, she still had internet friends.

And her mother had said, "I love you." That was huge.

Yes, Johanna was afraid. Some unknown enemy could be lurking in the shadows waiting for a chance to grab her and kill her. It could be anybody. For all she knew, her assailant could be somewhere in this very bus station, hiding behind a wall just waiting for a chance to put a bullet through her heart. How do you protect yourself from that? The thought made her jumpy. Gave her goose bumps. And she'd be living with that possibility, that fear, for as long as she stayed in the United States. In other words, for the rest of her life. 'Unlikely,' thought Johanna, to bolster her courage. 'They probably think I'm dead.' But the tingle of anxiety persisted. Well, she was afraid, but she was no longer running scared. She'd learned how to face fear. Sandy had taught her that. She was no longer a mouse, but a moose.

A moose at midday. Like Sandy.

Wobbly, quixotic, but a survivor.

And then, Johanna looked up and there was her mother, Martha Jacobson. Johanna could see that her mother had aged. So many new wrinkles on her forehead and around her eyes and her mouth! Was that from worrying about Johanna? Martha's hair was cut short now—lush, wavy, dark brown with auburn highlights. But the gray roots showed through.

Johanna jumped into the air and waved, both excited to see her mother and uncertain of the welcome she'd receive. Then Martha ran to her as fast as she could on three-inch heels. And she hugged Johanna hard, not caring who saw her.

<<<<>>>>

Johanna's first few days at home were idyllic. She had expected a barrage of disapproval from her mother. Instead, she and her mother reconnected, both as mother and daughter and as adult friends. They'd curl up on Martha's plush green couch in the evening, sipping hot chocolate and talking about everything and nothing—everything except the last year of Johanna's life. 'Denial isn't all that bad,' Johanna decided.

But inevitably a problem came up. "Johanna, my bridge club is coming to my house tomorrow," Martha said over a scrambled-egg breakfast. She picked at the hem of her blouse as she spoke. "And there's—well, there's something you need to know." Martha breathed a deep, dramatic sigh, gathering courage. "I told my ladies that you were one of President Bush's aides, and that you didn't come home often because you were busy flying around the country on various important assignments. I need you to back me up on this."

Johanna flinched. She hated lying, and she wasn't a fan of the president. Besides, it was such an outrageous story! Who in her right mind would believe it? She finally said, "I'm no good at fibbing, Mom. If I tried to lie, I'd probably start blushing and stuttering."

Martha wasn't listening. "You're a writer. You could say something like—oh, I don't know—like you helped broker a deal with the president of Belgium . . ."

"Belgium has a prime minister, Mom."

"You could say that you helped write an agreement that saved Belgium's floundering economy and cemented relations between the United States and five European countries." Martha smiled. "In a hush-hush story that never made the papers."

Johanna shook her head, but Martha persisted. "You're so talented." She put her hand on Johanna's cheek. "Just think of it as a writing assignment—writing a story for your newspaper. Only you'll be talking to my ladies instead of writing." She smoothed

Johanna's hair as she talked, tucking some strands behind Johanna's ears. "I know—pretend you're a television news reporter."

"Mom, you're not listening. I'm a terrible liar. I can't do it."

"Can't or won't?"

"Mom, please . . ."

Martha took her hand away. "But . . . but I already told the girls all about your assignments. I said our president would have been lost without you." She shrugged her shoulders. "You know how they are."

"Well, you'll have to take it back." Johanna reached her hand out tentatively. "Mom, I know how gossipy . . ."

Martha batted the hand away. "Well, I can't tell them you spent the last year in Iran as a hippie protestor working with some terrorists, and that you didn't even have the, the decency to write a note or, heaven forbid, call me to find out if I was still alive."

"Mother, I never flew to Iran. That's a mistake."

Now, Martha's voice was shrill. A year's worth of shame and worry were suddenly surfacing. "Oh, now you're too high and mighty to help your mother! You're fine with lying about doing who-knows-what in Iran, but you can't help your mother out with a perfectly innocent, white lie—a dignified lie about working for our president."

"Honestly, Mom, I've never been anywhere in the Middle East."

"Don't lie to me, Johanna. That's what the police told me, and they should know."

Johanna squared her shoulders. "Sandy taught me to face my fears. Maybe it's time to tell you about the last year of my life."

"And just who is this Sandy person?" Martha lowered her voice. "Did you have sex with him?"

Johanna tried to smother her laugh. It didn't work. "Mom, Sandy is a First Nations elder, probably about seventy years old. He took me in because I had nowhere else to go. He's a healer, not a gigolo."

Martha shook Johanna's shoulders. "You cannot tell my friends about this Sandy person. You hear me? A Protestant, I could understand, but a pagan! You absolutely cannot." Now she was yelling. "A healer! What did this Sandy person do to you? Did you worship snakes? Or eat peyote? What's become of you? I never should have let you go to college in Berkeley. That's where it all started."

"I don't think peyote cacti grow in Canada."

"Canada?"

"Yes. I had to . . ."

"Canada! My own daughter! A draft dodger, a criminal hiding from the law in Canada."

"Mom, you're kind of hysterical right now. And you're imagining things that aren't even real."

Martha wasn't listening. "A hooligan, a devil-worshipper!"

She moaned, her hand theatrically grabbing at her heart.

Johanna tried to calm her down. "I've never been a hippie. Women don't get drafted. I'm still a Christian and a Catholic. Although I did go on a vision quest, and Sandy did smudge me."

But Martha was swept away on a tide of emotions that had no place for reality. "No more. I can't take any more." She began to hyperventilate. "You just made me cancel my bridge club. I hope you're satisfied."

She walked away, still clutching at her heart.

<<<<>>>>

That night after dinner, Johanna approached her mother. "Mom, if you're ready to hear about it, I want to tell you what really happened."

Martha nodded quietly.

Johanna skipped through the abduction part as quickly as possible, and she minimized the threat to her life.

"So that's how I ended up in Canada," she said. "Oh, Mom, northern Canada is this magical place. The winters are unending. I didn't know so much cold existed. But then the snow melts, and it's a wild land with forests that go on forever. You can open your front door and see moose, and bears, and caribou. And you can walk for miles without coming across another soul."

"Why Canada? Why not come home to your mother?"

"I figured it would be . . . easier . . . until the whole mess got sorted out. And it was easier until . . ."

"Until?"

"Well, until I got deported."

"So, you ARE a criminal!"

"I didn't do anything wrong. Except that I entered Canada with a fake ID. But I didn't break any laws. I didn't do anything bad."

For a long time, Martha was silent. "Well, you're home now. I'm sure you're glad of that, anyway," she finally said.

That's when Johanna began crying. "Oh, Mom!" She reached for Martha's hand. "Oh, Mom!"

Martha just sighed and shook her head. "Who is he?"

"How . . . how did you know?"

Martha smiled. "Honey, it's always a man."

"He's a Mountie, Mom," Johanna sniffed. "His name is Will. Will Campbell. Sandy and I used to watch his kids."

"He has children?"

"Three of them. The middle kid, Emberlee, she's the first one who really got to me. She's smart and just this bubble of sunshine; you can't help smiling around her. She liked me—right from the beginning when I didn't think anyone could." Johanna blinked back her tears.

"Chioke's the youngest, still a baby, all snuggles, kisses, and hugs. But those hugs and kisses are to-die-for. And she's just beginning to develop a personality. I'd donate a kidney to get to watch her grow up." With the back of her hand, Johanna wiped away the tears that were running down her cheek.

"The oldest one, Liam, he's a teenager. He's a hard nut to crack, and at first, he scared the stuffing out of me. He still does a little, if I'm honest. But he can be charming—usually when he's up to something. Still . . . And he's so fiercely loyal to the memory of his mother, that I have to believe that there's something there worth knowing. Maybe, he's such a pain-in-the-neck pickle because he's still hurting from his mother's death. That's probably what's going on. Only now, I'll never get a chance to figure it out, let alone help him through it somehow."

"And Will?"

Mom, he's the kindest, most perfect person. When I'm with him . . . I mean, when I was with him, it was like, like I was surrounded by all kinds of love and happy." Johanna stared into Martha's face. "I was just a little kid when Daddy died, but I remember him; and Will sort of reminds me of Daddy."

Martha sighed with the memory of the man who'd made her feel that way long ago.

"At first, I was scared of Will. He was so official—a Mountie and all that. And then we got to talking. And we'd talk about things we cared about. And then . . ."

"You fell in love?"

Johanna nodded.

"You really love him?" Martha asked.

"I do."

"And he loves you?"

"Yes. At least he did until this whole deportation mess

happened. That's when he just blew up. Got furious. He can't stand being lied to, and he didn't believe my story. When he gets mad, he's not kind, gentle, or funny. He's the LAW."

Martha took Johanna's face in her hands. "If you really love this Will . . ."

"I do." Johanna was blinking back tears.

"Then fight for him. Write to him. Call him. He may have made up his mind; it may not do you any good. But fight for him anyway. If you two love each other, it's worth the fight. This Sandy person told you to face your fears. The risk of being hurt for love's sake is a fear worth facing."

They'd both told the truth, or at least part of it. But Johanna told her story as if it were no big deal, and Martha listened and reacted as if she wasn't afraid for her daughter.

<<<◇>>>

Using Martha's computer, Johanna logged onto her website, fairytalesfortherestofus. She chuckled, reading Brat's comments, and she pondered those that Shadow had written. But Sandy's last entry was the one that moved her to tears. "Jody, if you read this, know that you're a part of our family. You will be forever."

Johanna typed back: "I'm facing my fears. There are many of them. Sandy, thank you for that. Brat, don't ever change. Grow up, but don't ever change. Shadow, I wish you peace. To all of you, I love you."

Then she started typing a post to Will. She'd ask Sandy to

show it to him. But what could she say? He'd been so angry. Maybe she'd wait just a bit, let him cool down before she tried writing to him. Maybe she'd postpone facing that fear until a bit later.

<<<<>>>>

Back when she'd lived in Berkeley and her life had been normal, Johanna had written a column for The *Upstart Gazette.* She learned that her old editor, Ivan Buncheski, ran his own newspaper now. *The New Upstart.* Well, she needed a job. She couldn't sponge off her mother forever. Johanna got a cozy feeling remembering Ivan's bulldog face and his blustery way. Somehow, even at her most timid time, she'd always thought of him as a softie and a big brother. With a contented sigh, she looked up the phone number for *The New Upstart.*

"Hi, Ivan," she started. "It's . . . it's Johanna Jacobson. Remember me? I'm back in the United States, and I need a job. I'm not living in Berkeley at the moment, but I can move back"

"Lot of nerve—that's what you've got. A lot of nerve."

"But . . ."

"You disappear for months. You get me fired. Then you have the nerve to ask for a job."

"How did I get you fired? You never printed any of my controversial articles."

"You got me thinking. That's how. You got me sticking my neck out. The *Upstart Gazette* was the first newspaper to print the

Lidecker letter."

"The Lidecker letter?"

"A confession from Bush's top PR man. Usually, it's a good thing to scoop the other papers. In this case, it got me fired."

"I'm . . . sorry? So, um, since I got you fired, I guess there's no chance in hell of a job for me?"

"Getting fired was the best thing that could have happened," he grumbled. "Now I can print whatever I goddamn want. But as far as hiring you, I'm running the paper on less than a shoestring. There's just no money for another reporter."

"So, I shouldn't pack my bags and head for Berkeley?"

"Save yourself the bus fare. Here's what I can do. I'll read whatever you submit, and if I like it, I'll pay you top dollar. But as for a full-time job, I just can't do it right now."

<<<<>>>>

After striking out with some thirty-odd newspapers, radio stations, and television shows, Johanna decided to go for anything that paid a minimum wage. She almost went to work at Chubby Dog Diner, but Martha threw a minor tantrum. "You're not getting a job where everyone can see you. Waiting on tables, of all things! You know how people talk. I couldn't bear it."

"It's only temporary. Besides, I want to be a waitress, not a prostitute."

"But you used to work for the president."

"Only in your imagination. I never actually worked for

him. Remember?"

"But everyone thought you worked for him. In fact, they still do. If you must get a job, and I'll admit it—we could use the money. If you must get a job, find one where no one can see you."

After a lot of internet searching, Johanna got hired to work the graveyard shift at the Happy Valley Cannery. During the day, she tried to write articles for Ivan, but nothing grabbed her, and she only got one article printed.

Damn writer's block!

CHAPTER 12

Will's children still needed someone watching them occasionally, and Sandy was happy to help. Lately, they were a somber crew. Emberlee read a lot. When she wasn't reading, she was trying to entertain Chioke, but the little one fussed more than before. She cried more readily, and she kept calling out, "Mama."

"You have to expect it." Emberlee sounded like an adult. "Of course, she misses Jody, but she'll get over it."

Sandy nodded. "Thank goodness for pacifiers," he said.

<<<<>>>

After Jody's deportation, Will pretended that she had never been a part of his life. 'It's better this way,' he thought as he sat in front of his office computer trying to concentrate on the reports he was working on. The trouble was that memories of Jody kept returning unbidden. He stared at the computer and saw her face, imagined her brushing her hair from her eyes, kissing Chioke, and making the baby girl laugh. He could almost feel Jody's hand on his face, her skin against his, her kiss melting the hard edges of his heart, her body next to his making love. Deliberately, Will turned his attention to his work, but his thoughts had a way of circling around back to Jody.

Sgt. Hendricks, or the other hand, had been in a great mood ever since he'd learned that Jody was back in the States. "Good job, Campbell. The tipster was right about the phony ID. If he, or she, was also right about Jacobson being a terrorist, we dodged a bullet!"

"Yes, sir," Will said without feeling.

"Cheer up, Campbell. Supposedly, she was also involved with the drugs. If that's true, we'll be seeing fewer doped up kids."

"Hope you're right," Will said under his breath.

Three days later, Will responded to an emergency call in Dominion. A twelve-year-old girl, high on meth, was brandishing a knife.

Then weeks passed without any drug-related incidents. Will dared to hope that Hendricks was right—that they'd be seeing fewer cases involving methamphetamine. At the same time, he cringed at the idea of Jody somehow being involved in selling drugs.

<<<<>>>>

And then, early one Saturday morning, Will's pager went off. He rubbed the sleep from his eyes and checked his clock. Almost six a.m. He rolled out of bed and called into the office dispatch.

"A meth party gone wrong," said the dispatcher. Her voice

registered no emotion. "Get down to the office as soon as you can."

Sandy was the only one Will could ask to watch the kids on such short notice. He punched in Sandy's number wishing that Jody were there to help his father-in-law, but Sandy's voice was as placid as ever. "No trouble at all," he said.

Will hung up the phone and wished he weren't worried that they'd be too much for Sandy to handle without Jody.

A half hour later, Sandy met Will at the door, cinched the belt of his robe tighter around his waist, and held his arms out to Chioke. "Go. Do what you have to do. We'll be fine."

At Dawson's detachment office, Mounties were trickling into the conference room where someone had provided coffee, tea, and donuts. Gratefully, Will helped himself and sat down. He counted eleven officers seated around an oak table, and more were on their way in—a lot of manpower for a detachment as small as Dawson's. Something huge was happening.

Sgt. Hendricks stood up and rapped the table for quiet. Apparently, he hadn't gotten much sleep that night, as his eyes were red, his clothes were rumpled, and he needed a shave badly.

"Here's what we have so far. At five forty-six a.m., we received a call from Dawson's community hospital. A twenty-year-old male was brought in unconscious, probably OD'd on meth." Hendricks rubbed the stubble on his chin. "His comatose body was found a couple of miles outside of Dawson. Not surprisingly, the anonymous female who had called for an ambulance was nowhere to be seen.

"Minutes later, a couple of kids were rushed to hospital in restraints. Two males—seventeen and eighteen. One kept trying to fly away to Greenland—by flapping his arms. Claimed he had superpowers. Said he couldn't feel pain—which was probably true as he had gashes all along his arms and legs and didn't seem bothered by them. We don't have an ID on him yet.

"The other kid, Louis Westfall, was a bit more lucid. Was able to talk to the officers. Threatened to take on the whole mounted police force. Said *they* had come to conquer the world. When the officers asked who *they* were, Louis talked about a mega-party in the woods a couple of miles outside of Dawson. We couldn't get any more details on the location of said party or how many people a mega-party consisted of. He did say that he'd taken methamphetamine laced with PCP. This is consistent with the combative behavior and lack of sensitivity to pain."

Hendricks wiped his forehead with his badly rumpled handkerchief. "We had another case called in a minute ago. An adult female clawing at her face because she thought rats were eating it. I don't know how many more ODs we'll see today, but be prepared for hallucinations and violent behavior. And remember, if they can't feel pain, they'll fight harder. Try not to let them break any bones—either theirs or yours."

Will just shook his head. So, some lunatic had laced methamphetamine with angel dust for an ultimate high experience! It was going to be a long and miserable day. Situations like this always made him worry about his own kids—especially Liam. He wished that he didn't have to leave them alone so often. It was too easy for good kids to get into trouble these days.

<<<<>>>>

Will was teamed up with Spencer Wyatt, a good Mountie and a good friend. Spencer was tall, thin, and blond, and he had an easygoing attitude despite his youth. He had graduated from academy only a year ago, but he had the assurance of someone much more experienced.

The two spent most of the morning chasing, subduing, and arresting a rock-throwing teen who believed he was pitching for the Toronto Blue Jays, and a raven-haired horse thief claiming to be Lady Godiva. No, she wasn't wearing any clothes, and her hair was long, but not long enough for the part. By half past one, Will was ravenous. "Time for lunch?" he asked.

Spencer nodded, and the two got into their car, with Spencer driving.

"Ernie's pizza?" Will suggested.

"Works for me."

And with that, Spencer set out for Ernie's, while Will called into the office. Will's brain and his mouth were anticipating sausage and pepperoni wallowing in melted cheese.

"Check this one out first," said the cheery voice on the phone. "A disturbance. Someone screaming. No description, except that it sounds like a deranged young woman. Shouldn't take you too long. Talk to Andrew Sykes." The dispatcher rattled off an address on Rabbit Creek Road, and Spencer reluctantly turned the car around.

By the time Will and Spencer knocked on the complainant's door, everything was quiet except for a couple of crows cawing in the distance. Andrew Sykes' voice was low and raspy, and he talked slowly. "I couldn't see who was making that noise, but her voice scared me. It was— I don't know—shrill and human, but not exactly human. She sounded desperate one minute and overjoyed the next. And . . . okay, this going to sound weird, but it sounded like it was coming from up there." He pointed to the sky.

"You're sure it was a human voice?"

"Yes, I'm sure."

"Not a cat meowing? Or an excited rooster? Or maybe a peacock? Nothing like that?"

"No. It was a human voice."

"Go on. You said you heard a woman's voice."

"Or maybe a girl's voice. I couldn't be sure."

"Coming from your roof?" Spencer asked.

"No, I don't think so." Andrew took a long breath and ran his hands through his hair. "But maybe from somewhere out there . . ." He gestured vaguely to the trees outside his house.

"I'll look around," said Will. He left Spencer to finish taking the witness's statement, and set out to check the area surrounding the house. It consisted mostly of trees, brush, and a smattering of small houses set back from the road. Will figured that there was nothing he and Spencer could do. Whoever or whatever Andrew had heard was probably long gone, but they'd look around and check the trees for any signs that someone had climbed them.

Will looked diligently but didn't see anything unusual. He was famished. His mind was so set on a pizza with everything, that he almost missed the quiet sound of scratching coming from the roof of a nearby cottage.

He looked up. The roof was pitched, and the slope was steep enough to send shivers down Will's spine because a girl, perhaps a teen, was walking along the peak of that roof as if on a tightrope, occasionally stretching out her arms for balance. She was barefoot, and her pale, blond hair whipped wildly about her face. The girl wore only a purple T-shirt with matching shorts and seemed oblivious to the chill in the air.

'She's not much bigger than Emberlee.' That was Will's first thought.

Suddenly, the girl noticed Will. She threw back her head and crowed—a perfect imitation of a rooster; then she grinned and arched her back. The movement threw her off balance and she waved her arms wildly trying to regain her footing. Will reached out preparing to catch her if she fell, but the girl, unperturbed as far as Will could tell, steadied herself, arched her back again, and crowed.

"Get out here, Spence," Will whispered into his radio.

Turning to the girl, he said. "Don't be scared. No one's going to hurt you." His voice was soothing, unhurried. He spoke just above a whisper. "I'm Will. What's your name?"

"Peter," she answered.

"Peter," Will repeated.

"And I can fly." She crowed again. "I can fly like . . . I can fly."

"Peter Pan?" Will asked softly.

In response, the girl shrieked like a female peacock during mating season. Then she spread her arms out and jumped off the roof.

Will rushed towards her, arms outstretched and broke her fall. "You're okay," he said. "I have you."

"Let go," she screamed and twisted out of his arms. Her movements were quick and jerky like a weasel's. She screamed again, pulled a small knife out of the pocket of her shorts, and slashed Will twice along his right shoulder just as Spencer rushed over to help.

The girl fought with reckless abandon, thrashing, kicking, and waving the knife around furiously. Finally, she dropped it. Then her hands curved. Her fingernails reminded Will of an eagle's talons, and she clawed and scratched as if fighting for her life. She was only a wisp of a girl, probably weighing less than a hundred pounds, but her kick had the force of a stallion's. By the time Will and Spencer had restrained her, they were both breathing like marathon runners.

With difficulty, they packed the girl into the back seat of their vehicle while she kept on kicking, thrashing, and screaming threats and obscenities.

"She's such a tiny thing," Will mused, "and hardly older than Emberlee."

He turned to Spencer. "Who's driving?"

Spencer pointed to Will's shoulder. "Do you really have to ask? You're in worse shape than that flying wonder in the back seat. At least your shoulder is."

Will turned his head to stare at the blood seeping through long slashes in his shirt. His adrenaline was wearing off, and he suddenly became aware of the sharp pain in his shoulder. "I'm fine. Just a little blood," he mumbled.

Spencer shook his head. "Those cuts are deep. They're going to need stitches. And try to keep that arm still while I drive you to hospital."

<<<<>>>

By the time Will showed up at Sandy's door with his arm in a sling, the sun was setting, and he was exhausted. He left Spencer waiting for him in the squad car outside while he collected his children.

Sandy took one look at Will and shook his head. "Stay the night. Sleep off the painkillers. We'll sort out the rest in the morning."

"No, I'm fine," Will said. "It's just a scratch."

Sandy looked down at Will's arm but said nothing.

"Okay, maybe I'm not fine, but, Sandy, you've watched the kids all day."

Sandy raised an eyebrow and pointed at Will's injured shoulder. "Can you change a diaper? Can you get the little one dressed or undressed? Can you cook supper?"

"Emberlee can do it. Or Liam . . ." Will's voice trailed off.

Sandy shook his head. "You will stay here," he said.

"Thanks." Will gave up the bravado and sank gratefully onto Sandy's couch while Sandy signaled for Spencer to leave and brought out salami and crackers for the hungry children. Then he set about chopping up more vegetables. Without being told, Liam set the table, and Emberlee picked up toys.

'What a mess!' Will thought, watching his father-in-law cooking for his children because he, Will, was too broken to take care of them himself. 'If only Jody were still here.' There was no denying it. Will was stronger, kinder, happier, better with Jody around. 'Some father I turned out to be!'

After serving the kids dinner, Sandy brought tea along with bread and bowls of stew for Will and himself.

Will straightened his posture and assumed his Mountie persona—strong, capable, the man in charge. "The kids are doing better and better," he said, trying to make it sound as if everything was okay. "They seem to have gotten over Jody's leaving."

Sandy stared into Will's face, without a word. The look in his eyes said it all clearly—hogwash.

Will stared down at his mug of tea. "Okay, maybe they haven't gotten over Jody. When she first showed up in our lives, it seemed as if we were finally getting over the shock of Emma's death. I let my guard down. And then . . ." His Mountie persona was slipping. "Then Jody . . . got herself deported."

"You never believed her story," Sandy said gently.

"That's the trouble—I did believe it. I believed her at first. I made the colossal mistake of letting her into our lives." He clenched the fist of his good arm. "We were doing fine until she came along. And then I started to rely on her and care about her." He shook his head. "Big mistake. She wasn't Emma. No one can ever replace Emma. I should have left well enough alone."

"You and the kids weren't fine," Sandy said. "You were existing, not thriving. Emberlee missed her mother terribly and covered up her pain by taking care of you. Liam, on the other hand, hid his grief by attacking everyone and everything around him. He was heading for trouble. He still is."

"Liam's not as angry anymore. Jody's leaving was the best thing for him."

"No. He's still grieving for his mother, and he's hiding something. I'm not sure what it is." Sandy sipped his tea. "Why didn't you believe Jody?"

"Too many holes in her story. The fake ID for one thing. Then she claimed she'd never flown to Iran, yet airline records say she did. And that Homer Perlman who supposedly started the whole thing—surprise—he doesn't exist. On the other hand, that anonymous tipster—his information about the fake ID was accurate. It's a good bet the rest was true as well."

"That's the letter you showed me?"

Will nodded.

"Didn't it also say that you were acting real stupid and shouldn't be a Mountie anymore?"

Will gave a wry chuckle.

"Unless you're willing to hand in your badge, you have no business judging Jody on the strength of that letter."

Will sighed. "None of it matters anyway. My chief told me to talk Jody into leaving the country, and I did. I was following orders. That's what a good Mountie does. I didn't have a choice." His words had the hollow ring of a bad excuse, and Will was ashamed that he'd said them. "You don't believe her story, do you?"

Sandy nodded. "I do."

"Why?"

"This Homer Perlman character, or whatever his real name is, was in our internet chat room. He said Jody was in Berkeley with him at the time her supposed flight to Iran was departing. The fake ID is the only real evidence you have against her, and if she was afraid for her life, faking identification is understandable. You're the Mountie. Dig deeper. There's more to the story."

"What's the point? Jody's already gone, and the way we ended things, she'll never speak to me again."

"And if her story is true?"

Will turned his head away. He couldn't bear to look at Sandy. "If her story is true, then I destroyed the possibility of us loving each other, and love is something rare and precious." Will's shoulder began to throb; apparently, the painkillers were wearing off. He didn't reach into his pocket for more because maybe he deserved the pain. "I'd promised to stand by her. I told her she could depend on me. I said I'd never let her down, and then I tossed her out without a backward glance. I drove the last nails into her proverbial coffin." He shivered. "Even worse, if someone in the U.S. actually wants Jody dead, that coffin could be a real one. But that story just doesn't ring true."

Will waited for Sandy to say something, but Sandy was silent. Will had never run away from uncomfortable truths before today. He wouldn't do so now. He turned back to Sandy. "I'll dig deeper," he said.

<<<<>>>>

So, Will dug deeper. He found no evidence, no reservations in Iranian hotels, no car rentals, no credit card purchases, nothing that proved Johanna Jacobson had ever been in Iran. 'Doesn't mean all that much,' he thought. 'She could have used a different name. Or I could have just missed it.'

He searched again for a report of Jody's alleged kidnapping, and still found no records. Well, if everyone believed she had flown to Iran, there wouldn't be records. Such an unlikely story. Sandy believed Jody, but there was no way that Jody could have been kidnapped. There would be records . . . unless . . . unless she had been kidnapped by someone high up in the United States government. Unlikely. But if it were true, Will would need to get his hands on classified documents, which was impossible. Will shook his head. The facts just didn't support Jody's abduction story.

Will tried to put it out of his mind, but the nagging voice in his head persisted. 'You're overlooking the obvious, you bloody fool!'

<<<<>>>>

Two days later, as Will was taking a shower, his thoughts drifted unbidden to that horrible afternoon when he'd treated Jody like a two-bit criminal. The image of her face, deflated like a two-day-old balloon, replayed bits and pieces of their conversation. "I'll probably need a passport by the time Canada lets me back in."

Will dropped his soap. Bloody fool, indeed! The passport!

The first chance he got, Will checked U.S. passport records. Sure enough, no passport had ever been issued to anyone fitting Jody's description named Johanna Jacobson. 'How the heck did they let Johanna Jacobson—and that was the name on the airline records—how did they let her board a plane to Iran without a passport? Either someone was grossly negligent, or someone with enough clout to fake airline records was lying.

Or she'd faked a passport the way she'd faked her ID. Like a bloodhound following a rabbit's scent, Will kept digging.

He logged on to her website, <u>fairytalesfortherestofus</u>, and scrolled down to the first entry. The Jody who had created the website was a far cry from the Jody who jumped at the sound of a firecracker. The one on the website was fearless. "Beware the bureaucrat, my son," she'd written—a poem blaming mega-billionaires for California's energy crisis. She'd rewritten *The Emperor's New Clothes* with her president cast as the emperor.

'There's a fine line between freedom of speech and treason,' thought Will, somewhat shocked by Jody's stories.

Her stories about foxes and chickens accused the president's people of attempting to assassinate Senators Leahy and Daschle with anthrax-laced letters allegedly written by Osama bin Laden. There was more of the same.

'A loose cannon,' thought Will. This was no ordinary chatroom.

Further on, someone who called himself Spiderman joined the chatroom. 'According to Sandy, Jody used to have a crush on him. Spiderman had asked Jody to meet him in Berkeley to plan a peace project, and Jody had agreed.

Jody hadn't posted after that.

In Spiderman's final post, he had described trying to calm a hysterical Jody, who was insisting on flying to Iran.

Will felt deflated. He'd found no evidence for a government conspiracy and no evidence of a kidnapping—just a distraught hippie with an overactive imagination. And this was the same Jody to whom he'd entrusted his children. He'd been right to break off his relationship with her.

Will should have felt vindicated; he should have breathed a sigh of relief. Instead, he felt numb, crushed. Will kept on reading because 'hope springs eternal.'

Soon after Jody's disappearance, Ivan Buncheski, Jody's former editor, had joined the chatroom as Big Bad Wolf, worried because Jody hadn't shown up for work. It took a bit of doing for Will to find Buncheski since he'd been fired from his old newspaper, but Will finally got him on the phone.

"Ditzy female," Ivan grumbled. She's the reason I got fired."

'More ammo against Jody.' Will sighed. "What happened?"

"She got me thinking; that's what happened. So, I stuck my neck out, wrote what I thought, and got fired." He chuckled. "Best thing that ever happened. I'm running my own paper now, and I can print whatever I dadburn want."

"But what about Jody?"

"We all figured she'd been killed. Then, I got a call from her about a month ago asking for a job."

"She's been living in Canada," Will said, "watching my kids, and we . . . well, the kids got quite close to her."

"And?"

"Can she be trusted? Is she a victim or a traitor? The stories she wrote are . . . inflammatory to put it mildly."

"Is it treason if what she wrote was the truth? Give me an

email address, and I'll send you a copy of Alexander Lidecker's confession letter. He used to work for the president. The letter made quite a stir when it first hit the papers and airways. Then it fizzled and died like most news does. I'll email you some other articles as well. A lot of questionable shit went on. Johanna was the first to figure it out. That's how she got into all that trouble."

"Do you have a number for Alexander Lidecker?" Will asked.

"Lidecker's dead. He died in an African prison. Someone probably got to him because of that letter."

<<<<>>>>

Buncheski's email arrived a couple of hours later. Will learned that two of the letters laced with an American strain of Anthrax were mailed to Pat Leahy and Thomas Daschle, two thorns in the president's side.

Will kept reading. It chilled him to discover that, yes, the United States did torture suspected spies, and that it didn't take much evidence to be classified as one. With her dark complexion, Jody might even have been mistaken for a Middle Easterner. He'd said to Jody, "Maybe, if you came from some lesser-known African dictatorship. But the United States doesn't do that." And Jody had answered, "They do now."

Then she'd shown him the scars on her back.

Maybe he couldn't have prevented her being deported. But he could have stood beside her, supported her, and believed her.

Advocated for her. It might have made a difference. Oh, how he wished for a do-over!

He sent the information he'd uncovered to the immigration board. "Johanna Jacobson isn't a terrorist, and she's not a drug pusher. She entered Canada as a political refugee."

Then Will logged on to fairytalesfortherestofus as MountieDad: "Jody, you weren't lying. I should have believed you. If you never want to speak to me again, I understand, but please forgive me. I'm sorry, and I love you. I should have stood by you. I wish you were back here with us. I love you. I love you. I love you."

Will checked the website each morning, hoping to see a post from Jody. Even if it was to tell him he'd missed his chance. 'She must still be mad at me,' thought Will. 'Well, she has every right to be.'

He logged on to Jody's website again. "Jody, I love you. Please say something. Tell me you still care about me. Or tell me you hate me, but tell me something. I can't take the suspense."

He posted his comment. 'That sounds desperate,' he thought, but there was no way to take it back.

He waited for the reply that never came. And then an unsettling thought struck him. Jody's mother lived in Mississippi—where the hurricane had caused so much damage. 'What if Jody couldn't post anything because she was injured or . . . killed?'

CHAPTER 13

On Tuesday, August 23, 2005, the National Hurricane Center informed the United States that Tropical Storm Katrina would become a hurricane. As Katrina grew in strength, she became the major topic of the evening newscasts.

By Sunday evening, Katrina was predicted to be catastrophic. Watching the news on television, Martha and Johanna heard the reporter's dire announcement: "All residents of Pascagoula are urged to evacuate."

Martha made a face at the television. "We're not going anywhere," she declared. "They said the same thing last year when Hurricane Ivan blew through the gulf, and it was a big nothing. Before that, it was Hurricane Dennis. This year won't be any different. Trust me. The weather people don't know how to stick their heads out a window and look at the sky."

Johanna was inclined to agree with her mother. After all, she'd weathered a Yukon winter. How could a hurricane be any worse? "I'll finish boarding up the windows," she said. "We have enough food, water, and batteries to see us through at least five hurricanes."

<<<<>>>>

Katrina announced her arrival into Pascagoula with winds of over one hundred miles per hour. "See," Martha said with a fake smile on her face. "Nothing to it. We just ride out this wind in our house, safe and warm. We have plenty of food, a TV for entertainment, and each other for company. Too bad the windows are boarded up or we'd see some amazing sights."

Johanna smiled and nodded. She tensed up as the wind's howling increased and jumped every time something hit the side of the house, but she was glad that they hadn't joined that long, long line of people she'd seen on television, driving bumper to bumper on the jammed-up freeways, inching their way to safer ground.

To distract herself from the squalls outside, Martha poured Southern Comfort over ice cubes, and added a sprig of mint. "Just a drop of liquid courage," she laughed. "Nothing wrong with that."

Meanwhile, Johanna listened to the news and tried to ignore the sound of rattling windows. Of course, Katrina was the top story of the evening. Safe inside, Johanna watched the storm's devastation on the TV screen. Trees were the hurricane's first casualties. Katrina's rampage started with flying sticks and small branches. Rain fell sideways. But this was only the beginning. Katrina uprooted trees and smashed windows, even those that had been carefully boarded up before the storm.

Instead of reaching for Southern Comfort, Johanna picked up a pen and notebook. "I've always been terrified of storms," she wrote. "It's an irrational fear, I know. Still, it feels as if the menacing winds are threatening me personally. But a First Nations elder taught me to stand up to my fears; that's what I'm doing now."

The walls shook, and the windows continued to rattle. Johanna remembered pounding nail after nail into the boards covering the windows. She hoped she'd done a good enough job. Meanwhile, Martha poured herself a second glass of Southern Comfort.

"I'm impressed by the raw power of the winds," Johanna wrote. "Nothing stands in their way. Trees bend and break. Stop signs fly. Cars are overturned. These winds own the streets of Pascagoula." Johanna sucked on her pen, then continued writing. "I'm impressed, but I'm also scared."

A sharp crack, the noise of a kitchen window breaking, sounded above the wail of the winds. Broken glass flew across the room. The boards Johanna had carefully nailed over the window went sailing down the street. Johanna screamed. Martha dropped her glass.

"It's okay," Johanna said, trying to sound calm. "We're safe. We'll be a bit more uncomfortable because of the broken window, but in a few hours, it'll all be over."

But the wind, shrieking through the broken window, disagreed.

Martha didn't say anything. Instead, she went into the upstairs bathroom and shook two Valium tablets out of an amber vial. She swallowed them without water. Then she knelt before her statue of Mary and mumbled the words of the rosary.

"It seems as if it can't get any worse," Johanna wrote, "and then it does. Most of our windows are cracked now, and three are completely broken. I thought I'd boarded them up well enough, but the storm just knocked the boards clean off the walls. The air from outside tingles, and you can smell that fishy, algae smell of an angry ocean. I'm glad our house has a second story.

"On the positive side, now that the windows are broken, we can see what's happening outside. Many trees have been uprooted. The ones still standing are bent almost to ninety-degree angles. Trash cans, cars, chunks of houses get blown about like kites. Someone's roof just flew by.

"Maybe I'm better off not knowing what's out there.

"Our walls are shaking badly now. I hope they hold out."

Nothing else happened for a couple of hours. Johanna was hoping that they'd seen the worst of the storm. She was about to breathe a sigh of relief, when Martha started screaming. "The surge!" she yelled. "It's the surge! They warned us about it on TV. 911! Call 911!"

Johanna looked out a broken window and saw a wall of water half as tall as the house rolling towards her like a scene in a movie—unreal. It took a second for the shock to pass.

"Upstairs, Mom, right now," she screamed, but Martha was already climbing the staircase. A second later, Johanna was right behind her.

The shock of the wave hitting Martha's house almost knocked Johanna off her feet. At the first landing, she turned, and to her horror, saw water gushing in under the door and through the broken windows. 'Please don't go any higher,' she prayed as the water rose steadily up the stairs.

Seconds later, Johanna sat on her bed and punched 911 into Martha's phone, shaking with fear all the while.

It took a long time to get through. Finally, a woman's voice said the most wonderful words in the world. "911. What is your emergency?"

Johanna took a deep breath. "We need help. The water is rising inside our house. If it gets much higher, we won't make it." She tried to sound calm as she gave the dispatcher her address.

In a small voice, the dispatcher answered. "We can't do anything right now. Our copters can't fly in the storm. Sit tight. Get up as high as possible. We'll look for you as soon as we can." It sounded as if she were trying not to cry. "I'm sorry," she added.

Then the line went dead.

Martha shook Johanna's shoulder. "What did they say? When are they coming to rescue us?"

"Not for a while." Johanna shuddered as she said the words.

"You should have cried. You should have told them we're dying. You could have said I'm having a heart attack. Anything to move us to the top of their list."

"It's not that, Mom. They can't fly in the storm. They won't come until it's over."

Johanna braced herself for a bout of hysteria from Martha. It didn't come. "If I'm meeting God today, I might as well get ready," Martha said. She put her arms around her daughter, and the two hugged and hugged. Martha said the rosary; she didn't need her beads. Johanna prayed the way she always did. "God help me through this. And if I'm going to die, please remember the good stuff."

Johanna wanted to scream. 'Face your fears,' she told herself. It was becoming her mantra. Instead of screaming, Johanna looked about for her notepad, hoping to distract herself from the fact that she might die any minute. Besides, she wanted to capture the dispatcher's words and that sense of terror and being abandoned that followed hearing them. But the notepad was floating somewhere downstairs, and the ink, with all her words, had probably bled off the paper. That's when she lost it. She began to cry as if her heart would break wide open.

The stormwater rose to about two feet on the upper floor, causing Johanna's nightstand to swish back and forth with the current. The ceiling and walls shuddered, and Johanna prayed that the house would hold together. Then, with one long roar, a chunk of the roof blew away. Looking up, Johanna found herself staring at a wet, dark-gray sky. The winds howled and shrieked like banshees, while branches, bricks, glass, and other objects hurled themselves through the sky like missiles.

And all at once it was over. The rain stopped, and the water inside the house began subsiding. The silence was startling after the steady roaring of the wind. 'It's over.' That was Johanna's first thought. And then she figured it out. The hurricane's eye was passing over Pascagoula.

All too soon the pounding storm returned.

<<<<>>>>

Nothing lasts forever—not the good, not the terrifying. Gradually, the rain lessened, and the wind subsided, becoming an annoying, noisy chill. Then, over the noise of the storm, Johanna heard the heavenly sound of helicopter blades.

"How many people? Any injured? Any children?" A human, whom Johanna figured to be an angel, was talking through a bullhorn.

"Two adults. No injuries," Johanna yelled back, holding up two fingers. Then she cried with relief.

Getting hauled into a helicopter was another unnerving experience—being tossed around by angry winds and hoping that the cable holding the pitiful basket she sat in wouldn't snap. But the promise of rescue, of respite from the battering rain and winds—you couldn't see it as anything but a blessing.

<<<<>>>>

Eventually, Johanna and her mother ended up at Martha's sister's house in Colorado. Aunt Muriel was a pale, wrinkly woman in her late sixties, petite and unassuming. She scowled a lot, and made it known that Martha and Johanna were "inconvenient" but that she had to take them in because that's what Jesus would do.

<<<<>>>>

Johanna wrote her story of surviving Katrina and sent it in to Ivan Buncheski, who published it and asked for more of the same.

After a dinner of Kentucky Fried Chicken with all the fixings, Johanna announced her intentions: "I want to go to New Orleans, or as close as I can get to it. That's where the real stories are, and I want to be the one to tell them. Horrible as Katrina was, one good thing came out of it; this is the first time in forever that I've felt like an actual writer. I have some money saved, and if I don't do anything stupid, it should last me long enough to get some good reporting done. Aunt Muriel, thank you for your hospitality, but it's time I paid my own way, and this will be a start."

Martha burst into tears and left the table crying, "My baby! My baby!"

Aunt Muriel tried to hide her smile. "Whatever you think is right, dear," she said, and later that evening, she slipped Johanna fifty dollars.

The next day, Johanna left Colorado in a black Honda Rent-A-Wreck. Katrina's victims had been relocated from Louisiana's Superdome to Houston's Astrodome, so, Johanna figured that was a good place to stop first. Maybe some of the hurricane survivors would have stories to tell.

<<<<>>>

Johanna fell in love with Harriet the minute the old lady opened her mouth. Very thin, very black, Harriet had wispy, white hair, and a smile that could light up Louisiana. In spite of everything, she was smiling! Johanna turned on her tape recorder and let Harriet tell her story.

Harriet's story

"Now, I'm old—gettin' on eighty—but I ain't so old that I don't have at least some of my wits about me. And I heard what I heard, and I seen what I seen. And I ain't superstitious, but I know that there's more to this world than what you can kick with your toe or eat on a sandwich. I been believing in the Lord since I was four years old, and I ain't about to stop now.

"So, I was sleeping in my bed at the home. It's an old folks' home, and there's just no getting around that. So, I got used to it, and I didn't notice the smell of the pee no more, nor all the ceiling cracks, nor all the snoring and moaning that goes with an old folks' home. And that's just the way it is. You don't have to like it, but that's what it is.

"Anyway, I was sleeping in the bed, or at least trying to sleep. But the wind was howling something ferocious, like it was going to tear the home apart. Well, I ain't afraid of dying. Heck, I figured I've been hanging around this old world too long already. And it was about time that the good Lord took me. Now I ain't about to tell Him that. He's God and I'm me, and He'll come for me all in good time. But I figure, 'Lord, if it's all the same to you, could you make it sooner instead of later?'

"So anyway, I'm trying to sleep, and I'm listening to the wind whipping through the trees outside, and then it got even stronger, and there were all kinds of thumps of large and heavy things thrown about outside. And the rain was pouring! Lord, it was coming down like buckets and barrels! Now, I don't mind being dead. I'm ready for that. But the dying part, that's another story. I don't want to be bashed against the wall like no tomato ready for squashing.

"So, I'm listening. And then there's this roaring sound. No way I can describe it 'scept it was roaring. And there were folks suddenly screaming and hollering. And then the window just blew into bits and broke inward, and all this water swamped me. My roommate, Lucinda, she couldn't walk, and she just got caught in the flooding and I guess she must have died. But me, I was always a swimmer. And I'm stronger than most of the folk passing time at the home. I guess my instincts must have kicked in, and I held my breath and managed to kick myself up to where air was bubbled up at the ceiling. The room was almost filled with water. Like a fishbowl it was. Only I was the fish, and I wasn't fond of the feeling. When the room was mostly full of water, and it wasn't gushing so fast, I took a big old breath and swam for the broken window, and fought my way out of the room. Like a netted catfish, which is pretty much what I was, only in reverse—battling to get to the surface and breathe air instead of water. There I was, swimming for my life, and I managed to grab onto a tree that was floating by. Except it was really me that was floating by and not the tree. So, I found myself a perch above the water, kind of like a nest with branches holding me up. I sat there ready to wait out the storm.

"And all around me, folks was bleeding, and dying, and moaning, and shrieking, and it suddenly came to me. I asked the Lord, "Is this the end, Lord? Is this Armageddon?" I felt so old, and so . . . left. It seemed like everyone was caught in the rapture, and I was the only one left behind. And I asked the good Lord, "Take me, Lord. Take me." But He didn't. And I asked him again. And I thought maybe if I hadn't a swum out of the room, if I'd a stayed and drowned, maybe I'd be with God in his glory instead of stuck up a tree with the rain coming down and the wind blowing wild around me.

"I felt sad watching as everyone around me was caught up in the rapture.

"So, I stayed stuck in the tree for what seemed like forever, but it was really only about a day. And my mind was doing tricks all the while, and I figured it was the rapture, and I had been left behind. All because I was a good swimmer. And that didn't seem like a good reason to leave me.

"So then, sometime later—I kind of lost count, because I was feeling poorly and passing in and out of consciousness. Anyway, this guy with a bullhorn was floating by on a raft, and he spotted me, and he told me to hold on, and that help was a coming. So, that's when I figured it wasn't the rapture, but just an old regular storm. But, by all that's right and holy, that weren't no ordinary storm. If the end of the world is any worse than that, well, I hope I'm good and dead before it happens.

"Then this helicopter comes flying over me, and they're yelling at me with the bullhorn again, and telling me that help is coming, and to hold on. Well, I been holding on for more 'n a day now. I wasn't about to let go just when someone's seen me. Then this rope comes down beside me, and this young 'un climbs down this ladder, and they sit me in this basket, and they reel me up like they was fishing. They haul me into this 'copter, and they check me out; they say I'm fine, and in the end, they leave me with a mess of other people who were hot, sick, and fed up like me.

"I find out later it's the Superdome, and they dumped the lot of us there. They had cots for us to lie on, and at first there was food and water, but later they must of run out. And I wasn't doing much of anything but lying around, so, it weren't no different from the home. 'Scept, it got blazing hot. There's nothing like a Louisiana summer day to drain the tiger right out of your tank."

It didn't need much editing. Johanna typed it up on a library computer and emailed it to Ivan.

"Yeh, I can probably use it," Ivan typed back. He was never one for showing enthusiasm.

<<<<>>>>

Driving her rented Honda, Johanna reached the outskirts of New Orleans after most of the floodwater had been pumped out of the city. The city was bizarre, disjointed. The smells of ocean, garbage, and death were everywhere; sometimes the odor was just a whiff, but sometimes the smell was strong enough to make Johanna gag.

Katrina had reduced houses to untidy woodpiles; she'd turned cars upside down and left them to rust in roadside ditches. Johanna stepped over and around uprooted trees, unidentifiable trash, a stop sign, and a tattered beach umbrella as she made her way through the city looking for a good topic for her next article. A bloated rat's body lay in a ditch. Johanna gagged but kept on going.

People were coming back into New Orleans and taking stock. They rolled up their pant legs, took off their shoes and socks, and waded through sludgy puddles looking for something worth salvaging, looking for pieces of their former lives.

It was a city of heartache, but also one of hope. Along with the casualties and looters, there were people offering food, shelter, medical attention, and, best of all, kindness. That's what Johanna wanted to write about. Among the wreckage that was Katrina's aftermath, Johanna wanted to find goodness. She wanted to find the love.

CHAPTER 14

As she searched for a story, camera in hand and a tape recorder in her purse, Johanna noticed a flyer taped to a leaning telephone pole:

THE PAWS CAUSE

I've always had a thing for animals. Just a part of who I am, I guess. So, when I found out about all the critters left homeless after Katrina, I knew I had to do something. At first, the situation was desperate. They were just shooting the animals rather than letting them drown, starve to death, or worse. Animal shelters and rescue organizations were overwhelmed. So many animals needed homes and medical attention. I figured I'd just be minding the pets for a few days until they could be reunited with their families.

But, even if they learned where their pets had ended up, most of the families were suddenly homeless and couldn't take care of their faithful, furry friends. That's where I came in. Well, I had to do something. I don't have a lot of room, but I figured I'd do what I could.

First there was this golden retriever, half drowned and so waterlogged I almost couldn't pull him out of the flood waters. But I managed to get him into my skiff and take him home. Well, after that, I knew this was my thing, my way of helping. I took off each day, looking for animals in need. I tried to find their owners, which was almost impossible.

So now I'm just caring for a mini zoo until the owners appear. I have some property out by Colyell, and it's a temporary home for a parrot, twenty-five cats, thirty-two dogs, including a Great Dane and a Saint Bernard, assorted chickens—I forget how many—a rabbit, and a very old pony. It's costing a fortune to feed them all, and I'd appreciate any help I could get. My P.O. Box number is 4397 in Colyell if anyone wants to throw a couple of coins my way. Checks can be made out to The Paws Cause.

Thanks for any help you can give, and God bless.

Nick Underhill

Johanna found an open motel in Colyell and got a room there. Then she wrote to the P. O. number asking Mr. Underhill for an interview. "People might see my article and send you some money," she wrote, fingers crossed.

Mr. Underhill happily agreed to the interview. For once, everything was going Johanna's way. They met for lunch at Harry's Diner, a cheery café with an eclectic décor of ferns and neon beer signs. If Harry's had air conditioning, it wasn't working, but an overhead fan pushed the muggy air around enough for Johanna to feel comfortable.

Mr. Underhill turned out to be a Grizzly Adams sort in blue jeans and a T-shirt with a brown pelican printed on its front. Black hair, a mustache, and a beard hid most of his face. "Call me Nick," he said in a lazy Southern drawl and smiled a smile that lit up the diner. Instead of a handshake, he hugged her as if they'd been friends from kindergarten.

Johanna ordered hamburgers, fries, and coffee for the both of them, and while they waited for their food to arrive, Nick began telling his story into Johanna's tape recorder. "It's what I was meant to do," he said. "I love animals, and it broke my heart to see them suffering. So, if there was some way I could help, well, of course I had to do it."

He smiled and tapped his chin. To Johanna there was something endearing about this man. And so familiar! Had they met before? The conversation was as comfortable as chatting with a best friend around a campfire.

The meals were served, and Nick frequently waved a French fry around as he spoke. "My hardest rescue was a spectacularly stubborn billy goat." He shook his head, "Gaw-lee." He slapped his thigh and Johanna laughed. "This sucker had the biggest set of horns I've ever seen on a goat. He'd somehow gotten himself tied up to a telephone pole by a fallen wire, and I had a devil of a time getting him loose. The poor guy was terrified and kept trying to butt me. My thanks for rescuing him was a seat so sore that, the next day, I just about lost it every time I sat down."

Nick had a homey laugh and expansive gestures. "You're a kindred soul, I think," he said and causally touched Johanna's arm.

Excited sparks flew—so suddenly and unexpectedly that she almost dropped the hamburger she was holding. She had a tremendous desire to kiss him. Clearly, there was something magical about this guy. With everything that was happening around her, how could she be thinking about sex? With a sigh of regret, Johanna controlled her impulse. After all, she barely knew the man. Besides, she was a reporter, and kissing the interviewee was highly unprofessional. 'Shame, shame on me.' She nodded to Nick, encouraging him to keep going.

But . . . her arm was warm where he had touched it. This was the happiest Johanna had been since, well, since she'd been with Will. She hoped this interview would last a long time.

Nick seemed oblivious as he talked about waterlogged cats and a half-starved beagle.

"Can I see your place?" Johanna asked after regaining some composure, "and take a few pictures of the animals?"

"See my place?" Nick's eyes grew wide, and beneath the beard and shaggy hair, his face had turned pale. You'd think she'd pointed a gun in his face. You'd think she was asking him to shoot his best friend or burn down his house. "I, I really can't let you do that," he stammered. "It's too dangerous. It's too dangerous. There's . . . there's been some . . . some storm damage on my property . . . A lot of damage. Besides, the animals are nervous. They don't know you, and they're likely to kick or bite."

But Johanna was so eager to get her story that she didn't pay attention to Nick's agitation. 'Reporters are supposed to be pushy,' she figured. "I'll risk it. And I'll be careful. Please. It would add a lot to the story. A picture's worth a thousand words and all that. Just a couple of quick snapshots and then I'm gone."

Nick scowled. 'What now?' He didn't want to make her angry because he wanted her to write the article. He needed the money. God, but he needed the money! His brain raced, searching for good excuses as to why she couldn't take any photographs. He shook his head in frustration. "No! No friggin' way," he finally blurted out. He sighed in exasperation and took hold of her hand—an earnest gesture. "Look I'd love to let you see the animals, but . . ." He looked into her eyes. "You see . . . ." He kept searching his mind for more excuses but found none.

For several seconds, Nick stared into Johanna's eyes. Then he jerked his hand back as if he'd burned it.

"What's the matter?"

"Gotta use the john," he mumbled and sprang up from his seat. "Gotta go bad."

'He's a character; that's for sure,' Johanna thought as she watched Nick walk away. 'A little weird, but definitely one of the good guys.'

<<<<>>>>

In the men's room, Nick splashed water on his face. This reporter—she looked just like that nosy liberal he'd run into ages ago, the woman who somehow had found out secrets she wasn't privy to. But those secrets were a part of a different lifetime, a time when he'd been someone. Back then, he'd had style and class . . . and money instead of a conscience. But she was supposed to be dead. It couldn't be her. Could it? Fuck! Now what was he going to do? Had she recognized him? Probably not. She didn't act like it. If she wrote an article about the Paws Cause, it would net him some money. And he could certainly use it. But if she had recognized him . . . what then? He'd never actually killed anybody—with his own hands, anyway.

He sighed and said, "Remordia," his sort-of magic word. It wasn't really magic, but somehow, whenever he said it, he felt a surge of power shooting through him; and then people believed whatever came out of his mouth, and his problems resolved themselves. Well, if she recognized him, he'd have to kill her. Too bad! He thought he was through with facing the consequences of things he'd done back when he'd been a White House hotshot; but somehow, no matter where he went, his past just kept finding him.

"Remordia," Nick repeated. And with that word, the last vestiges of his conscience died.

Was she or wasn't she that reporter? Well, he certainly couldn't shoot her in Harry's diner. So, he'd take her out into the bayou, he decided, and he'd let her talk; that way, he could learn how much she knew. If she seemed harmless enough and wasn't the one who'd smeared his secrets all over the internet (actually, all over her pathetic little website, but that had started things rolling), he'd make up some excuse and take her back to her motel. But if there was any chance she recognized him, well, he'd have to dump her into the river. It would be weeks before anyone found her body.

He wiped his hands on a paper towel and headed back to the table, wearing the happiest of grins on his face. "You know what? Maybe I can show you my place after all. Just give me a day to put stuff away and make sure it's safe for company. Could you do that?"

"Of course."

"Then you can take your pictures of my babies. Take all the pictures you want. But I should warn you—seeing some of the critters will break your heart."

CHAPTER 15

Shortly after sunrise, Nick showed up at Johanna's motel in a muddy, red Dodge Ram truck. "Get in," Nick said and gestured at the passenger door. "It'll be easier if I drive. My place is considerably off the beaten path." She hopped in, and a cloud of dust rose from the seat as she sat down. She buckled her seat belt, and they took off.

"Did I tell you about the horse that I pulled out of the bayou?" Nick asked. "He was stuck in quicksand and thrashing around. It was out by Alligator Bend, I think, and he was up to his neck in the muck. I was afraid he was a goner. But, never say die—that's my motto. All I had was my bare hands and a rope. So, I grabbed the horse by the mane, and tied the rope around his neck; and I hauled and hauled. We were almost out of the muck. I started to breathe easier, when what do I see just across the water, but a family of alligators! They don't call it Alligator Bend for nothing. Two of them spotted us and started swimming toward us. Well, I wasn't giving up on the horse. Not after all that pulling and hauling. I just kept throwing rocks at the gators until they gave up and swam away. I tell you, it's a miracle I'm still alive."

"Wow!" That was all Johanna could think of to say.

"Short cut," Nick mumbled and turned the wheel sharply. Soon they were driving along a road with ruts deep as wading pools. Nick's truck was covered by even more dust. "Where are we going?" Johanna asked. She didn't want to complain, but all the dust in the truck was making her eyes water.

"Into the heart of Louisiana. It's wild, and it's beautiful, and I'm blessed to live there."

After a half hour, Nick veered back onto a paved road, and minutes later, he stopped for gas. As Johanna watched him filling the tank, she tried to fit together the pieces of the puzzle that was this man. He felt familiar. It was like déjà vu. She was almost sure that she'd seen him somewhere before, but, of course, that was impossible.

"Do you want anything from the snack bar?" he asked.

"Maybe a Coke. And a box of tissues, if they sell them. And if they have anything for allergies."

As Nick began walking away, that flash of recognition hit Johanna. "Homer? Are you Homer Perlman?" she asked. "AKA Spiderman?"

Without answering, Nick headed for the minimart, mumbling something under his breath. So, she WAS the nerdy reporter, and she'd recognized him. Too bad for her.

Inside the store, Nick stared at the candy bar display and considered Johanna's words. Well, he knew what he had to do.

He'd keep up the Louisiana charm, and he'd take her far enough upriver that no one would hear anything or find her body for a long time—if ever.

Meanwhile, Johanna's eyes kept itching, and her nose began to drip unprofessionally. She had no tissues in the fanny pack she'd brought with her, so, she wiped her nose on the back of her hand.

It made sense. Nick had to be Homer Perlman, the guy who had logged onto her website as Spiderman. That seemed a lifetime ago. Back then, she'd pegged him for a hero, someone who stood up for honesty and was willing to risk his life for what he believed. And he was someone she'd had a monumental crush on. Nick had to be the same person. No wonder she felt all that chemistry when he'd touched her hand.

But Sandy had told her that Spiderman was responsible for her kidnapping, and that Spiderman was the one who had told the chat room she'd flown to Iran. She remembered the way Homer had talked. He was so, so genuine. The man was good and honest. He couldn't have had anything to do with her abduction. And if Nick was the same person, then he had to be good and honest as well. 'For heaven's sakes, he rescues animals!'

And then there was the magic when Nick had put his hand on her arm, and the world turned rosy. She thought about that touch, and she imagined kissing him, a friendly, no-big-deal and thanks-for-everything peck on the cheek. No, she imagined lots more than a peck. She imagined the whole deal. Dang, why did he have to be so sexy?

Well, Sandy didn't know everything. No, Nick wasn't a villain. He probably had a good explanation for whatever had made Sandy suspicious. Anyway, she wasn't going to make any snap decisions. 'Nick's one of the good guys,' Johanna decided and crossed her fingers. 'He just has to be.'

As she mulled over the mystery that was Nick Underhill/Homer Perlman, her allergies began to bother her again. Maybe Nick had tissues or something in his glove compartment. 'Here's hoping,' she thought and opened it.

Inside, she found a rental agreement signed by Nick Underhill as the renter. 'Rental truck? Weird!' thought Johanna and began rummaging through the rest of the papers inside. Under the rental agreement and an owner's manual, Johanna discovered a stack of driver's licenses.

Curious, she looked through the licenses, which were issued from various states. Each had a different driver's name. She expected to find Homer Perlman's name, but it wasn't there. 'Maybe that one's in his wallet,' thought Johanna. One of the licenses was issued to Alexander Lidecker, and the name rang a bell.

Guiltily, she looked around to see if anyone had noticed her snooping. Nick was returning from the store, so, she quickly put all the licenses back in the bottom of the glove compartment and closed its door.

Was she in horrible danger? Should she get out of the truck

immediately and run? But where to? An icy chill of past nightmares shot through her. No, she was probably overreacting? There was that moment of indecision, and then Nick was back behind the wheel, and they were off.

"Yes, I'm really Homer Perlman," Nick said. "I changed my name. I had to." Nick shook his head, and his sigh conveyed volumes of pain. "You deserve to hear the whole story, but it's going to be hard to listen to. That night that we hung the signs, I was so focused, so sure that I was doing something good, something worthwhile. Well, I was concentrating on hanging my signs, and I wasn't watching what was happening around me. And I was attacked."

"Oh my gosh, how awful. Who attacked you?"

Nick gulped. "I never knew who or what attacked me. I was drugged." He took a deep breath. "This is hard to talk about. They held me for months and kept asking who I'd been talking to. Well, you were the only one I'd ever talked to, and I'd never give out your name. I'm just not that kind of guy."

He brushed his hand across his eyes. "Pretend you didn't see that. Real men don't cry." He looked down. "They beat me a lot. And starved me. And, and in the end, I was so broken that all I wanted to do was die. I still have nightmares. I dream of chains, and whips, and hoses. I wake screaming and spend the rest of the night pacing, trying to soothe my nerves—which never works."

Nick wiped the sweat from his forehead. "I've never told this story to anyone before." Johanna had a surge of sympathy for

Nick and for all he had gone through. He was telling the truth. He had to be. The story was fantastic, but it was the same as her story. No one believed her, and she knew what that felt like. She couldn't do the same thing to Homer. Or Nick.

But there was still one thing bothering her, and she had to harden her heart and summon all her strength to ask it. "I'm so sorry . . . that you suffered all that. And I'm even sorrier for what I'm going to ask you. But I have to know. Why did you tell everyone that I'd flown to Iran?" She watched his eyes, hoping, oh so hard, that he had a good explanation. Because, damn it all, she liked the guy.

He gave her a look like he'd just been stabbed. "That wasn't me," he finally said. "I never logged onto your website after our Berkeley meeting. I'd written the name of our website on a scrap of paper which I kept in my wallet, and when they kidnapped me, they went through my stuff. They must have been the ones who made up the story about you flying to Iran."

"How did you get away?" she asked.

"By pretending I was dead. I know some yoga, and I know how to stop my heart. So, they thought I'd died. They wrapped me up in duct tape and threw me into a trash dumpster. When I finally got loose, I changed my name, grew the long hair and beard, and moved to Louisiana. But what hurts the most . . ." 'Hot dog, but I'm good at this,' he thought and managed to keep from smiling. "What hurts the most is that you don't believe me. You're the one person in this whole, messy, Godforsaken world that I thought I could count on, and you're asking questions."

Johanna turned away. She felt so mean, so guilty for questioning him after all he'd been through. She looked at Homer's face and saw such pain, such sorrow! "I do believe you," she said finally. To change the subject, she asked, "So, what should I call you?"

"Call me Nick. It's best." He smiled and reached for her hand. "Don't worry. You're safe here with me."

That smile was charming, so warm and genuine! Johanna took it all in and was happy.

Nick pulled out of the gas station and a half hour later, turned onto a dirt road. Minutes later, they arrived at a harbor so small it had no name. "Anyone home?" Nick called, but no one answered. A shack with no roof, three docks, a cement ramp for launching boats, and a ten-foot motorboat tied up to one of the docks were the only indications that humans had ever been here. "Welcome to the bayou, my home and the most beautiful place on earth."

"You're a Louisiana boy?" she asked.

"Born and raised."

They jumped out of the truck, and Nick offered Johanna his hand to steady her as she stepped aboard the motorboat. She didn't actually need any help, but she took his hand anyway, enjoying that gesture of Southern manners and the warmth of his fingers.

The boat was an aluminum skiff with an Evinrude outboard engine—none too powerful, but more than adequate for cruising the bayous. Nick gave the starter cord three pulls, and the motor came to life with a reluctant rumble. Then he pulled up an anchor and guided the skiff out into the center of the river.

Johanna had spent her childhood in Mississippi, and the swamps and bayous had that "coming home" feeling for her. She'd whiled away many hours fishing and boating in the wetlands. A few places were stagnant and smelly, but most were breathtakingly beautiful. This stretch of river was one of the beautiful ones. She took a big breath. The air carried the scent of damp earth and lush vegetation. Yes, she was back home in bayou country. Wisps of fog danced on the water, hiding a world of critters from view. Plant mats floated serenely, poking their leaves up above the fog like islands in miniature. Fairy islands, Johanna used to call them. And those crazy, bald cypress trees! They stood above the water on fat pyramids of ropey roots, with Spanish moss hanging like spiderwebs from their branches. Gorgeous and spooky at the same time. Stories of witches and voodoo came from here, as well as tales of Rougarou, Louisiana's werewolf. Johanna listened to the river's gurgling and the shrill chirping of birds and insects, barely discernable above the engine's thrum. Somewhere in the distance, something made a splashing sound, probably a fish jumping to catch a snack out of the air. She listened and sighed a happy sigh. She was home.

"Those trees are mangroves," Nick told her. "Some grow to be a hundred years old."

Johanna smiled. 'Louisiana boy doesn't know his botany,'

she thought, but she didn't bother correcting him. Why spoil the moment?

"I remember one time." Nick tapped his chin. "We had a pier just a couple of hundred feet away from my house, and I used to ditch school to go fishing. There was one time I hooked this huge catfish." Nick held his hands about three feet apart. "So, I'm bringing in this catfish, and he's putting up a hell of a fight. Then suddenly, there's a ripple in the water, an enormous vee, and, at the tip of the vee, a gator nose aiming right at me."

"Is this a fish story?"

"Swear to God." Nick made the "scout's honor" sign. "Well, I couldn't tell if he was going after the fish or my leg. I started throwing rocks at his big, ugly snout. Luckily, I'd pitched for my school baseball team, so, I was a pretty good shot. He kept on coming, and I kept pelting him with stones, but it didn't stop him."

'Again, with the rocks,' thought Johanna.

"Finally, I picked up this huge rock, almost a foot across. I threw it into his mouth, and it stuck in his throat. That's when he lunged at my leg. I could see this big arc of teeth all jagged and aiming right at me. Then he went for my stomach, and I thought I was a goner, but that rock kept his mouth open." Nick stopped to wipe his forehead, although the day hadn't heated up yet.

"And? Then what happened?"

"I took off for home and had catfish that night for dinner."

"I'll bet you brought a rifle with you the next time you

went fishing."

Nick shook his head. "Never carried a gun. Never will. I don't believe in them."

Johanna loved the story. It was ridiculous, and she didn't believe it; but he was trying to impress her, and that made her day. This funny, sexy, rescuer of animals was trying to impress her! That was all she wanted. He noticed her. He cared about her enough to make up outrageous alligator stories. Nick reminded her of a rooster strutting around the barnyard trying to attract the ladies, and she was going to enjoy every bit of it.

'I'm really happy,' she realized. 'I haven't been this happy since Will.'

From throwing rocks at an alligator, Nick segued into a story about rescuing a calf from a school of piranhas.

Johanna was supposed to be awed by the story. Instead, she laughed. She couldn't help it.

Too late, Nick realized his mistake. Piranhas live somewhere in South America. He'd gotten carried away. "Remordia," he mumbled. He said it quietly, but Johanna heard the word anyway.

"What was that?"

"Just my lucky word."

"Remordia." She repeated it under her breath.

"Sorry, I got confused," Nick admitted. "Ever since the kidnapping, I sometimes get stuff mixed up. You know how it is. I'll bet the same things are happening to you. Weird dreams, flashbacks of being tortured." He made a face. "And all those drugs! My brain's roasted. Probably, yours is too. Heck, some of those drugs don't even have names—just numbers." He slapped the side of the boat with his hand.

Johanna kept smiling, but, inside, she was frozen as if she'd been sitting on a block of ice. She'd never told Nick, AKA Homer, about her kidnapping. While he talked, she replayed all their conversations in her head. No, she was sure she'd never told him she'd been tortured. And how did he know she'd been drugged, let alone what drugs she'd been given? And when he denied telling the story of her flying to Iran, he'd known that the story was posted on her website. How had he known that? "Have you ever eaten alligator?" she asked, hoping to change the subject. He grinned and talked about gator on the barbie, while Johanna tried to make sense of what she'd just heard.

Facts vs. feelings—that was the question. Should she go with her heart or her head? 'Go with your heart, of course,' she told herself. That's what every movie she'd ever seen said to do. Nick was nothing but goodness—pure, basic, heart-on-your-sleeve goodness. Everything he'd said, everything he'd done had been kind. He rescued animals. He'd suffered for his convictions. He told goofy stories to impress her. Maybe she could even fall in love with him someday. She certainly had a crush on him. He was one of the good guys. She was sure of it.

But what if she were wrong? Johanna shuddered to think about that.

"Lots of butter and lots of garlic. That's the secret. Then you just let the coals do the rest."

Johanna laughed. "Sounds terrific. How about water moccasin? I'll bet you've never eaten snake."

As Nick rambled on, another unpleasant thought popped into Johanna's head. 'Back in Berkeley, he hadn't talked with a Louisiana drawl.'

He wasn't born in Louisiana, and most of his stories were full of mistakes. But did that actually mean anything? Lots of people enjoy telling tall tales. Since the beginning of time, males have been doing outrageous things to impress females. So what if he had some fake IDs? That didn't prove anything. Johanna had used a fake ID to get into Canada, and she was basically a good person, no matter what Will thought.

But somehow, Nick knew she'd been attacked. How had he known? Maybe, she'd told him about that and then forgot. No, she'd made a point of letting him do the talking. Well, maybe he'd just assumed she'd been held captive because he had been. Or maybe he read the posts on her website. That was probably it. Only, was there anything about her abduction on the website? And he said he hadn't checked her website since his abduction. Rats! It was hard to think and to pretend to listen to Nick's stories at the same time.

<<<<>>>>

The fog was burning off, and Johanna looked about her. They were far upriver now, and the water was shallow enough for Johanna to see the rocks on the bottom. To her right, a gator was sunning itself on a rock. On her left, a heron stepped daintily among the cattails looking for small fish to spear. It was all perfect. Then she looked up to see the muzzle of a pistol pointed at her face.

"Why?" She froze. "What did I ever do to you?"

Nick shook his head. "You didn't do anything. And you don't know how sorry I am that it has to end like this. You didn't do anything, but my friends and I, we did a lot. We created an energy crisis that almost bankrupted California and got the governor recalled. No one else knew about it, but somehow you figured it out. Because you're a frickin' genius? No, there had to be a snitch.

"I used to be a hotshot in the White House. We started the anthrax scare and blamed it on Bin Laden. Everyone else bought the story. Everyone except you. Supposedly, you were smart enough to figure it all out, yet you weren't smart enough to keep quiet about it." His gun hand shook a little bit.

"And 9/11. . . I knew about it, and . . ." His voice quavered as he spoke. "And I let . . ." His voice trailed off.

Images of the towers falling and people screaming and jumping out of windows flashed before Johanna's eyes, The memory was a stabbing hurt, almost as painful as when she'd seen the disaster happening on television. She wanted to weep.

Was Nick remembering 9/11 too? Was that why he trembled? Johanna stilled her feelings and tried to think. For this one moment, Nick was vulnerable. This was her chance. Johanna looked around for something to throw at Nick's gun. There was bottled water in the bottom of the boat. Johanna reached down for a bottle.

Nick kicked it out of her hand. He grinned. Apparently, he was in control again. "I did a lot. It was all classified, yet somehow you figured it out."

"That's why you kidnapped me?"

"It's why I had you kidnapped. I had to. To find the leak, the snitch. But apparently there was no snitch—only you." Nick pulled on the motor's handle to guide the boat around a patch of plant material. "And then I felt guilty. For everything. Stupid! Stupid! And I told the truth, which was even stupider, and that's how I pissed off a lot of other hotshots who would be very unhappy if they knew I was still alive."

'He wouldn't be telling me all this unless he planned to kill me.' The steely gun muzzle that was pointed at Johanna's face jumbled her thoughts, and she shivered like a mouse staring at the fangs in a snake's mouth.

He looked sad. "Never tell the truth. I learned that the hard way. The rich and powerful people I know didn't get rich playing by the rules. Unfortunately, you recognized me, somehow. And now you're trying to find a way to rat me out. I can tell by the confused look in your eyes. You're deciding what to do next."

'I so need a lucky word right now,' thought Johanna. 'Remordia.' That was the word Nick had mumbled. 'Remordia.'

She felt something akin to power as she thought it. She chuckled. "Actually, I was looking at you because I thought you were cute. I was trying to come up with a way to get you to ask me out."

He laughed too, and with that laughing, the tension broke.

Johanna turned to look upriver. Spanish moss hanging off the cedars brushed her head as they passed under the trees. The stream was narrowing. 'If I have to die now,' she thought, 'this is where I'd like it to happen.'

"BOULDER AHEAD!" Her high-pitched scream startled Nick. In that second, Johanna turned back and lunged at him. Off balance, Nick pulled the trigger, and the gun went off just as Johanna's head butted into his stomach. She screamed again as the bullet lodged in her left shoulder. She swung her right arm wildly, and the gun flew out of Nick's hand and into the river. He punched her stomach. Pumped up on adrenaline, Johanna barely felt it.

Then, she jumped into the water.

'Narrow waters run deep.' Johanna hoped it was true here. She dove under the boat, and kicked its bottom to propel herself downward as deep as she could. Her foot barely cleared the propeller.

Nick waited for Johanna to surface, but she didn't. As his eyes swept the water's surface for a sign of her body, the boat nosed into the bank with a jarring thud that almost knocked Nick off balance. He steadied himself, then kept on scanning the water all around his boat, and still there was no sign of her. Suddenly, an almost imperceptible movement in the water ahead caught his eye.

With a sick feeling, he watched an alligator upstream slip silently into the water. Quiet as death. He grimaced, picturing the alligator tearing his victim apart. 'She didn't deserve this. Not any of this.' But sympathy was an unpleasant emotion for Nick, one that interfered with what he had to do. He stifled it.

"Remordia." He said the word out loud, and somehow, he knew everything would turn out all right. He sat back down on the boat's seat, closed his eyes, and let out a comfortable sigh. Johanna had to die. He was going to kill her anyway. A bullet into her heart would have been less painful, but she still needed to die.

In fact, the alligator was about to do Nick a favor. It meant that Nick didn't have to look for her to finish her off. The gun had been knocked out of his hand. He sure as hell wasn't going to go wading in the bayou trying to find it, not with an alligator swimming somewhere nearby. Even without the alligator, Nick wasn't about to poke around for his gun in the muddy water, infested with who knows what. No, he had to believe that if Johanna weren't already dead when she hit the water, the gator would finish her off. And what would Nick have done with her body anyway?

Luckily, the gun wasn't registered. In the unlikely event that someone found it, the gun couldn't be traced to him. Besides, as far as anyone was concerned, he was already dead.

Nick slapped a mosquito that had landed on his arm, and he smiled with satisfaction. 'No worries. It's like it says in the song—if the damn 'skeeters don't get her, the alligators will.' He turned the boat downriver. 'Time for a few scotch-and-sodas in the old motel room,' he figured.

<<<<>>>>

Johanna held her breath and swam underwater with the current for as long as she could. Then she surfaced, gasping, about twenty feet from Nick's boat. Quickly, she took another breath, ducked under the surface, and swam some more. Adrenaline dulled the stinging in her shoulder. In a fog, she paddled slowly downstream. Shock had settled in. Johanna felt as if she were detached from her body. Her thinking was muddy. Like walking through glue.

Eventually, Johanna found a rocky clearing where she was able to pull herself up out of the water using her good arm. She turned her head upriver, scanning the water for a glimpse of Nick's boat and listening for the sound of his motor, terrified that his skiff would appear. But the water was calm, and the only sounds she could hear were insects buzzing, birds chirping, and somewhere in the distance, a heron calling out a rusty squawk. The thought of Nick coming after her was a sobering one. Sadly, she looked at the puddle she'd left behind her when she'd climbed out of the water and wondered how she could hide it. She pulled at some vines and kicked the dirt a bit, but soon, she gave up on the idea. 'Maybe he'll think an alligator left it,' she hoped. 'Better to just get as far away from here as possible.' And she started to make her way through tangles of vines, roots, and grass, following the river as well as she could.

As she stumbled over a cypress root, Johanna looked down and noticed a trickle of blood flowing from her shoulder. She pressed her blouse against the wound to staunch the bleeding. Still foggy, she trudged on.

The shock was wearing off now, and Johanna became aware of the stinging in her shoulder. The wound had probably become infected. 'Oh, well.'

She trudged on. The vegetation was thick, jungle-like; she wished she had a machete to hack down the branches blocking her way.

Cautiously, Johanna pushed aside a thick patch of tule grass; and not ten feet ahead of her, an alligator sat sunning itself on a patch of exposed rock, staring directly at her. She suppressed a scream and gently moved the grass back, unnerved to see one so . . . so up close and personal. The gator was probably a female; it was only about five feet long.

Alligators seldom attack humans. Johanna knew that. Even humans who smell of blood, as she did. Still, Johanna was spooked. What if the gator was guarding a nest! She skirted around the alligator giving it as wide a berth as possible. Worries of Nick finding her faded into the back of her mind, replaced by images of snapping teeth. Then she half walked and half jogged until she had put a good distance between herself and the alligator. The effort tired Johanna, and she sank down on a patch of vine-covered ground, resting her head in her hands. She wanted to lie down, but there wasn't enough room for it. The wound, the walking, and the extra exertion of avoiding the alligator had taken their toll.

'I should get up,' she thought. Instead, she stared at the tangle of vines ahead of her, remembering the encounter with the gator. Scary, yet she'd remained calm. 'Downright impressive,' thought Johanna, 'I'm a friggin' lightning storm. But if I'm so amazing, why did I fall for Nick's lines?' She actually chuckled in spite of how miserable she was. Funny how charming Nick was— charming and deadly. He didn't just bend the truth; he broke it, shattered it into splinters.

His alligator stories were pure bunk. Even in water, alligators usually ignore humans; they eat smaller prey like water birds, fish, and rodents. But it wasn't just the gator stories. It was the serious lies—the ones about being her ally, and being kidnapped, and whatever had come before. When everything in front of her had told her that he was lying, Johanna had put aside common sense and believed him. 'Stupid, stupid, stupid!' She'd thrown aside logic and believed Nick.

'No,' she thought, 'I'm not stupid. Not really. I'm just human. So often, people do just that—watching the news, hearing a loved one's excuses. I guess, in the end, we believe what we want to believe.'

The truth. Such a concept! Johanna had always respected truth. For her, the biggest insult, the greatest act of disrespect, was a lie. What is truth? "The self-expression of God." That's what Jesus had said. You couldn't get around that.

But in Canada, she'd told the truth, and no one had

believed her. They had deported her anyway. On the other hand, she'd neglected telling Will about Liam's back talk, and it had saved all of them grief.

When she'd screamed, "Boulder ahead," she'd told another lie; it had saved her life. That lucky word, Remordia, had certainly been lucky for her. Of course, she had a bullet in her shoulder, and the wound was stinging a lot and probably massively infected. But the lie had worked. And there was something else.

She remembered, so clearly, the feeling she'd had when she'd mumbled, "Remordia," shouted, "Boulder ahead," and then knocked the gun out of Nick's hand. It was a flash of power surging through her. She'd outsmarted her killer; she'd overcome the man holding the gun. Just for a moment, she was the conqueror, the winner. And it had felt good. There really weren't any words large enough to describe the rush.

Reluctantly, Johanna stood up. Philosophical musings would have to wait for another time. Right now, she needed to find civilization before it got dark.

Johanna kept walking and trying to ignore the pain which was getting worse by the hour. She was able to keep the river in sight, so, she knew she was heading in the right direction; and she kept a sharp eye out for alligators, water moccasins, and wild boars. As long as she didn't surprise any of them, she'd be okay. At least, she hoped she'd be okay. She'd been in the bayous many times on field trips or with friends, but always in a boat or fishing from a pier—never making her way through overgrown wilderness on foot alone.

A patch of blackberries caught her eye. Johanna wasn't hungry, but she ate a handful of the berries anyway. Most were sour, but they seemed to give her strength, so she picked as many ripe ones as she could fit into her fanny pack. The berries were the only safe source of water she could think of. She figured she'd eat a couple every time she got thirsty, and hopefully they'd last until she got back among people. She'd drink from the river if she had to, but that was only a last resort. And if she did drink the river water, she knew she'd pay for it later on—big time.

After filling her fanny pack, Johanna pressed on following the river. The afternoon was hot and muggy, and her blouse was soaked through. She was sweating as if she had a fever. She probably did have a fever.

Johanna kept on going, trying to ignore pain and nausea. She tried not to imagine her lifeless body torn apart by scavengers, but her mind seemed to fixate on dying. Just how far had they travelled upriver? Two miles? Five miles? Probably more than five. Johanna wished she'd paid more attention when they'd started out. Whenever it all seemed hopeless, she slipped a berry into her mouth, and thought, 'Please, God, help me.' Then, she reminded herself that she'd just outwitted a killer. That thought gave her courage, gave her strength to keep moving forward.

<<<<>>>>

She ate the last of her berries, and minutes later, was thirsty again. 'Maybe there'll be some more berries up ahead,' she hoped and kept walking, watching eagerly for that harbor where they'd gotten into Nick's boat earlier in the day.

As the sun sank lower and lower in the sky, Johanna grew anxious, imagining herself sleeping amid prowling animals. She'd be okay as long as she made it out of the bayou before dark.

A second blackberry patch beckoned, and she stopped to eat and to replenish her supply. 'The berries have to be a good sign,' she thought. 'The harbor couldn't be too much farther ahead.'

But all too soon, the sun began its dip below the horizon, and the first tinges of pink appeared in the heavens. 'Maybe I really will have to sleep here tonight,' she thought and immediately shrugged away the idea. 'What if I stopped, and it turned out that the harbor was only a hundred feet away? How sad would that be?' She looked around for signs that humans had been by, but there were none. 'It can't be too much farther,' she decided and willed herself to keep going.

Now the shadows were long, and the sky was blazing an angry orange. The sun had almost disappeared, and there was still no sign of civilization. She'd have noticed the harbor; she couldn't have walked past it. Or could she? No, even if she'd missed the harbor, for sure she'd have noticed the road. Johanna tried to walk faster, but she'd been walking all day and there was hardly any strength left in her body.

And then there was no strength at all.

She'd have to spend the night in the bayou. It was that

simple. She sank to the ground under a cypress and covered herself with her jacket.

The sky had turned dark purple. She tried not to think about prowling alligators.

Rougarou, Louisiana's werewolf, also prowled the bayous at night, looking for lapsed Catholics to eat. Johanna shook her head. 'Superstition and nonsense.'

She said ten Hail Marys before she fell into a restless sleep. Just in case.

<<<<>>>

The next morning Johanna woke up swimming in pain. Reluctantly, she sat up, dreading the minutes, or more probably the hours, of walking ahead of her. But as soon as she stood up, the ground seemed to sway under her feet, and she sat back down. Nauseated and disoriented, she pulled herself up onto her knees. Maybe, she needed food. Or water. Even though Johanna didn't feel hungry, she unzipped her fanny pack, pulled out a handful of berries, and put them into her mouth, one by one. Then she ate a few more, hoping they'd give her some strength. Now that there was a real possibility that she could die, Johanna realized how precious her life was, and how badly she didn't want it to end. She ate a few more berries, saving a handful of them for later. Hopefully, they'd last until someone found her. She struggled to her feet and discovered that she could walk, albeit very slowly.

She started on her way again.

Two hours later, Johanna reached the boat harbor and the dirt path which led to civilization. She'd made it out of the bayou. She'd have cried with relief if she hadn't been too tired and dehydrated. The harbor was deserted, as it had been the day before. Johanna shrugged. She ate the last of her berries and started walking, figuring she had to get to a paved road for any chance to be noticed.

Johanna trudged on. The day was heating up, she was, oh, so tired, and her spirits sank with each step. Mostly, she stared at the ground in front of her feet. But then she looked up and saw eddies of hot air rising ahead of her.

Rising up from asphalt!

Never had asphalt looked so wonderful. It spelled hope. Just a few more steps.

And then she made it! She relished the feeling of smooth paving under her feet and the odor of petroleum fumes; both promised rescue. She dragged herself a bit farther to a venerable pine tree which offered some shade and sat down under it to wait for a car.

<<<<>>>>

Johanna didn't have long to wait. Soon after she'd sat down, she heard the rumbling sound of a motor in the distance. Full of hope, she stumbled to her feet and stuck out her thumb.

John and Vera, a couple of pensioners, spotted Johanna. John was in the driver's seat of a green Datsun pickup, and he applied his brakes as his truck approached Johanna.

"What are you slowing down for? We don't know that woman," Vera said. "Keep driving. It could be a setup. Maybe someone's hiding behind the tree, waiting to rob us."

"But she looks like she's in trouble."

"Just keep on driving."

"I'll call the cops when I get to a place where there's cell phone reception," John said.

Vera shrugged, and Johanna turned her head as she watched the car pass her and keep going.

Defeated, Johanna sat back down in the dirt. Her shoulder was throbbing like bongo drums now, and the pain was making her dizzy. With a great deal of effort, she peeled back her grimy blouse and turned her head to examine the wound underneath. The blood had clotted, but the wound was oozing a yellow liquid, and the area around it was red and swollen.

'Why am I sitting when I could be lying down?' she wondered. So, she lay in the dirt by the side of the road in the shade of the pine tree.

CHAPTER 16

Zeke and RJ, a couple of teenage brothers driving toward the bayou in the hopes of snagging some catfish for dinner, were the next people to spot Johanna. "Zeke pointed at her with his elbow. "What do you think—sick or wasted?"

"Not sure. Either way, she looks like trouble."

"You want to stop and check her out?"

"Naw. We got places to go and fish to catch."

"Bet you'd stop if she was a dog."

"Look, little brother, sometimes life's a whole lot simpler if you just mind your own business." He pressed down on the accelerator and drove on past Johanna.

"Just go back and let me see if she's okay." Zeke scratched the back of his head. "Pop would have tried to help."

RJ hesitated. "And what's in it for us?"

"Bragging rights. Come on. You ain't scared of that little, white lady, are you?"

"It's the fuzz that goes around protecting little white

ladies—that's who give me the heebie-jeebies." Zeke didn't say anything. With a long sigh, RJ pulled the car over to the side of the road. "The fish won't be biting for another couple of hours, anyway."

Their car was a ten-year-old, white Honda. RJ put it into reverse and backtracked down the road to where Johanna was lying. "If she's dead, we're out o' here. Two black kids drivin' west o' nowhere find a body. You know we'll be the first ones they suspect."

"She ain't dead. I saw her move," said Zeke.

RJ pulled the car up next to Johanna, and Zeke jumped out. "Hey, lady, you okay?'

Johanna raised her head. "Please help." Suddenly moving seemed hard.

RJ reached into a cooler in the back seat and pulled out a bottle of water. He lobbed it to Zeke who unscrewed the cap and gave it to Johanna. She drank the water slowly and felt her strength returning a bit.

"Do you think you can walk?" Zeke asked.

Johanna nodded. She struggled to her feet, leaned on Zeke, and managed to climb into the back seat of the Honda.

"She's wounded," said RJ. "That a gunshot?"

Johanna nodded.

RJ rolled his eyes. He gunned the engine, U-turned the car, and headed back toward town. "Shit," he said. "Do us a solid. Don't tell 'em we picked you up. They'll think we the ones who shot you. Say it was some white guy that shot you. Tell 'em that."

"Okay," she agreed.

"There's a hospital in Prairieville," RJ said. "I think I can find it. But we ain't gonna stick around."

"I get it." Johanna spoke slowly. "I've been accused of things I didn't do."

Zeke reached into the cooler. "Want a Moon Pie?" he asked.

Johanna shook her head, then thought better of it. She hadn't eaten anything all day except for a handful of berries. "Yes," she said. "And thanks. For stopping."

"That better not be my Moon Pie," RJ grumbled.

While RJ drove, Johanna nibbled on the cookie and took small sips from the water bottle. No one wanted to talk. Zeke turned on the radio, and they listened to hip-hop all the way to the hospital.

<<<<>>>

Prairieville Family Hospital was a one-story, tan-colored building with white trim and a ledger-stone façade accent—not a big building as hospitals go. It reminded Johanna of a Kmart store. "Their plants look healthy," Zeke said hopefully. RJ drove to the emergency entrance at the rear of the building where Zeke nudged Johanna out of the car, and the two brothers made a hasty retreat. Johanna stumbled inside the hospital on her own steam.

The hospital was crowded. Hurricane Katrina had left a lot

of human suffering in her wake. Nevertheless, Johanna was rushed almost immediately into a treatment room.

Dr. Rodriguez, a balding Hispanic with a no-nonsense attitude was her attending doctor. Soon, Johanna was lying on a hospital bed in the ER with an IV needle pumping fluids, nutrients, antibiotics, and painkillers into the back of her hand.

"As soon as she's hydrated, take a blood sample and crossmatch it for a transfusion," he told the attending nurse.

"Yes, Doctor."

"I'm injecting lidocaine to numb the wound," said Dr. Rodriguez, and Johanna felt a burning needlestick in her shoulder. He began cleaning the wound while Johanna grimaced and cried out despite the painkiller.

"Hold on. Just a bit more."

To Johanna, it seemed like forever.

"Is that a gunshot?" he asked.

Johanna sighed.

"Is it?"

"Yes," she admitted, and Dr. Rodriguez jotted down some notes but made no further comment about the gunshot. "As soon as your labs are back, we'll put you under, and I'll remove the bullet," he said. "Is there someone we can call?"

"My mother. She's staying in Colorado with my aunt." Johanna gave his nurse the phone number.

The painkillers were kicking in. She felt pleasantly sleepy watching the room twirling and tilting like a ride at Disneyworld.

'A quick nap would feel great,' she thought and closed her eyes. Soon after that, Johanna was in surgery.

<<<<>>>>>

Several hours later, Johanna woke up in a hospital bed, groggy and confused. An annoying needle was stuck into the back of her hand. She stared at it for a second, looked up at the ceiling, then went back to sleep.

Eventually, her foggy mind cleared, and she could focus on two uniformed police officers standing beside her bed—Landry and Kirshner, according to their badges.

"Do you feel up to talking?" Kirshner asked.

"Sure." Johanna nodded. Whatever they'd given Johanna left her drowsy but contented. The pain had subsided to a dull inconvenience. She could handle anything. "This interview is being recorded," said Kirshner, and set a small tape recorder on the tray next to Johanna. "Now, tell us what happened." He was the taller of the two, with hefty muscles that suggested hours spent lifting weights.

Johanna told her whole story, starting with her abduction almost two years earlier, and ending with Nick shooting her. She frequently stopped talking and stared into the faces of the two police officers. Her speech was slurred, and she kept repeating herself and losing her train of thought. "He goes by Nick Underhill, but he's probably—you know—that Alexander something. Alexander Li . . .Lidecker." Johanna closed her eyes for a few seconds. "At least, that's what one of his driver's licenses says. And he's the one . . . who—you know—all that stuff I told you about before."

"Rest now. We'll talk to you later," said Landry. He adjusted wire-rimmed glasses as he spoke. The two officers whispered as they left Johanna's room. Johanna could only make out the words, "Fifty-one fifty," and, "I thought Lidecker was dead."

'No.' Johanna sighed with frustration. 'Fifty-one fifty. Mentally incompetent. Why doesn't anyone ever believe me?'

She didn't have much energy, but with the little strength she had, Johanna was mad. She'd told the truth. Supposedly, a good thing. And nobody had believed her, and the cops thought she was crazy. In Nick's boat, she'd told a lie, and it had saved her life. Not only that, but there had been this giddy, intoxicating feeling of power when she'd yelled, "Boulder ahead." She'd been resourceful, quick-witted. She'd outsmarted a spin doctor at his own game.

If truth was like a glass of water, then lying resembled Southern Comfort; if truth was a walk on the beach, lying was a weekend in Vegas.

Her passion for truth? Well, perhaps it was a bit childish, too naïve for the modern world.

Maybe she should grow up.

<<<<>>>>

Early the next day, the two officers came back.

"Feeling any better?" Landry asked in a mellow voice. His eyes and his smile were kind.

"Much." Johanna was sitting up now. The color was back in her face, and her speech was almost normal. "I need to tell you what happened."

The two officers nodded.

"I met this guy in a bar." She paused. "This is kind of embarrassing. He was all Southern charm and, well, I don't usually fall for a pickup line, but I did this time. He told me about this great fishing spot, and he said he'd take me there. Like I said, I'm not usually so gullible, but—I hate to admit it—he had blue eyes, and I'm a sucker for blue eyes. And then he described the boat he'd just bought, which was a spiffy cabin cruiser. I'm also a sucker for boat rides. Anyway, long story short—he took me upriver, and he started putting moves on me. I said, 'No,' but he didn't care. There was no one around to hear me screaming. He told me to relax and enjoy it. Only I didn't relax. Instead, I struggled. Then I lucked out; I got in one good kick where it counted—in his privates. And he doubled over. Then he called me every disgusting name he could think of, shot me, threw me over the side, and took off."

"Can you tell us what he looked like?"

"Medium height, medium build, Caucasian." Johanna stopped to think. "He had dark, dark hair, almost shoulder length, a lot of beard, and a mustache. You couldn't see much of his face.

Except for the blue eyes. Oh, and he was about forty because he was starting to get gray hair."

'At least the description is true,' Johanna thought.

Landry cleared his throat. "What about the kidnapping by government officials and being mistaken for a spy?"

"Oh, my gosh!" Johanna covered her face with her hands. "Tell me I didn't say that! A few days ago, I was watching old spy movies on TV, and one of them must have stuck in my head. I probably sounded like a nut case." She giggled behind her hand and almost managed a blush.

Kirshner shook his head.

"I'm sorry. They gave me a lot of painkillers yesterday. I remember talking to you, but that's all I remember. If I said anything weird, I apologize."

"Don't give it another thought," said Landry. They talked a bit more.

Kirshner winked and grinned. "We'll catch that guy. Don't you worry. We'll get him, and we'll make him pay. You have my word." He laughed. "If you can't trust a cop, who can you trust? Right?"

Johanna smiled back. Her smile looked genuine.

As the officers got up to leave, Landry patted her good shoulder. "Feel better," he said.

Once outside Johanna's room, Kirshner dropped the smile. "Her description is pretty generic. We won't be able to do a damn thing about this one. Especially with all the confusion following

Katrina."

Landry nodded emphatically. "And if he shaves off his beard and mustache and cuts his hair, he'll look completely different. My money—he goes free unless he nabs a smarter chick. Eventually, most rapists do something stupid and get caught."

After the two had gone, Johanna thought about the conversations. They hadn't believed the truth, but they bought the story about the rapist in the bar. 'What's wrong with this picture?' she wondered.

And then, it seemed so obvious. Familiarity. The rapist-in-a-bar story was familiar. They'd heard it hundreds of times. They could understand it. They could believe it. The other was far-fetched. It happened to be true, but it wasn't believable.

From there, her thoughts turned to Will. He'd dealt with hundreds of liars and criminals. Maybe he'd dealt with actual terrorists, maybe not, but their existence was believable. And her story wasn't. Her truth wasn't believable. And Will had to protect his kids. 'I get it,' she told an imaginary Will. 'You couldn't stand up for me. It was me or your kids, and you had to choose your kids. I would have done the same thing.'

That's when she was able to forgive him.

<<<<>>>>

A funny thing! After her encounter with Nick/Homer/Alexander, Johanna was no longer afraid. Her assailant wasn't a part of some mysterious, all-powerful alliance, so far above the law that kidnap and murder carried no punishment. No, he was just one shaggy individual. He was a bad liar, presumed dead, who couldn't tell a cypress from a mangrove. She knew what he looked like. She remembered his cleanshaven face from their meeting in Berkeley when he'd used the name Homer Perlman. And she'd outwitted him. Twice. Plus, he probably thought she was dead. Of course, he could still come after her, but the odds of that happening were slim. Johanna took a deep, relaxing breath. That horrible, helpless sensation was gone. And as soon as she got back into Canada, he wouldn't be a threat at all.

<<<<>>>>

Soon after, Johanna's mother appeared at her bedside. Johanna wasn't alone anymore. She cried with relief. "Mommy."

The questions would come later. Martha leaned over and kissed Johanna's forehead. "Be well," she said and then turned away to brush a tear from her face. She sat down on the edge of the bed and took Johanna's hand in hers. Neither spoke. They didn't need to.

CHAPTER 17

It seemed as if it took forever before Martha's house was livable again, but the day finally came when Johanna and Martha entered their Pascagoula home, each dragging two wheeled suitcases behind them. Many of Martha's belongings had perished in the hurricane, but most of the house had survived. Now, it was time to rebuild their lives. Over the next few weeks, they restocked their new cupboards and refrigerator. They bought food, furniture, clothes, and blankets. They started with necessities, like a computer, then added gadgets and splurges like curtains and hand cream.

More importantly, rebuilding meant rebuilding friendships. It meant endless cups of tea and coffee, and endless glasses of soda, lemonade, and Southern Comfort, as friends hugged, and cried, and told their stories.

For Johanna, rebuilding meant rebuilding her life in Canada with Sandy, Will, and the kids—assuming Will and Canada's immigration authorities would accept her.

Using the name Jody, Johanna logged onto fairytalesfortherestofus and found Will's posts. Will had said he loved her! Her heart all but exploded with wave after wave of happiness. Then she danced around the room, fist-pumped the air, and hugged her computer. Suddenly, her day was better than Christmas morning. He wanted her back. Well, she wanted to come back. Badly!

"I love you too, Will," she typed, not caring that anyone who logged on could read her post. "It should be scary to say it, and even scarier to mean it, but I do love you with all my heart. Whatever else happens, loving you has been the best part of my life." She sighed wistfully remembering her head on his shoulder and the feel of his hand on her cheek.

"Of course, I forgive you. I couldn't at first; I didn't understand. Now I get it. I do. Your kids have to come first. But make a place in your heart for me too, because in your heart is where I want to be; it's my idea of heaven. Sometimes, I reach my hand out into the air, wishing I could touch you. I remember the feeling of your arms around me, and I want that again—that and more.

"Please call me at my mom's house." She typed in the number. "I want to hear you actually talking to me—not just to read typed words on a computer screen. Hearing your voice is still not enough, but in the meantime, it'll have to do.

"Now, I have to figure out how to get back into Canada, if

you and Canada will have me. You said you still want me. Please don't take it back. I love you so much. Jody."

<<<<>>>>

Will hesitantly punched in the phone number Johanna had given him. What do you say to the woman you love whom you treated shamefully? He needn't have worried. She was deliriously happy to hear his voice and told him so in as many ways as she could think of. Will apologized, stumbling over his words. 'I sound like an idiot,' he thought.

"Too much mushy stuff," said Emberlee. "Let me have a turn." She told Johanna about her new best friend at school and all the words that Chioke could say now. "We missed you, especially Chioke, but I knew you'd come back. When are you coming back?"

"That's a hard question. As soon as Canada lets me back in, I suppose. I'll be working my hardest to do everything they want."

Emberlee put the phone next to Chioke's ear. When the little one heard Johanna's voice, she let out a loud giggle and a stream of baby talk that not even Emberlee could understand.

"I want to be with all of you," Johanna told Will when she finally got to talk to him again. "Tomorrow, I'll start reestablishing my identity. Fingers crossed it'll all go smoothly."

They ended the call with some long-distance smooches. She heard Emberlee's voice in the background saying, "Gross and mushy," and then Johanna hung up the phone, tipsy with happiness.

<<<<>>>>

The next morning, Johanna began a list of what she'd have to do to reestablish her identity. 'Did my old landlord throw all my stuff away?' she wondered. At lightning speed, Johanna rebuilt her life, or at least most of it. Soon she had a social security card, a driver's license, and a passport, all issued to Johanna Jacobson. Thanks to her Katrina articles, she had earned a decent reputation as a freelance writer, and she even had a shaky income. Johanna could live anywhere she wanted; well, she wanted to live in Canada. She'd saved a tidy sum while staying with her mother, enough money to see her through tough times or a spell of writer's block. "Canada, here I come!" she told the computer.

As her first step toward reentering Canada, Jody requested a "rehabilitation application." Rehabilitation—the word was cringeworthy. 'I never did anything wrong. I don't need rehabilitating.' Nevertheless, she filled out the form, mailed it in, and waited for IRCC (Immigration, Refugees, and Citizenship Canada) to reply. Their answer came a week later. They thanked her for her application and told her that there was a ten-year waiting period after rehabilitation before she could be readmitted.

"No fair!" She screamed; then made a fist. "No fair!" She missed Will and the kids something fierce! She reached her arms out and hugged empty air, pretending she had all of them in her embrace. She ached for more evenings with Sandy. Thinking about the old man got her teary. Sandy, her mentor, her friend, the grandfather figure she'd never had. By the time Canada let her back in, Sandy would be . . . She choked on the thought. He would probably be dead by then. Will would be remarried and would have forgotten all about Jody, the pitiful ragamuffin whom Sandy had taken in. And the kids! Johanna pictured them ten years from now: Liam—a grown man with a job and family of his own, Emberlee—graduating high school, and Chioke—a preteen. 'No. Unacceptable!' But what could she do?

She held off telling Will about the ten-year wait. Anyway, he probably knew about it, being a Mountie. There had to be something else. She contacted an immigration lawyer, who was useless.

Johanna was tired of feeling small and helpless. Heck, she was anything but helpless. She'd chopped wood, weathered blizzards, survived a hurricane, and made it out of a wilderness— with a bullet in her shoulder, no less. She'd written fierce stories, important stories; her writing was better than ever. And she'd outwitted a would-be murderer—twice! No, Johanna wasn't helpless; she wasn't a victim; she was a courageous survivor, a conqueror, a frickin' human lightning storm. She'd been through worse challenges and triumphed. She'd make it through this one.

'I tried the truth, and no one believed me,' thought Johanna. 'Time to try something else.' "Remordia." She said the word out loud for luck. Then she started another letter to Canada's immigration office.

Please help me. I fell in love with a man who later turned out to have Mafia connections. When I refused to marry him, he put a contract out on me.

No. Canada might not want to give refuge to a Mafia target. Besides, she'd have to provide her killer's name, and she wasn't sure what it was. The rapist-in-a-bar scene had worked before. 'Remordia.'

I met a man in a bar who called himself Dave Stanton, all Southern charm and so handsome it took my breath away. He offered to take me on a boat ride and show me a great fishing spot. Even though I barely knew him, I agreed. He seemed harmless enough. So, Dave took me to a secluded spot far upriver on some Louisiana bayou. Suddenly, the Southern charm disappeared, and he started tearing off my blouse.

I said, "No. What the heck?" but he didn't care.

He did this disgusting, leery thing with his tongue, grabbed me, and punched and slapped me. "Relax and enjoy it, or I'll have to rough you up again," he said. "You might as well; there's no one around to hear you scream."

Instead, I struggled. Then I lucked out; I got in

one good kick where it counted—in his privates. He doubled over. He called me every filthy name he could think of. Then he shot me, threw me over the side of his boat, and took off.

I thought the nightmare was over, but then the threatening letters started. I had unwittingly told him where I live. The last letter was tied to the tail of a dead cat.

I notified the police; they were sympathetic but said they couldn't do anything since I don't know his real name. I'm enclosing medical records of my bullet wound and copies of the letters I've received. Please help. I'm desperate. If Canada won't accept me, I'll be dead in a matter of weeks.

Respectfully,

Johanna Jacobson

She clipped words out of newspapers to create three threatening notes:

That's NOT *ketchup*. It's **blood**. Next time it will be yours

I'm watching *U*, BitCh. It's just a matter of TIME Rest with worms

The wait seemed forever, although only a week passed

between her writing to IRCC and receiving their response.

Your ten-year wait period is suspended due to extenuating circumstances. Welcome to Canada!

Johanna breathed a sigh of relief. The deranged-man-in-the-bar story was so good, she'd almost believed it herself.

CHAPTER 18

The Yukon forests put on a spectacular show of flame-colored autumn for Jody's return to Canada. Her heart beat with happy thumps as her Air North plane taxied to a bumpy stop on Dawson City's gravel airstrip.

Inside the tiny terminal, Sandy and the Campbells had turned out to welcome her. Chioke had a balloon reading, "Welcome Home," tied to her wrist. Emberlee held out a chocolate cake topped with "Welcome home, Jody" piped in shaky lettering. Liam said, "Welcome back," and smiled. He didn't actually look happy to see her; it was more as if he were showing a dentist his teeth. Still, Jody appreciated the effort.

Then Sandy and Will held out their arms, and soon Jody was surrounded by hugs; and when Jody figured it couldn't get any better, Chioke said, "Mama."

<<<<>>>>

Jody hadn't planned on staying with Sandy for more than a week at most, but it turned out that he needed her. His steps were slower, and he tired more easily. When she'd first moved in with him—it was almost a year ago—he could cut an armful of wood in the time it took her to split one log. She'd wear out before the afternoon was over, while Sandy could keep going as long as there was light in the sky. Now, he got winded after an hour of chopping. So, she moved into her old spot, sleeping on Sandy's couch, watching Will's kids, and helping with whatever he needed.

Liam and Jody mostly ignored each other, and when Liam had to say something to Jody, there was always a bit of a disdainful sneer on his face. Jody tried talking to him, but it always failed.

Until, one day, it didn't.

<<<<>>>>

Jody saw her chance to get through to Liam one afternoon when Will dropped the kids off at Sandy's cabin, and she smelled aftershave on Liam's face. Jody resisted the urge to laugh. There had never been anything on Liam's face to shave. Nevertheless, it gave her an idea of how to reach him.

"What would you think if your father and I became a couple?" she asked. She'd never had the nerve to broach the subject to him before.

The answer jumped out of Liam's mouth like a bullfrog on steroids. "You'll never get him. He's not that dumb."

"But I will." She dropped her voice to a whisper. "You see, I'm a witch."

Liam sneered. "Ha!"

"I've given him a love potion. It works slowly, but it works. There's nothing anyone can do to stop me now. Unless, of course, they use the spell to disenchant."

It only made sense to Liam. There was no way Jody could have competed honestly with his mother. It had to be witchcraft. Well, Jody wasn't all that smart, bragging about her love potion spell like that. Liam's brain switched into overdrive. How could he use this information? Blackmail Jody? A possibility. But what would she do to him if he made her mad? No, he'd have to be nice and win her over to his side. Besides, he could get her to teach him that love-potion spell so he could be irresistible to girls.

"I learned a lot while I was in the United States," said Jody. "After the hurricane, I spent some time in Louisiana. And . . ." Jody smiled and slowly poured water into a kettle. She set it on the stove and changed the subject. "I'm making tea. Do you want a cup?"

Liam shook his head impatiently. "And what?"

"And I learned voodoo."

Slowly, deliberately, Jody took a mug down from Sandy's cupboard. She removed a teabag from a Lipton's carton, then put it back and instead, spooned loose tea into Sandy's teapot.

"You and I—we'll be seeing a lot of each other. We can be friends. I can teach you things. I can help you. And if you ever want someone to fall in love with you . . .," Jody laughed. She stopped talking, letting the words soak in. "I can make it happen."

She brushed imaginary crumbs off Sandy's table. "But should you make me angry . . ." For a moment, her face flashed with the piercing stare of an enraged murderer. Then the look was gone. "Well, you don't want to know what I can do. Think it over." It wasn't the words that scared him. It was the look on Jody's face. Fury—then the trace of a smile on her lips that told of secrets only she was privy to.

Liam smiled. "We were always friends. I'm just a quiet kind of kid. That's all."

"I thought as much."

"Um, Jody, maybe I would like a cup of tea after all."

They sat down at Sandy's table, and Jody watched Liam fidget as he sipped his tea.

"Were you in Louisiana during the hurricane?" he asked.

Jody smiled. Louisiana was a segue into the realm of voodoo, no doubt. "I was in Mississippi when the hurricane hit. It broke windows and blew part of the roof off our house, and it filled the bottom floor with water. We were rescued by helicopter." Jody frowned, remembering those terrifying days. "My mother and I were two of the lucky ones. Many people died. So many more were seriously injured." As she talked, she watched Liam's face. Clearly, he couldn't have cared less about the hurricane.

"But how did you learn the voodoo?"

"After things had settled down a bit, I drove to Louisiana in search of stories for my newspaper and magazine articles. That's when I ran into Harriet." Jody paused for dramatic effect. "A voodoo priestess."

Liam was holding his breath. "What did she look like?"

"She was tall, well over six feet. Her skin was midnight black and glistened like an olive dunked in oil. I don't know what color her eyes were. I didn't dare look into them; they could see inside my soul. Her clothes were made of loosely-woven cotton— bright, bright orange shirts and matching skirts, both trimmed with aquamarine figures. Her belt and her necklace were chains of chicken bones, and they made a sound like a death rattle when she moved. In her right hand, she carried a cedar staff, as tall as she was, topped by . . . a human skull."

Jody sipped her tea slowly, enjoying Liam's attempts to act casual. At last, she put her cup down. "We became friends. I gave her a carton of cigarettes and a bottle of vodka; in exchange, she taught me some of her spells."

"Including the love potion?"

"Including the love potion. Her most powerful spell. It works slowly. But once it's cast, its magic holds the victim prisoner under your spell forever."

Liam gasped. His eyes were fixed on Jody's face. "Can you teach me the love potion spell?"

"Have you done your homework?" Jody stared into his eyes, as if she could see into his soul.

"I was just taking a break. I'll finish it now." And he was gone.

Jody laughed to herself. It was all too easy. What would

Harriet, a gentle Christian soul, think if she knew Jody had just described her as a voodoo priestess?

Unfortunately for Liam, before he could get his homework finished, Will came to pick up the kids. The love potion spell would have to wait until another day.

<<<<>>>>

"Before I can make this love potion, I need to know a few things," Jody told Liam. "The magic will be stronger that way. First of all, what's her name?"

"Yvonne."

"Good. What does Yvonne like to do?"

"She's really hot, and she already has boobs. So, she probably likes kissing."

"Kissing is already built into the spell. What else does she like?"

"Is that really necessary?"

"If you want the spell to work."

"Okay, I'll ask her."

<<<<>>>>

Liam came back a few days later, disillusioned with his prospects. "She plays the violin and writes poetry. She's a total nerd. I don't care about any of that stuff. I just want to make out with her."

"Patience, Liam. You don't want a total nerd hopelessly in love with you. You'll get tired of her, and then you're stuck with the lovesick geekette following you around, writing poems which you'll have to read, and playing the violin for you when you'd rather be with someone else. It's not worth a kiss and a quick feel."

"Oh. I didn't think of that."

<<<<>>>>

Jody didn't hear any more about the love potion for several days. Then one afternoon Liam shyly tapped Jody on her shoulder. "Jody, can I talk to you? It's kind of important."

Jody smiled. "Of course."

"So, there's this girl, Jessica. Before you ask, my homework's done. Anyway, I asked Jessica what she likes, and she's into hiking, and she knows how to fish. She likes science too, which is kind of nerdy, but I'm okay with that. I think she's the one. So, I'm ready for the love potion."

"Then I'll prepare the spell."

<<<<>>>>

Liam waited impatiently for three days before broaching the subject of the love potion, "So, um, Jody." He stared at his shoes. "Did you, um, have time to make me that love potion? I mean, if you have the time and everything."

Jody put her finger to her lips. "I have to gather the ingredients, and the potion has to be prepared on the night of a full moon. I should have it ready at the end of next week."

"Next week? Can't you make it any sooner?"

"You can't rush these things. You make one mistake, and the potion doesn't work."

Liam rolled his eyes, and Jody hid her smile. Funny how Liam seemed so much younger lately, now that he'd dropped all that anger and bitterness.

By the end of the following week, Liam was ready to explode. "Do you have the potion ready now?"

"I do."

"Finally. Man, this voodoo stuff takes forever."

Jody led Liam into the kitchen and brought out two raspberry muffins. One of the them had a piece cut off the side.

"Now, here's what you have to do. Give her the whole muffin and you eat the one with the piece cut out of it. Then give her a present, a bracelet or a card. Something you made yourself is best. Then—this is very important—ask her a question about fishing or science or hiking, or anything else, but it must be about her. Listen hard to what she's saying. Ask questions. Make comments. If either of you gets bored, she's the wrong girl, and the spell won't work. But if you're having a good time, and she keeps talking until the muffins are both eaten, then the potion probably worked, and you've got yourself a girlfriend."

Liam's brows were furrowed in concentration; he took in every word Jody said. "Do the muffins taste weird or anything?"

"No, they taste like regular raspberry muffins."

"Wow. Love is hard."

"But it's worth it. And whatever you do, don't breathe a

word about the spell to anyone. Not to your dad, and, especially, not to Jessica."

"I'm not that dumb, Jody."

"And don't tell any of your friends about the potion either. They'll swear they won't tell anyone, and then they'll let something slip, either accidentally or on purpose, and pretty soon the whole school will know about the spell. Including Jessica. And if Jessica finds out, believe me, she'll be furious. This is strictly between you and me."

Liam walked away smiling.

So did Jody. It was so easy!

<<<<>>>>

Liam was still smiling the next time he saw Jody. "The spell worked. She can tie flies, you know, for flyfishing. And later she passed me a note in history class. I think she likes me."

"I told you—it's a very powerful spell."

"If she asks me something about, say, basketball or, you know, something that I like, can I talk about it?"

"Sure. You're an interesting person. You can talk about anything you want. Let her get to know all about you. Just don't hog the conversation."

"It won't wreck the spell?"

"It won't wreck the spell."

Liam walked away whistling, and Jody marveled at Liam's gullibility. Liam smiled a lot these days.

Will was happy too. "I don't know what you said, Jody, but whatever it was, it worked like magic. Liam is back. My sunny, goofy kid is back. You can't know how worried I was. I didn't think that chip on his shoulder would ever disappear. Now, suddenly, he's your best friend! Thank you. How on earth did you manage it?"

Jody wanted to laugh badly. "He's in love. I just gave him a few pointers. That's all."

Will winked. "I need details," he said and put his arm around her. "There's someone I want to impress." Then he kissed her. Not a friendly, just-a-bit-more-than-a-handshake peck. This was a steamy kiss that left Jody starry-eyed, slightly wobbly, and breathing in whispers.

They sat on Sandy's couch with Jody's head lying in Will's lap. "Jody told Will everything she knew of Liam's crush, only leaving out the bit about the voodoo love potion. Then they shared the stories of their own first loves and first heartaches. They talked about anything and everything. Wrapped in a bubble of happiness, Jody told Will about the hard things as well—her father dying, her abduction, getting shot in the bayou. For the first time in a long time, she felt as if she belonged somewhere. She was safe; she was loved. She could be vulnerable.

"Dad, are we ever going home? I'm hungry." Emberlee's voice popped the bubble.

Will checked his watch, as he and Jody stood up, and he kissed Jody's lips. "In a minute, Kit-kat," he said.

<<<<>>>

Love was in the air. You could see it like soap bubbles, smell it like honeysuckle, taste it like chocolate.

Will came home from work each night smiling. Somehow, the bad guys he arrested weren't so bad after all. And when his chief went on a tirade, with veins standing out on his neck and forehead, Will shrugged off the angry vibes without a qualm.

One day, Liam strutted into Sandy's kitchen like a rooster entering a chicken coop. He kissed Chioke on top of her head, put a cookie into her hand, and took a bite off another one. "Jessica let me touch her boobs," he told Jody. Almost overnight it seemed, he'd turned into this funny reservoir of human kindness who helped Emberlee with her homework, and gave Chioke piggyback rides, and even changed her diapers a few times without being asked.

As for Jody, she walked on clouds and never stopped smiling. And she wrote; she wrote story after story, and got to see most of them in print—under her own name now, not Sandy's.

<<<<>>>

It was a time of magic, a time when anything was possible. Love was in the air.

As Will dropped the kids off, clouds of good karma seemed to follow them into Sandy's cabin. Emberlee, always a happy, giggling bit of sunshine, was happier and gigglier than ever.

One evening, when Will came to pick up the kids, he gave

kisses to the girls and a hug to Liam. "Come to dinner, Jody," he said. "My way of saying 'thank you' for everything."

Emberlee bounced and laughed with a hand covering her mouth. "Jody's coming to our house. Jody's coming to our house."

"Sure. Why not? Thank you," Jody said and reached for her parka. Outside, the ground was dusted with snow, but true winter with howling winds and blinding snowstorms hadn't hit the Yukon yet.

Jody had been inside Will's house only a few times. She remembered it looking like a typical single-dad pad. Except for the photographs on the wall, which Emma had probably hung years ago, there were no homey touches. A couple of old newspapers and a few kids' toys strewn about the furniture and floor were the only signs of life in the otherwise spartan rooms. It wasn't filthy or badly cluttered. There just wasn't much love evidenced there. In other words, it was a house, not a home. Jody didn't care. It was the people she loved, not the building. Will and the kids—they were what was important. She followed Will inside.

And Jody gasped as Will smiled and Emberlee giggled, because all the toys, papers, and miscellaneous scraps had been put away. The house was as neat as the proverbial pin. Bunches of wildflowers arranged in Mason jars decorated bookshelves and end tables. The aroma of something heavenly wafted out of Will's kitchen.

"I hope you're hungry," Will said.

A six-foot-long, oval table covered by an embroidered

tablecloth was the main feature of Will's dining room. A centerpiece of wildflowers and candles ran along its length. At one end, the table was set for two people.

"We get to eat by the TV," said Emberlee, while Liam lit the candles.

Will seated Jody at the table, then went into the kitchen and emerged with a green salad and a covered casserole dish. "I made coq au vin. I hope you like it. It's the only thing I know how to cook."

Jody knew for a fact that the Campbells subsisted mainly on sandwiches, TV dinners, soup, and an occasional steak or pork chop. Jody wanted to peek into the kitchen, oh, so badly, but of course, that would have spoiled a lovely moment. Instead, she took a bite of velvety chicken in a rich, delicately-seasoned wine sauce. "It's not my birthday," she said. "Why all this? Which is wonderful, by the way." She took another bite. "Did you really cook the chicken?"

Will held up three fingers. "Mountie's honor."

Liam turned on a CD player, and soft violin music hummed in the background.

Will sat down, tasted his meat, and let out a sigh of relief. It had turned out all right. He took another bite. Suddenly, he realized how hungry he was.

As they ate their meal, Jody could hear whispers and giggles. Occasionally, Emberlee peeked out of the doorway.

"I made a chocolate cake for dessert," Will said. Many

more giggles erupted as he got up. Emberlee and Liam appeared to clear the table. For a minute, the dining room was empty; then, one by one, the kids emerged from the kitchen followed by Will. Chioke toddled in first with a nudge from Emberlee. Emberlee followed, then Liam, and finally, Will. Each held a balloon with one word written on it. When they stood in a row, the balloons read, "Will" "you" "marry" "us?" Will held his balloon in his left hand and a small box in the other. He opened the box to reveal a ring with a pear-shaped diamond lying on a rose-gold maple leaf.

Overwhelmed with happiness, Jody jumped out of her chair. She hugged Will hard, and then she hugged each of the children. "Of course, of course, yes, yes, yes," she said, and Will put the ring on her finger. It was a time of magic, a time when anything was possible.

<<<<>>>>

One day, the magic broke. "She isn't speaking to me anymore," Liam told Jody. "She said I'm a jerk—just like all the rest of the jerks she's known. She wrote, 'Liam is a lying, two-faced moron' on my locker in lipstick. I hate being in love." He stomped around Sandy's kitchen like a gorilla on steroids.

"What did you do?" Jody asked.

He bit his lip. "I didn't do anything."

"Did you brag about kissing Jessica?"

"Maybe."

"You didn't tell anyone about the love potion, did you?"

"I only told Steve, and he swore he wouldn't tell anyone."

Jody sighed an exaggerated sigh. "You broke the spell. I told you not to tell anyone."

"You never said it would cancel out the magic. I never want to see her again. Except, I think my heart is breaking. Can you die of a broken heart? Because I think I'm dying."

Jody put her arm around Liam as he struggled not to cry.

<<<<>>>>

Liam walked around for days afterwards, head down and sighing like a martyr every time he opened his mouth to speak. No one had ever suffered such agony. And then he perked up. Maybe there was a spell to win Jessica back. You'd think Jody would have volunteered that information without his having to ask her. Women just weren't that smart.

"Um, Jody, is there a spell to undo the undo spell? I mean, is there a way I could get her to like me again?"

"Did you try apologizing?"

"No, but I told her she was missing out on something good. Why should I apologize? I'm not the one who broke us up. Besides, it took me a long time to clean the lipstick off my locker door."

Jody put her hands on Liam's shoulders. "When Jessica found out about the love potion and that you'd bragged about kissing her, she probably felt betrayed and manipulated. She felt the same way you're feeling now. Someone has to be first to apologize. It may as well be you."

"Is there an apology potion I could use?"

Jody was thinking fast. Would a teenage girl forgive an idiot boy who had supposedly cast a voodoo spell on her? The odds were good that she wouldn't, especially if she actually believed that he'd practiced voodoo on her.

Jody squirmed. Apparently, that love-potion story was a mistake. She wondered how Liam would react if she told him she'd just made up the bit about the voodoo. Would he turn back into the angry, rebellious teenager who hated her guts? And how would Will react if he ever found out what she'd done? Well, she was in too deep to back out now.

"Do you really care about this girl?" Jody asked. "Or is this just about wanting to feel her breasts?"

Liam looked straight into Jody's eyes. "At first, yeah, it was just about the boobs. But then something happened. I can't explain it, but it was, you know, it was nice hanging out with her, and I liked giving her stuff and making her happy. And yeah, I still want to feel her boobs, but I guess there's all that other stuff too."

"And do you think she cares about you? Did she like you before she found out about the love potion?"

"I think so."

"There's a chance," Jody said, "but this time you absolutely have to keep quiet. Have you learned your lesson?"

"My lips are sealed. I won't tell anyone anything. They can torture me. They can kick me in the nuts. I won't say a word."

"There's a . . ." She furrowed her brow. "There's a . . . de . . . denoxifying spell." With a straight face, she went on. "Yes, a denoxifying spell. But I've never made it before. I can't guarantee it'll work." If Jessica were to forgive Liam, Jody could take credit for it with the spell. If not, well, she'd warned Liam it might not work. At the least, it would buy Jody some time.

"Please make me some of that, Jody. I'm desperate. I'll try anything."

"Okay then. While I'm cooking up the potion, you write her a note each day. Pass it to her in homeroom or slip it into her locker. Tell her you're sorry. Tell her that the voodoo story is just something your stupid friend made up. Tell her you really like her, and that you want to start over. You can put a small present in with the note, if you want. Something you made is best—like a card or a cookie or something. Denoxifying spells are tricky, and a lot depends on you. In fact, how you treat her is more important than the actual potion."

"Thanks Jody. You're the best," said Liam, and he walked away hopeful.

<<<<>>>>

"I think it's working," Liam reported two days later. "I made her a bracelet, and she was wearing it in homeroom."

"That's a good sign," Jody agreed with a perfectly serious expression on her face. It hadn't dawned on Liam that Jessica hadn't consumed any "denoxifying potion" yet. Jody figured she'd use two chocolate cupcakes to denoxify Jessica. Making up voodoo stories was entertaining. 'Definitely,' she thought, 'truth is overrated.'

Liam's next news, however, was discouraging. He'd put a snickerdoodle on Jessica's desk in homeroom, and later he found it on his desk squashed to crumbs along with a note: "How do I know you didn't poison the cookie?"

Liam scowled at Jody. "You and your stupid spells. Because of you, I'll probably die of a broken heart." He stomped out of the room, appearing more angry than heartbroken.

'I'm a heel,' thought Jody, considering the stupidity of what she'd done.

<<<<>>>>

'Jody and her dumb advice,' Liam grumbled to himself. Well, there were other ways to get a girl to like you. Jody didn't know everything. Heck, when it came to women, Jody didn't know anything. Steve never had trouble getting girls, and he didn't use love potions, or write sappy cards, or make stupid bracelets. Steve got girls because he had pockets full of cash, and Liam did know how he could get his hands on money. It would take a bit of daring, but true love was worth it.

CHAPTER 19

"Sandy . . ." Will's voice over the phone was shaky.

"What's wrong?"

"Is Liam at your house by any chance?"

"No. Why do you ask?" It was obvious why Will was asking, and his shaky voice conveyed just how worried he was.

"He hasn't come home yet."

Sandy looked out his window. The sun had already set, leaving that last glow of light before nightfall.

"I've already called all his friends' houses," Will said. "No one has seen him. Earlier, when I called the school, the secretary told me he'd handed in a note, supposedly from me, asking them to let him leave early. There's probably a good explanation. He probably got stranded somewhere without money to call home. I know I shouldn't worry, at least not yet, but I have a horrible feeling in my gut."

<<<<>>>>

"I don't need no magic to get Jessica to like me again," Liam muttered. He'd forged a note from his father excusing him from school early, and he had hitched a ride to a place not far from Sandy's house where a path led away from the main road and into the forest. From there he trudged purposefully through the trees, kicking up puffs of snow as he went.

<<<<>>>>

The next day, there was still no sign of Liam. "Sandy, can you watch the girls today?" Will's voice betrayed the strain he'd been under. "It really looked as if Liam had turned a corner, gotten his act together, and now . . ."

"Of course. When will you bring them over?"

"In about an hour. I have a couple of ideas of where Liam might have gone."

An hour later, Will came over with Emberlee and Chioke. The kids seemed to have picked up on Will's nervousness. Emberlee couldn't stay still; she looked as if she were about to jump out of her skin. Even Chioke was more fretful than usual. Jody set about playing with the kids, but it was a halfhearted attempt. Emberlee kept looking at the door as if she expected Liam to waltz in with some crazy explanation.

At noon, Jody made sandwiches and cut up some fruits and raw vegetables for Sandy and the girls. She poured out milk.

Everyone ate in silence, and Jody savored the peace. She knew it wouldn't last.

"Did you just give Chioke cow's milk?" Emberlee asked.

"I did," said Jody. "Look how well she's handling her sippy cup."

"You can't do that." Emberlee grabbed the cup from Chioke, who began to cry. "She's allergic to it. The last time she drank cow's milk she threw up all over everyone."

"Oh, no!" Jody took the cup from Emberlee. "I was worrying about your brother and just forgot." She unscrewed the lid and looked inside. It was almost empty. She ran to the kitchen, rinsed out the sippy cup, and filled it with water for Chioke. An hour later, true to Emberlee's prediction, Chioke simultaneously threw up and messed her diaper, along with her clothes, some toys, and Sandy's floor.

"I'll take care of the little one," Sandy volunteered, picking Chioke up in his arms. "You clean up the mess here."

Jody began soaking up the vomit and poop with a sponge. Emberlee, who was usually quick to help, put on her parka and mittens, grabbed her backpack and a flashlight, and ran out the front door, slamming it behind her.

Jody looked up, puzzled. This wasn't the Emberlee she knew. For a few seconds she just stared, frozen. She called Emberlee's name, but the little girl didn't answer. Not knowing what else to do, Jody put down the sponge and went outside after her.

She found Emberlee staring at the house from about twenty feet away. "Come on back inside," Jody said in her most authoritative voice. "It doesn't smell that bad." But Emberlee just shook her head, shifting her weight from one leg to the other.

"Please come inside," Jody said. "With Liam gone, everyone is nervous, and you're not helping."

"Come get me," Emberlee taunted, her face set in a determined frown. She crossed her arms in front of her. "I'm not coming inside."

Jody was stunned. Emberlee was usually so sunny, such an easy kid, and now she was acting like a miniature version of Liam in a snit.

"Stop it, Emberlee. Right now."

Emberlee began skipping towards the road that passed by Sandy's house. "Make me."

Not knowing what else to do, Jody went inside for her parka and trotted after Emberlee, who was now jogging down the road.

"This isn't funny! Your father is going to be furious when he hears what you're doing."

Emberlee ran faster, then turned off of the road and onto a dirt path sprinkled with snow.

"Emberlee, please stop."

Emberlee ducked under a branch and kept running.

By the time Jody caught up to her, they were almost a mile away from the house. Jody grabbed Emberlee's arm and began dragging her back to the cabin until Emberlee dropped to the ground. "Are you strong enough to carry me all the way back to the house?" Emberlee asked. "I'll bet you're not."

Jody plopped down on the ground beside Emberlee, still holding onto her arm. "Sandy and your Papa are going to be worried. And furious. First your brother and now you."

"Sandy won't be worried. I left a note saying that we had to go to Laurie Moffit's house. I said her mother had an emergency and asked us to watch the baby for her." Emberlee smiled at her cleverness. Then she burst into tears. "Oh, Jody, please don't be mad."

"What's going on?" Jody put an arm around Emberlee. "Why are you running away? Does it have something to do with your brother?"

Emberlee wiped her eyes. "I know where Liam is. I have to get to him and bring him back, but he won't listen to me. And besides, I'm scared. I need you to come with me."

"Honey, if you know where your brother is, you need to tell your father. He's the one who should be dealing with this—not me and certainly not you."

"I can't tell Papa. Liam will kill me if I do. No one likes a snitch." Emberlee stuck the end of her braid into her mouth and looked away. "It's all my fault that Liam ran away. He'd stolen some beer, and I threatened to tell on him if he didn't let me play with his Game Boy." She brushed a tear from her eye. "Oh, Jody, it's been so good around the house lately. Liam's happy. Papa's happy. Or at least they were until Liam got poopy and decided to take off. And before, remember how it used to be, Jody? Everyone was yelling at everyone. It was like the air was full of bad-feeling germs, and instead of making us sick, they were making us yell at each other. You never knew what to say, and sometimes, even if you didn't say anything, Liam's head would explode. And Papa was always sad. Sometimes my stomach used to hurt so bad I couldn't go to sleep."

"Oh, Sweetie, come on back to the cabin and tell Sandy what you know. This is a job for grown-ups."

"You're a grown-up."

"Yes, but . . ." Jody felt horribly guilty. This wasn't Emberlee's fault; it was Jody's. Liam was dealing with his first heartbreak, and all because of her malarky about voodoo and love potions. Maybe he'd have gotten his heart broken anyway, she thought, then mentally kicked herself for trying to rationalize away what she had done. Yes, this was all Jody's fault. Of course, it was her fault. But if she and Emberlee could find Liam, it would surely be a good thing. "How do you know where your brother is?"

Emberlee looked down at the ground and sucked on her braid. "Remember that time when we ran away and got our clothes all wet and dirty? That's where he is. It's a secret place not far from here. But you can't tell Papa."

"We have to."

"It'll be okay. Honestly. But you can't tell Papa. Promise?"

"Okay, I promise," Jody said, knowing she'd break that

promise the minute she saw Will. 'This is probably the worst decision of my life,' thought Jody as she got up from the ground and brushed herself off.

On the other hand, would it really be that bad? Maybe, after spending the night in the woods, Liam would be ready to come back with just a bit of persuasion. Maybe he'd be cold, hungry, and scared. Hopefully, if they found him, he'd be the sunny, gentle version of Liam and not the sullen, angry boy who'd given her so much trouble when she'd first come to Canada.

And maybe she wouldn't feel as if she had to tell Will about the voodoo.

But what if he were dead? The thought sent shivers up and down Jody's spine. 'Don't even think it,' she told herself. After all, she'd spent three days in the woods by herself without incident. She forced a smile for Emberlee's sake. "Okay, let's go," she said, and the two set off with Emberlee leading the way.

A short walk brought Jody and Emberlee to a boarded-up opening in the side of a mountain. "This is the old Devil's Haunt Mine," Emberlee told Jody. "It's been abandoned for years. No one's supposed to go inside." She tugged at one of the boards until it gave way, revealing a gaping hole and a tunnel leading into the heart of the mountain. "They didn't do a good job of boarding it up. Liam showed me how to move the boards."

Jody was tempted. It seemed a shame to turn back after they'd come all this way. You don't start climbing a mountain and then turn back ten feet from the top.

Could she talk Liam into returning home with them? He was a gentler Liam these days, and he believed that she could perform voodoo. That gave her some power over him. Maybe, she could still convince him that she had a spell to win Jessica back. Besides, Jody hadn't actually given Liam the cupcakes with the denoxifying spell yet. And if the first ones didn't succeed, she could always whip up a second batch of denoxifying cupcakes. Liam was fourteen years old, for Pete's sake. How long would it take before he forgot about Jessica and fell for a different girl?

While Jody considered ignoring Will's warning about abandoned mines, Emberlee was pulling a second board free from the mine's opening and then a third one.

"We can't go in there," Jody sighed. "You heard what your father said about mines."

"Okay, just let me move the boards back to where they were." Emberlee pushed her braids back behind her shoulders. But instead of replacing the boards, she squeezed through the opening. "Come on," she said, "Liam says it's not really haunted, and I brought a flashlight. It'll be okay. I promise."

"Emberlee, get back here this minute. You father will be furious. Besides, I thought you were scared."

But Emberlee was already making her way farther into the mountain. "You make me brave," she called over her shoulder.

"Emberlee, come back here." Jody expected Emberlee to mind, but Emberlee didn't turn back. It wasn't like her to be this stubborn. "Come back right now. I mean it."

Instead, Emberlee clicked on her flashlight and kept walking.

Jody felt helpless. She wished she could project Will's Mountie voice. In the end, Jody had the option of following Emberlee or leaving her alone in the gold mine. "At least wait for me," she yelled and squeezed between the boards. "And don't think there won't be consequences when all this is over."

Walking into the mine, Jody felt as if she'd stepped into an Edgar Allan Poe story. The air was humid, and the mine's darkness seemed smothering. At first, Jody couldn't see anything ahead of her except the beam from Emberlee's flashlight. As her eyes adjusted, Jody could make out the sides and ceiling of the tunnel. They were solid bedrock. A pair of metal rails ran along the ground; they'd probably been used to convey carts in and out of the mine, back when it was in operation. She hurried her pace to catch up to Emberlee.

A few meters in, the floor of the mine became muddy; a bit farther and Jody stepped into a puddle of water. By the time she caught up to Emberlee, who had paused to wait for her, Jody's boots were soaked through. Jody decided that the mine was aptly named; it looked like a place the devil would enjoy haunting.

Jody reached for Emberlee's hand, and Emberlee held on tightly as they walked deeper into the heart of the mountain above them.

They'd only gone about a hundred meters into the mine, but to Jody it felt like miles. The weak beam from Emberlee's flashlight seemed ineffective against the smothering darkness. Jody pulled Emberlee's hand. "This is a bad idea. We need to get out of here and let your father and the Mounties search this cave. If he yells at your brother, so be it. I'd yell at him if he were my son."

"Please, Jody. It's just a little farther. And I brought extra batteries, just in case." Emberlee tugged on Jody's hand. "Come on. I'm not scared. Are you?"

"No," Jody lied. They walked on in silence. All the while, Jody was thinking about Will's warning—no, his order—to stay out of mines. Still, if it meant getting Liam back, the risk was worth it. Jody looked over her shoulder and was relieved to see a skinny shaft of daylight coming in through the entrance. As long as they didn't venture too far into the mine, everything would be okay.

The path branched into two tunnels. Emberlee paused and shone her light into both sides as she decided which one to take.

The passageway on the left was straight out of a horror flick. Instead of bedrock, the walls and ceiling consisted of mud and boulders. Rotting timbers kept the whole mess from caving in. In fact, a few feet beyond the fork, two of the timbers had given way, and several boulders lay in a muddy pile blocking more than three quarters of the tunnel.

"It's this way." Emberlee pulled Jody toward the tunnel on the right. "And we're almost there. Honest."

With her free hand, Emberlee put the end of a braid into her mouth. Jody looked back over her shoulder. The light from the adit was barely visible. 'If it's only a little bit farther, we won't get lost,' Jody thought. A few more steps, and the light from the mouth of the cave was gone.

Emberlee's flashlight gave off so little light! They trudged on, trying not to stumble on the rocks, metal tracks, discarded tools, and other hazards that littered the mine's floor. The darkness was unsettling. Jody's feelings sank. It was silly; she knew it, but she couldn't help imagining vampire bats, broken legs, cave-ins and other unlikely disasters. She even imagined snakes, spooks, and devils. But of course, she didn't want to share her feelings with Emberlee. Instead, she squeezed Emberlee's hand and continued on.

And then, like the promise of a happy ending, a comforting light appeared in the tunnel up ahead. It was probably a long way off. The distance was difficult to estimate in the dark, but the light was brighter than Emberlee's flashlight, and it signaled an end of their journey into the Devil's Haunt.

"Liam." Emberlee shouted. "Liam, Liam. I knew you'd be here. Guess what—I'm not scared. Don't run away." She dropped Jody's hand and broke into a run.

Jody took heart.

<<<<>>>>

"Walk; don't run," Jody shouted. Emberlee slowed down and took Jody's hand once Jody caught up to her.

As they walked towards the light, Jody debated what to say

to Liam. She felt ashamed, guilty. Liam wouldn't have run off if she hadn't made up that stupid story about knowing voodoo. She should come clean, admit that she'd been lying. Jody knew that, but the mine wasn't the place to explain everything. Right now, the important thing was to get Liam to come home. She could pretend she remembered a super-powerful spell guaranteed to win Jessica back. That would probably work. It hurt knowing that, up until a few months ago, she'd prided herself on being honest. Now, she was a liar. Oh well, that would all have to wait until later. As she'd told Emberlee, there would be consequences.

Jody and Emberlee walked on, still holding hands. Suddenly, Jody became aware of a faint smell in the tunnel, something out of place. It made her think of a rotting piece of fruit, but, no, that wasn't it at all. It was a sweet odor, something she'd smelled once a long time ago. Jody tried to think. Where had she smelled it?

And then she remembered. She'd been writing an article about illegal drug labs—a lifetime ago, it seemed—and had been interviewing an undercover policeman back in Berkeley. He was tired, but he'd taken the time to talk to her anyway. He'd had a weird, sickly-sweet smell on his clothes—the same odor that she was now smelling inside the mine.

The officer had smiled ruefully as he told Jody that he'd just come from a drug lab bust. "The odor you're smelling is p2p," he'd said, "an intermediate in the making of methamphetamine, and it'll be a royal pain to get that smell out of my clothes." He'd knocked over a Tupperware container, spilling its contents, and in spite of the fact that he had on a Tyvek suit and Tyvek booties, the chemical had somehow contaminated his jeans and shoes.

Jody stopped in her tracks and pulled on Emberlee's hand. That's what she was smelling, p2p! "We have to get out of here right now," she whispered. "Don't ask; just walk quickly back the way we came."

Emberlee turned to face Jody. "Why are we whispering?" she asked. Her voice was louder than Jody would have liked.

"Someone in there has been making drugs. That's what we're smelling. I hope it's not Liam, but this is dangerous, and we need to get out of here fast. Before whoever turned on that light notices us. Can you be very brave and very grown up for the next few minutes?"

"But we're almost there, Jody. No one knows about this place except Liam and me. We can't leave now. It'll be perfectly safe."

Emberlee thought back to the day when she and Liam had explored the mine together.

Up ahead, the tunnel widened as if someone had scooped out some of the rock. Emberlee didn't remember much about it, except that there had been a ton of dirty containers. Probably, someone had eaten lunch there months earlier and left all their garbage. And she did remember a gross smell; she'd figured it came from the rotten food in one of the containers. So maybe someone had been there once, but it was a long, long time ago.

That odor was the same as what she was smelling now, except a lot stronger. Maybe Jody was right. No, she had to be wrong. There couldn't be anyone there except for Liam. Emberlee looked towards the light one more time just to reassure herself.

"Uh oh," she whispered. This time she saw a man's shape outlined by the light in the tunnel.

Jody saw the man too. He was bigger than Liam both in height and bulk, and he was heading towards them. "Run," she whispered to Emberlee and dropped her hand. "Fast as you can."

The two raced toward the mouth of the mine, Emberlee pointing the flashlight at the muddy ground ahead of them. They could hear their feet sloshing through puddles as they ran, and the splashing was frightfully loud in Jody's ears.

Jody turned one more time to see what was happening behind her. The man was still far away. She and Emberlee were going to make it. Or at least, they'd make it out of the mine. Everything would look better once they got into the forest where they could hide behind rocks or trees. But then her foot landed on one of the metal tracks that ran along the tunnel's floor. It was submersed in a puddle; that's why Jody hadn't noticed it. Her foot slipped off the metal with a wrenching sensation that almost made her cry out. She stumbled and fell headlong into the muddy water, breaking her fall with her hands. She managed not to scream despite the pain.

'Okay, we can still make it,' Jody thought, as she stood up; she tried to run and almost fell to her knees.

Emberlee stopped to see what was wrong. "Keep running," Jody said. "Quick as lightning. Run to Sandy's. Get help."

For a second, Emberlee stood staring, her eyes wide and her hand covering her mouth. Then she nodded and took off.

As Emberlee's form retreated into the distance, darkness settled around Jody, and hope seemed to vanish along with the beam from Emberlee's flashlight. She took a tentative step forward, placing her right hand against one of the sides of the tunnel to guide her out since she was now walking in complete darkness. Was the ankle sprained or broken? She took a few more steps. It wasn't too bad. She was limping and her ankle hurt, but she could walk. If she had to, she could walk all the way to Sandy's house. It would hurt a lot, but she could do it.

And suddenly, the wall that she'd been using to find her way out of the tunnel wasn't there anymore. Jody groped in the darkness feeling for the tunnel's side. At first, she panicked; then she smiled. Jody was at the place where the tunnel forked. She was getting close to the mine's entrance. She looked up and saw a thin strip of daylight ahead of her. Maybe she'd come out of this alive, after all.

She took a few more steps. The tunnel narrowed, and Jody's hand connected again with the rock wall. Using the tunnel's wall as a guide she limped towards the adit as best she could.

A rough hand grabbed her shoulder. "What the hell are you doing here?"

CHAPTER 20

Jody looked up at the man who'd grabbed her. His body made Jody think of an ogre. With his free hand, he swung an axe about as if it were made of cardboard.

Jody froze. "N-nothing," she stuttered. 'Please, God, help me,' she said in her mind—probably, the prayer God hears most often.

"Lady, I'm in no mood for games. What the hell are you doing snooping around here?" He threw the axe against the stone wall, and a deafening clang echoed through the tunnel.

Terrified, she stared up at her attacker. He had a fat face with a crooked nose and coal-black eyes. His jaw was square-shaped, like a pit bull's. She opened her mouth to speak, but no words came out.

"I'm waiting." He slapped her. "And I'm not a patient man."

Jody put her hand to her cheek. She didn't know what to tell him. Had he seen Emberlee? Had he heard her shouting Liam's name? Probably. Emberlee had been loud. He must have heard it. "Well . . ." She was stammering, stalling for time. He slapped her again.

'Remordia.' The word played inside her head. "Okay, okay. I—I heard there was still some gold here, and, and I need money. So, I thought if I could find maybe a couple of small nuggets . . ."

"You had a flashlight a while ago. Where's your flashlight?"

Maybe he hadn't seen Emberlee. "I dropped it."

"Why did you run?"

Jody looked down at the ground. "You startled me. I was . . . This is embarrassing. I thought you were a ghost."

"Quit fuckin' around. I don't believe a word of your story." He shook her shoulder roughly. He slapped her again, harder this time. "Now tell me, real nice, what you're doing down here."

Jody couldn't say she was looking for Liam. If Liam were here somewhere, and this gorilla didn't know it, Jody wasn't about to tell him. "I told you, I wanted to find some gold. But it was a dumb idea. I thought the gold would be, I don't know, all shiny. I thought you'd be able to see it lying in the dirt, but it's not like that at all. I can't see a thing, especially without my flashlight. It was a stupid idea. So, I'll just go back out and leave you alone."

"I don't think you'll be leaving anytime soon."

Her voice got higher and squeakier. "Honest, whatever you're doing, I won't bother you. If you're stealing gold, I won't tell anyone." Ack! She shouldn't have used the word, "stealing." "I mean, it's not really stealing. The mine's abandoned, and, and heck, I'm not supposed to be here either." Jody was babbling, her mind on autopilot. Words stumbled out of her mouth—hopefully, the right ones. "I'm supposed to be at work, but I called in sick. I'll be in a world of trouble if anyone finds out I'm here. So, whatever you're doing, your secret's safe. I'm no threat to you." She tried to pull her arm away, but he held on tightly. "Just let me go. We'll pretend that none of this happened. We never met." Jody tried for a winning smile. She ended up with a sick grimace instead.

"Look," Jody tried a different tack. "You'll be in a lot more trouble if I don't show up at home and people come looking for me. You don't want that, do you?"

The thug let go of Jody. Maybe he was going to let her leave. Jody allowed herself to hope.

Then a voice sounded from behind her. "Does this belong to you?" Jody turned to see a man's figure approaching from the mine's entrance hauling a squirming Emberlee by her arm.

He was young, probably in his late teens, and so thin that it frightened Jody. He reminded her of a starving refugee. She wished he'd stand still, but he kept twitching. 'The look of meth,' thought Jody. How the heck had she and Emberlee wandered into this mess?

Jody took a deep breath to calm herself. It didn't work. She felt as if her heart would explode right out of her chest. She took another deep breath. She couldn't panic. Because now, she had Emberlee to consider.

"Let's try this again." The ogre feigned patience. "What are you doing here?"

"Like I told you . . ."

"And how many of you are there?" He pinched Jody's face with his massive hand.

"Just us two. There's no one else. We were only looking for gold."

"You wouldn't be holding anything back from me, would you?"

Jody shook her head.

"You'd better not, because . . ." He yanked her arm behind her back and pulled up hard. Jody let out a scream. He dropped her arm.

Jody rubbed her shoulder. "Let the girl go. She's no threat to you. You can use me as a bargaining chip, or whatever. Just let her go. She won't say anything to anyone."

"No!" Emberlee stamped her foot. "We're a team. I left you alone before, and look what happened." She tried to hide her face in Jody's parka, but skinny held onto her arm so tightly that she couldn't reach Jody.

The two men burst out laughing.

"She's crying!" the huge one taunted.

"No, I'm not."

"Brat's crying." The ogre laughed harder.

"You better let us go, or you'll be sorry," Emberlee threatened.

"Hear that, Shrek," said the skinny one. "The moppet's gonna get us in trouble."

The one called Shrek pointed at Emberlee. "What should we do with this one?"

"Feed her to Wendigo," the skinny one said, and he stuck his grinning face right up against Emberlee's nose, making her shriek. "Grief, but she's noisy." With his free hand, he scratched his arm and rubbed his nose. "Seriously, the moppet is Liam Campbell's bratty sister, and their father is a Mountie. She probably knows who I am."

"No, I don't," said Emberlee. She'd wiped away her tears with her jacket.

"Then we got no choice," said the ogre. "A man's gotta do what a man's gotta do."

Abruptly, the skinny one stopped laughing. "Wait a minute. She's just a kid. We can't—you know."

"We gotta. It's like I told you—this ain't no job for sissies. You said you could handle the heat." Shrek's eyes flashed anger. He'd stopped laughing, and in the dim light of the cave, his face took on an eerie pallor. "Hold tight onto that one," he said, pointing at Emberlee. "The other one's not going to leave without the brat." He yanked the flashlight out of Emberlee's grasp and stuck it in Steve's free hand. "Besides, she's got no light, and she's limping."

"You're hurting me," Emberlee complained, as Steve tightened his grip on her arm.

A decrepit mine cart lay on its side in the left fork of the tunnel. It must have weighed a few hundred pounds. Shrek hauled it out as if it were made of plastic, turned it upside down, and wedged it into the space alongside of Steve, effectively blocking the way out. "You guard the pass," he said. "No one gets by you."

Emberlee was still crying; Jody put her arms around her while Shrek turned back toward the inside of the mountain.

"I'm trying to be very brave like you said." Emberlee swiped at the tears on her cheeks. She looked up at the skinny one. "You're Steve, aren't you?"

Steve nodded. He stared at the ground.

"Liam's friend?"

Again, he nodded.

"Is that guy's name really Shrek?"

"It's his tag. His real name is Montford."

"Yuck," said Emberlee. "And he wants to . . . to kill us?"

Steve looked away. "Of course not."

Emberlee looked up at Jody's face for reassurance. It wasn't there. Emberlee let out a long, loud shriek and began crying again.

Steve shifted his weight from side to side. "Bloody hell! Cut it out. It'll be okay, kid."

Emberlee kept crying, and Steve grimaced.

"Shrek's not really a bad guy. Come on, kid, let's see you smile." He turned to look into Emberlee's face. He smiled. At least he tried to. Emberlee continued to sob as if her heart would break.

'I can't do this,' he thought. "Either of you guys know any good jokes?" he asked.

Jody was silent. Emberlee stopped crying long enough to whisper, "No." And then there was nothing but silence except for the whimpering of a small child.

Steve coughed and twitched. He scratched his head. "Come on. Everything's fine. No one's gonna hurt you."

More silence.

All the while, Jody had her arms around Emberlee trying, in vain, to comfort her. 'Totally useless. I'm no lightning storm,' she thought sadly, remembering how powerful she had felt at the end of her quest. 'I'm more like a couple of raindrops falling on a banana slug.' Her ankle was aching, and she longed to sit down, but wouldn't let go of Emberlee.

The more Emberlee cried, the more Steve twitched and scratched.

"Hey, you want to dance?" Steve asked as if coming up with a brilliant idea. He pushed Jody aside, and, still holding on to Emberlee, he began hopping and swaying in place, nodding his head in time to a beat that only he could hear. His free arm waved about wildly, and the flashlight he held cast eerie moving shadows on the walls of the mine.

Suddenly, Emberlee pointed to the shadow and began shrieking.

"Now what?" Steve asked. 'How the fuck do you get this kid to stop screaming?' he wondered.

"Wendigo!" She pointed at the shadow on the wall and screamed again. "He's gonna get me! Don't let him . . ." She wrapped her arms around Steve's waist.

"There's no such thing," Steve said. "I made him up." But Emberlee was beyond reasoning.

Steve tried to unwrap Emberlee's arms, but she clung to him as if her life depended on it.

"I was just kidding. There's no Wendigo."

"He's just a superstition." Jody added.

"See, the shadows move when the flashlight moves." Steve demonstrated. The shadows twisted and flickered, and Emberlee screamed again.

Steve put the flashlight down. "See? Now, the shadow's not moving." Emberlee continued to cry. "Candy! You want some candy?" He let go of Emberlee to check his pockets.

Pumped up on adrenaline, Jody grabbed one of Emberlee's arms and tugged hard. Ignoring the child's screaming, she pulled Emberlee free from Steve's waist. Jody wasn't thinking clearly. In fact, she wasn't thinking at all, except that they had to get away from Steve. With one hand, she scooped up the flashlight, and with the other, she pushed Emberlee, who was still screaming, toward the left fork of the tunnel. Perhaps there was a second way out of the mine. Most mines had more than one adit, didn't they?

Emberlee scrambled around the pile of boulders which were blocking most of the passageway, climbing with the speed of a Tasmanian devil. She was probably more afraid of Wendigo than of the men. Jody followed limping. Then, they walked down the passageway as fast as they could, given Jody's sore ankle.

The left side of the mine's tunnel was different from the right one. Instead of bedrock, the walls and ceiling were mostly dirt, mud, rocks, and boulders shored up by huge logs. Many of the logs were rotten and some had rotted all the way through. Some were lying on the ground with nothing obvious holding up the earth above them. Here and there, rocks of all sizes had come loose from the walls and the top of the tunnel. Visions of a cave-in crept uncomfortably into Jody's mind.

A smaller tunnel led away from the path on which they were walking, and Jody steered Emberlee along the wider, better-defined path on the right. A bit farther on, the tunnel split again into a Y, and again Jody chose the wider right side. She'd have to be careful. It would be easy to get lost, especially if she panicked. She hoped they'd find a second way out of the mine. If not, she figured they'd wait a few hours and then maybe the coast would be clear for them to leave by the way they came in. She couldn't imagine Steve and Shrek patiently waiting by the mine's entrance. The ground beneath them was damp, but they had fewer puddles to wade through than before. At least they had that going for them.

<<<<>>>>

For a minute, Steve did nothing, relishing the quiet. Then, he muttered a curse word and started down the left fork following Jody and Emberlee. When he got to the blockage, he stopped in his tracks and sighed, thinking, 'How did I get into this mess? How the fuck did all this happen? I ain't no murderer.' For a minute he stood there staring; then, with another sigh, he began making his way through the rubble, but his steps were slow, halting. Truth be told, he wanted Jody and Emberlee to get away. He'd never killed anyone before, and he wasn't ready to be a party to murder now, especially to the murder of a child. Also, he didn't want to enter the mine's left fork with its loose earth and other unknown dangers.

"Fucked up again, didn't you?" Shrek's booming voice sounded behind him.

Steve jumped a mile and cringed, expecting pain.

Shrek grinned. "Never mind. Let 'em go. It's better this way. That tunnel is a dead end. It splits into dozens of shafts and branches, but none of them lead out of the ground." He stuffed the pistol he was carrying into his belt. "When they find the brat and her sidekick, if they ever find them, there won't be no bullet holes or signs of foul play, just the bodies of two idiots who got lost in an abandoned mine. Happens all the time."

With those words, he picked up the axe he'd previously thrown against the tunnel's wall. Grimly, he walked over to the pile of rubble blocking most of the left fork and attacked what was left of the timbers holding up the mud and rocks above the rubble pile. Shrek swung that axe fast and hard. Soon, he was sweating and drooling. With bulging eyes and his mouth set in a madman's grin, Shrek reminded Steve of a rabid animal. Rotten wood and boulders the size of tree stumps crashed onto the floor below. Steve backed away, afraid that the whole mine would collapse on top of him, but Shrek kept swinging the axe until mud, dirt, and rocks reached all the way to the top of the tunnel.

Shrek wasn't done. He kept on hacking, and his grin became a leer as more and more dirt, rocks, and boulders fell to the floor of the tunnel. Finally, when the tunnel's left branch was completely blocked so that not even light could get through, he threw the axe to the side and wiped his forehead with the back of his hand. "Wish I had cement," he said.

<<<<>>>>

After Jody and Emberlee had figured out that they weren't being chased, they slowed their steps, then stopped to look around.

"I don't hear anything," Jody ventured. She turned off the flashlight and peered into the darkness. "I don't see any light behind us. I hope that means that they've gone."

"But, but it's dark. And, and we can't see . . . Wendigo!"

"Honey, please believe me. There's no Wendigo. The idiot just said that to scare you." Jody took Emberlee's hand and squeezed it. "Honest."

"Maybe. But I saw him."

"Wendigo is just a stupid thing that boys say. It's like when Liam set off the cherry bombs. Remember?"

Emberlee squeezed Jody's hand." But I saw him."

"Here. Take the flashlight. Make goofy shapes on the walls.

That's what you saw."

Emberlee took the flashlight and waved it around. She sucked on her braid, "Let's get out of here. I hate this place."

"Let's wait just a bit. To make sure they've gone."

What was worse, Jody wondered, getting shot or getting lost inside a mine? She listened for footsteps but there weren't any. Then a clod of dirt fell on her shoulder. Emberlee jumped. Jody took Emberlee's flashlight and pointed it at the top of the tunnel. There was nothing shoring up the ceiling above her. While she was staring at the mud over her head, a fist-sized rock fell to the ground. That did it. 'Cave-in trumps bullets as a bad way to die,' Jody decided. "Me too. Let's go back," she said out loud. "Maybe those guys were just trying to scare us. If they'd really wanted to kill us, they'd have caught us by now."

"That's not comforting," said Emberlee.

"But we have to be as quiet as mice." Jody whispered. "In case they're waiting for us."

They walked back in silence, worried that their footsteps and their breathing were too loud.

They needn't have worried.

"It's all blocked up," said Emberlee and began crying as she sucked on her braid. "How are we going to get out?"

Jody put her arms around Emberlee, trying to comfort her. "It'll be all right. Shh. Don't cry." She dried Emberlee's eyes with the back of her hand. 'We should have tried to get over the mine cart,' she thought. She imagined herself boosting Emberlee over it.

If only she'd done that instead of leading her into the heart of the mountain! Emberlee might have made it out even if Jody couldn't. "Let's see how far this mess goes," she whispered. With bare hands, she pulled a clump away from the dirt mound, which was a wall for all intents and purposes.

A minute later, Emberlee joined her. "Ugh, I hit this huge rock, and I can't move it," she said.

"That's okay. Dig away the soil around it. Move what you can. Then I'll help you with the rock."

"Yuck. My braids taste like mud." Emberlee scooped out a disappointingly small clod of dirt. "I wish Papa was here. This is too hard, and my hands are dirty, and my jacket's a mess." Emberlee began crying again.

"Be brave just a little bit longer," Jody said. "When we get out of here, we'll both cry."

"It's not a rock; it's a friggin' boulder," Emberlee mumbled.

Jody stopped working and took a critical look at the wall of rocks and dirt. "I wonder how much farther this goes," she said. Jody also wondered if Shrek and Steve were waiting on the other side of the blockage, but she didn't want to say it out loud and scare Emberlee. The poor kid was already scared enough. Instead, she faked a smile. Then with Emberlee helping, she went back to work scooping away pebbles and dirt. Finally, they'd exposed as much of the rock as they could. It turned out to be a boulder about three feet across. Pushing it didn't do any good. "Grab it here, and we'll both pull as hard as we can. Pretend we're giants."

They pulled, tugged, and grunted. "It's . . . it's not working," Emberlee sobbed.

Jody wanted to cry too. "No, it's not. I wish we had some tools. We'll have to think of something else." She wiped her hands on her parka. "There's probably another way out of here. This side of the tunnel has a lot of branches. We'll have to explore them, but very carefully."

They left the pile of rubble Shrek had created and turned to wander deeper into the mountain. "We'll be okay," Jody said. "I've been in worse messes before." But she didn't believe it.

<<<<>>>

At least the tunnel wasn't leading them downward. They came to the first spot where the tunnel split into two branches. Emberlee shone the flashlight into the channel on the left and found that it came to an end only a few feet beyond the fork. "Rats!" Jody mumbled. They went on.

They came to the second fork, and it seemed to hold more promise. Jody tried to sound as if everything was okay. "This side is going uphill, and the timbers holding back the mountain look sturdier. Let's give it a try." They walked side by side, with Emberlee holding the flashlight. 'Brave little kid,' Jody thought. 'Somehow, someway, we have to get out of this horrible mine.'

Emberlee was shining the flashlight's beam along the sides of the tunnel, hoping to find—well, she wasn't sure what she was hoping to find. Some way out of the mountain. "That pile of rocks looks weird," she said. "I'll investigate." She approached it. Then she screamed. A loud, piercing scream.

"What?" Jody knelt next to Emberlee. And froze. There, among the rocks, a grinning, human skull seemed to stare at her through hollow eye sockets.

A hatchet stuck out from its forehead.

Jody's blood ran cold, unnerved by the sight of death. This had once been a living person. Jody and Emberlee could end up just like it. She shuddered, momentarily unable to pull her gaze away from the hatchet. Finally, she took a deep breath for courage and peered farther down the passage. It was also blocked.

Emberlee threw her arms around Jody and shrieked. "I don't want to die."

"Shh. We're getting out of here," Jody promised and led her back to the main part of the left fork.

Timidly, they walked farther into the left fork of the mine.

"Oh, no! No, no, no. The flashlight's growing dim," Emberlee whispered. "I brought extra batteries. What if they go out too?"

Jody didn't say anything. There was no good answer. Soon after, the light went out completely, and Jody felt inside Emberlee's backpack for the spare batteries. Replacing them was tricky; she was working in complete darkness. Finally, she got them into the flashlight lined up the right way, and, encouraged by the light, they went on with Emberlee shining the beam on the ground ahead of them.

Emberlee saw it first. Or rather, she stumbled over it. Predictably, she screamed.

"DEAD BODY!"

She screamed again, clinging to Jody's waist. She let out two more screams. "It moved." She pointed at the body. "It's not dead!" Jody looked down to see a human form lying on the ground, its head hidden inside a sleeping bag.

CHAPTER 21

The body spoke. "Emberlee?" A head peeped out from the sleeping bag. "What the bloody hell?"

Jody took the flashlight from Emberlee and shone it on the ground in front of them. "Liam?"

The tunnel had widened with a sort of niche scooped out of the wall on the right side large enough to house a couple of minecarts. Liam lay on the ground inside this niche with his head on his backpack and his legs sticking out into the middle of the tunnel.

"Liam?" Emberlee stopped screaming and stooped to wrap her arms around her brother.

He rubbed his eyes. "Was that you making all that noise? Bloody hell. Can't a guy get a little sleep around here? What are you doing here anyway?"

"Looking for you, stupid." She socked him in the arm. "We

have to get out of here. I'm scared of Wendigo, even if he isn't real. Papa's going to be so mad! He's going to ground you forever until your hair turns white."

Liam crawled out from his sleeping bag, stood up, and stared at his feet. 'They probably want to know what I'm doing here,' he thought but didn't say anything.

Emberlee socked him again. "Let's get out of here. This place gives me the creeps."

"I was looking for gold," he said.

Jody hugged him. Liam probably didn't want to be hugged. She hugged him anyway. "Let's get out of here," she said.

"We were lost," Emberlee told him, "and I tried to be brave, but I was really scared. You have to get us out of here."

Liam started to protest, but seeing Emberlee's terrified face, he stopped. Then with a shrug, he rolled up his sleeping bag and threw his backpack over his shoulder. "How the heck did you two manage to get lost? Any moron could figure out . . . Oh, never mind. It's this way." With those words, he turned to go back through the tunnel. Jody followed, happy to know that there was a way out, and happy to let someone else be in charge.

For a while, they walked, not speaking. Then Emberlee broke the silence. "Where are we going?" she asked.

Liam sighed. "Go back by the main path, and when you get to the Y keep going. As long as you don't take any of the side tunnels, you'll be fine. Jeez!"

Jody's heart sank, and Emberlee kicked Liam with the toe

of her boot. "We can't go back the way we came," Emberlee said, "on account of all the mud and rocks. It was your friend Steve and that bozo he calls Shrek. They knocked down half the mountain, and we can't get out that way anymore."

"Shit," said Liam.

They walked to the wall of rubble Shrek had created. With his hands and a pocketknife, Liam tried to dig a tunnel through it. He made a gallant attempt but had to admit defeat. He could move the dirt, but not the boulders. They were trapped.

Emberlee's lip trembled. "Now what?"

"Back to where I was sleeping," said Liam. "At least it's dry there."

"No, back to exploring. There must be another way out." Jody shook her head. 'I'm such a liar,' she thought.

"That's how people get lost," Liam muttered, but he couldn't come up with a better idea.

They walked farther along the tunnel for another hour and cautiously checked the smaller side tunnels. There were many of them, some with branches. A few turned away from the heart of the mountain, but non led to a way out.

After all the adrenaline surges of the day, Emberlee was exhausted, and Jody wasn't in much better shape.

"I'm really tired," Emberlee whined. "Can we please rest?" The three went back to Liam's niche. He put his sleeping bag down on the ground for Emberlee, and she fell asleep almost immediately. Jody lay down in the dirt beside her, imagined herself pushing Emberlee over the minecart that Shrek had used to block the way out, and, within minutes, was also sound asleep.

"Bloody hell," said Liam and lay down in the dirt next to them.

<<<<>>>>

Hours later, a small clod of dirt fell on Emberlee's head.

Emberlee screamed.

She grabbed Jody around her neck. "Someone's on the ceiling! Wendigo found me!" There was a faint noise, almost like a claw scratching on cellophane. Almost, but not quite. "Don't let him eat me!"

Jody heard it too. She turned on the flashlight and looked up. A crowd of black, fury bodies hung from the top of the tunnel. "Shh. It's nothing. Just a small colony of bats. No big deal." But she got up and moved away from them anyway.

"Make them go away. I hate bats."

"There's nothing to be scared of," Jody said in the most soothing voice she could muster. "It's just a few little bats."

Now more bats were stirring, wakened by Emberlee's screaming. "Bats are creepy," she sniffed. "I really hate them."

Jody wanted to admit it—the bats were creepy. She imagined spraying them with something and watching the little bodies falling to the ground. Instead, she told Emberlee, "They're God's creatures too, and they're probably just as scared of us."

"They couldn't be. Nobody could be as scared as me.

Besides, they stink. They stink worse than Chioke's diapers and throw-up."

Emberlee began jumping up down, and flailing her arms about. "Go away. Get out of here! I hate you, bats." Something dropped on her head, and she screamed again. "I hate, hate, hate, hate bats. They probably pooped on my head while we were sleeping." More bats began to stir as Emberlee kept on screaming. Soon, there was a confusion of dark wings above their heads as the last of the bats woke up from all the noise.

"Go away, bats." Emberlee reached for her flashlight. "I don't want them flying into me."

"They won't," Liam scoffed. "They have bat radar. They can find their way in the dark."

"Well, their radar isn't working," said Emberlee. "If they're trying to get out of the mine, they're flying the wrong way."

Jody looked up quickly. "There's another way out of here, and they know where it is."

Liam grabbed his flashlight and backpack. "Let's just not get into more trouble than we're already in."

They followed the bats through some twists and turns. Every time they came to a fork, Jody dragged her feet through the dirt leaving marks to hopefully keep from getting lost. The tunnel's height was decreasing as they walked.

"At least we're going uphill," Jody said. "That's a good sign, right?"

Finally, the stream of bats disappeared through a hole in the tunnel's ceiling. Liam turned off his flashlight, and the three looked up to see a patch of waning light and a flutter of black wings flapping out into the evening sky. "There IS another way out!" Jody almost cried with relief. "There had to be another way out. I knew it." She breathed out a delighted sigh. "No, I didn't, but I hoped."

'Thank you, God,' she added silently.

"I think I like bats now," said Emberlee. "They can even poop on my head while I'm asleep if they want."

After the last bat had left the cave, Liam turned on his flashlight. A log had rotted out and fallen from the top of the tunnel resulting in the narrow opening through which the bats had flown. He aimed his light at the space between the remaining timbers. The tunnel's ceiling was only a few inches above Jody's head, but from there, they'd have to dig through about fifteen feet of dirt to reach the earth's surface; and the opening wasn't more than a few inches wide at its narrowest parts, certainly not wide enough for any of them to squeeze through. Still, it was the closest they'd come to finding a way out.

"Heck of a lot of dirt to move," Liam grumbled. "I guess we'd better get started." He took out his pocketknife and began scraping away at what he could reach. "This won't be no picnic, and I don't know what we're going to do about the stuff we can't reach, which, by the way, is most of what we have to dig through. Any ideas, ladies?"

Jody was saved from having to come up with an answer,

for, just then, the dim light of Liam's flashlight went out.

CHAPTER 22

Liam felt around in his backpack. "I only brought one spare set of batteries," he said. He looked accusingly at Jody. "I wasn't expecting to be stuck here until the next snowmelt." After fumbling with the batteries, he attacked the dirt on the ceiling like a prizefighter in a championship bout.

"I have a flashlight too," Emberlee said.

Liam didn't say anything more, but he felt about to explode. He was furious at Jody and Emberlee—furious at them for wrecking his plans and furious at them for getting him trapped in this bloody mine. And furious because now they were his responsibility, and he had to get them out of this somehow.

He tried to hold onto the anger.

Because being angry was better than being afraid, and men weren't supposed to get scared.

'Stupid women!' Liam thought. Maybe they figured he

could just dig a way through all the dirt and rock above him. He had to act like it was no big deal, as if it weren't any harder than digging through sand in a sandbox, but he knew the job was impossible.

And he couldn't tell them that.

Emberlee held the flashlight. For a while, there was only the sound of Liam and Jody grunting and scraping the dirt and rocks above them.

"Wait," Jody said. "This is going to take a while. Let's work during the day. There might be enough light coming in from the hole above us to see. We should save the batteries for as long as we can."

They followed the marks Jody had made with her shoe and were able to find their way back to where they'd left Liam's sleeping bag and Emberlee's backpack. Liam picked up the sleeping bag, Emberlee slung her backpack over her shoulder, and the three returned to the space under the opening through which the bats had flown.

It was dark outside by the time they got back to the opening. "Can't see a thing without the flashlight," Liam grumbled. "We can't dig anymore until morning if we want to save the batteries."

"I'm hungry," Emberlee said suddenly.

Jody looked at Liam.

"Don't look at me." He turned away and stared at the wall. Then he shrugged. "Bloody hell." He picked up his backpack. "I brought two bottles of water, a cheese sandwich, four granola bars, two chocolate chip cookies, and an extra-large Snickers. I wasn't planning on running a catering service," he griped.

"We haven't eaten anything since lunch," Emberlee whispered.

"Jeez." He took out one of the water bottles, the sandwich, and the cookies. "Save the rest for later," he said. "Like four granola bars, a Snickers, and a bottle of water are going to last all that long," he mumbled.

Jody took a pinch of the sandwich and a couple of sips of water. "You two take the rest. I'm not all that hungry," she lied.

"Bloody martyr." Liam mumbled. He pulled the sandwich apart and handed a half of it to Emberlee, along with a cookie. "Go easy on the water," he told Emberlee and she, reluctantly, passed him the bottle after she'd drunk enough to wash down the sandwich and cookie.

After they'd eaten, Liam returned the half-full water bottle to his backpack and spread the sleeping bag down on the ground. Even though they were all still hungry, the three fell asleep almost immediately.

<<<<>>>>

Liam, Emberlee, and Jody were awakened at dawn the next morning by their empty stomachs. The kids each ate a granola bar for breakfast and they all took a sip of the water. Jody had a couple of bites off of a third bar, then handed the rest to Liam and

Emberlee saying she didn't want any more.

"I'm still hungry," Emberlee whispered.

Liam shook his head and reluctantly returned the rest of Jody's granola bar to his backpack. "Let's get this over with." He took out his knife and began scraping away the dirt on the tunnel's ceiling. After a few minutes, he threw the knife at the ground in disgust. "Too slow. At this rate, we'll still be here next year. If Dad had given me that hunting knife I'd asked for, maybe we'd stand a chance, but with this piece of shit . . ." Liam stopped in midsentence and turned away from Jody and Emberlee. He hadn't meant to blurt out the obvious truth. He didn't want them to realize how hopeless this all was and freak out. Although they'd probably figure it out eventually, anyway.

Jody was thinking the same thing. All they had left was a bottle of water, a couple of granola bars (minus two bites), and a chocolate bar. They could drink the water on the ground and get sick later. That would buy them a little time. Maybe someone would come by the hole they were trying to widen, and they'd be rescued. They couldn't have left any tracks on the road by Sandy's house, but maybe someone would find tracks where she and Emberlee had left the paved road. Or maybe they'd end up like that skeleton she and Emberlee had come across the other day.

The skeleton with the hatchet in his skull.

"How about a hatchet?" Jody asked.

Liam rolled his eyes. "Where are you going to find a hatchet?"

"It's probably dull, but it'll be better than what we have now."

"Ewe, it's in the head of a dead guy." Emberlee pinched her

nose. "Hurry up and get it." They set off for the tunnel where they'd found the skeleton with Emberlee leading the way.

<<<<>>>>

Liam smiled for the first time since Emberlee had tripped over him. "More power! More power!" he whooped and made swinging motions with his arms, pretending to be more excited than he really was. Well, maybe it would work. Anyway, it had to be better than the stupid pocketknife.

When they got back with the hatchet, Liam wanted the first turn with it. He took a swing at the earth above him, and a satisfying dirt clod almost the size of a soccer ball fell to the ground. He let out a Neanderthal grunt and beat his chest.

"Hey, go easy. Save your strength," Jody said, but Liam wasn't about to. He swung the hatchet like a folk hero; more dirt and rocks came crashing onto the ground. He whooped with real joy and kept on swinging the hatchet while Jody and Emberlee pushed the fallen rubble to the side.

Liam stared at all the dirt above him. "Go big or go home!" he yelled and struck one of the remaining timbers holding up the ceiling.

"Don't!" Jody cried. "You'll bring the whole thing down on your head!"

But Liam was hacking away like a man possessed, attacking the log closest to the hole. The wood was rotten. It gave way and fell to the ground with an ominous thud, taking a hefty chunk of mountain down with it. Then Liam went after a second log.

"Stop," Jody yelled. "You'll cause a cave-in."

332

Liam ignored her. With more Neanderthal grunts, he jammed the hatchet into the rotten timber. As he pulled the hatchet out, the log creaked and began to give way. He tugged at the wood as it crumbled in his hands. "Still too slow," he grunted, hacking away at the rotten logs, aiming for the weakest wood.

"Look out!" Emberlee yelled, staring at the ceiling with wide eyes.

Liam jumped out of the way nimbly as a huge piece of timber crashed down, missing his head by inches. Moments later, dirt and rocks rained down into the tunnel.

"Now that's what I'm talking about," he said. He went back to work whistling.

"Be careful, Liam," Jody cautioned. She felt obliged to say it, but, in truth, the sight of all that fallen debris made her hopeful. Maybe they'd get out of this mine after all.

<<<<>>>>

Determined to prove himself the man to depend on, Liam hacked away at the earth over his head with gusto, yelling like a samurai warrior with each swing. But eventually, his enthusiastic blows slowed down, and his karate shouts gave way to grunts and sighs. "Take a break," Jody said. "Let me have a turn." Reluctantly, he handed over the hatchet.

Jody swung hard at the dirt above her, then ducked as, predictably, dirt clumps and rocks poured down onto her back.

Liam rolled his eyes. "What a wuss!"

"I'm just warming up," Jody said and went back to work while trying to avoid getting dirt in her face. Doggedly, she attacked the earth above her. Soon her arms and shoulders ached, and she stopped to rub them. She'd put as little weight on her sore ankle as possible; consequently, her back hurt from the unnatural stance.

"Can I have a turn?" Emberlee piped up, and Jody handed over the hatchet.

Liam lifted his sister up, and she swung at a soft spot. A blob of dirt fell on her nose with a wet smack. "That's disgusting," she said.

Liam put Emberlee down. "My turn with the hatchet," he said quietly.

If Liam was tired, he didn't show it. He just kept swinging away at the ground above him. And he whooped with genuine pleasure as a boulder the size of a basketball fell to the earth. "Move those logs over here for me to stand on. I can't reach anything anymore."

Jody and Emberlee pushed logs and dirt over to where Liam had been standing, and they piled up rubble around them while Liam surreptitiously rubbed his arms and shoulders. The logs gave him a few more feet, and he went back to swinging the hatchet.

After what seemed like forever, Jody called up to Liam, "Do you want to take a break?"

"I'm okay," he answered, but it was obvious that Liam was exhausted.

"My turn," Jody finally said, and Liam didn't argue.

Jody worked until she couldn't reach the dirt above her anymore. Then Liam boosted her up, and Jody worked her way into the opening that she and Liam had enlarged, positioning herself with her knees resting on Liam's shoulders and her back against dirt. She swung the hatchet, dislodging three small rocks which bounced off of Jody's shoulders and hit Liam's head.

"Ow. Hey watch it," he yelled.

"Shut up and quit wiggling," Jody quipped, because laughter felt better than panic.

"I would, if you'd quit stabbing me with your knees. Go on a diet when we get back home." Liam was almost happy. He was obviously the strongest one of the three, the man of the group, the leader of the pack. Plus, there was a real chance that they'd get out of the mine alive.

"Funny man." Jody swung the hatchet until she could barely move her arms. "I'm done," she gasped. "Get me down from here."

Liam obliged and tried to help her gently to the ground. Instead, his hands slipped, and she ended up falling the last few feet.

"You okay?" Emberlee asked.

Jody brushed herself off and nodded. "Everything's still working."

"Then, please, can we eat something? I'm starving," said Emberlee.

Liam pulled the Snickers bar and the last water bottle out of his backpack. "Candy for lunch. All right! Something excellent had to come out of all this." They each had a few sips of water, leaving the bottle half full.

Jody took a pinch off the Snickers. "That's all I want," she said.

Liam rolled his eyes. "Starting that diet now, I see." He split the rest between himself and Emberlee.

"I made a step," Emberlee said, pointing to the pile of rubble she'd amassed on top of the logs and dirt they'd piled up earlier.

Jody patted her on the back. "Good job."

Gingerly, Liam climbed onto Emberlee's step. "It helps," he admitted. "Now hand me the instrument of destruction."

He hacked away at the earth above him. "Now I'm hitting roots," he announced, "and a couple of them are pretty fat."

"Leave some of them," said Jody. "We'll need them to pull ourselves out of here."

"I knew that," said Liam.

It wasn't long before he'd brought down everything he could reach. "Bloody hell," he mumbled.

"Do chin-ups," Emberlee yelled.

"This isn't gym class."

"So you can sit on that big fat root."

"I knew that," Liam grumbled. He grabbed it and pulled himself up off the ground.

Then, legs dangling, he called down to Jody. "Give me a boost."

She'd been sitting. She stood up and dusted off her seat. "Hurry up. My arms are about to fall off. Jeez!"

Finally, he got his body settled on the fat root and braced himself against the dirt surrounding it. "Bloody thing's poking into my butt," he complained and began chopping at the dirt above and around him.

Jody took a turn but had a hard time swinging the hatchet while keeping her balance, and her progress was slow.

Liam watched her shaking his head all the while. He

wanted to be up there attacking the dirt, but he needed the break. He rubbed his arms and what he could reach of his shoulders when he figured Jody and Emberlee weren't looking at him.

"I'm done," Jody finally admitted and, with the help of the fat root, lowered herself to the ground.

Liam resumed his place in the shaft they were enlarging, and refreshed, he tackled the dirt with a vengeance, cussing each time a rock hit him. He worked his way up. Bracing himself against the dirt around him, he stood on one of the roots and cleared away the rocks and dirt above his head.

"Watch out. Don't fall," Jody yelled.

In response, Liam backed away from the wall and balanced on the root as if it were a tightrope.

"Quit showing off. You could hurt yourself."

Liam lifted one leg up in the air. Then he looked down and began wobbling. He reached out an arm at the surrounding dirt to steady himself. "I'm okay," he yelled. "What a man!"

"Knock it off," Jody yelled back.

Liam smiled and took a bow. One of his feet slipped. "Oh, shit!" He grabbed at the roots around him to slow down his fall, and landed hard on his butt.

"I'm all right. No big deal." But he looked away as he said it.

Jody and Emberlee didn't say a word. It was better not to.

Liam climbed back up with a boost from Jody. Then, with less bravado, he attacked the dirt around him, widening the shaft that led to the outside world. He worked hard, only taking short breaks to rest his arms and shoulders. Finally, he was close enough to the top to stick the hatchet up above the ground.

"Only about a foot to go," Liam announced. "We're really close. Awesome!"

And then in a more subdued tone: "Bloody rock's in the way." He hit it hard with the hatchet.

"Careful." Jody whispered it to herself.

'Friggin' rock's huge. I'm gonna take out the dirt around it. No way this thing's gonna stop us now. We're too close."

Without warning, the rock came loose—a boulder almost two feet across. It hit the side of Liam's head and knocked him off his perch. He landed on his back in front of Jody's startled eyes with a resounding thud. The rock teetered a bit on the roots, then crashed to the ground below, missing Liam by inches. A barrage of dirt followed.

Jody and Emberlee jumped back, but Liam was right in the line of fire, and within seconds, he was covered by a mound of dirt.

Jody froze. "Liam, are you all right?" She ran over to him. He didn't move. Not sure what to do, she brushed dirt away from his face. "Please be okay."

"Is he breathing?" Emberlee asked.

Jody didn't answer. She tried to scrape some of the dirt out of his nose to clear an airway.

"Get your fingers out of my nose," Liam said. He stood up, sneezed, and shook a cloud of dirt off himself. Still sneezing and coughing, Liam pulled handfuls of pebbles and dirt out of the neck of his shirt. He poked his fingers into his ears and rubbed his face. He felt the sore spot on his head. There was blood on his fingers.

"You looked like the mud man," said Emberlee.

Liam just grinned and pointed to the space above his head. "Now that's what I'm talking about!" Jody and Emberlee looked up. The shaft was now wide enough for the three to climb out of the cave.

<<<<>>>>

Jody was the first one out. She squinted from the brightness of sunlight compared to the darkness inside the tunnel. 'I'll never take sunshine for granted again,' she thought. She took in three long breaths, enjoying the scent of clean air and pine resin. Then she leaned into the hole they'd created, waiting to pull out the backpacks and sleeping bag.

Liam boosted Emberlee to where she could reach the lowest root, and minutes later her head popped up above the hole they'd created, a big grin on her face.

Finally, Liam pulled himself up and out of the tunnel. He stood panting, hands on his thighs as if he'd just run a marathon.

Emberlee tugged on his sleeve. "I'm hungry," she said.

They split the last granola bars, drank the rest of Liam's water, and started home.

"I just thought of something," Emberlee squeaked and clapped her hands to her cheeks. "Papa! Oh, my goodness! He's going to be so mad!" She shook her head. "There will be consequences."

CHAPTER 23

First, there were happy tears, exuberant hugging, and high-pitched squealing on Emberlee's part. They were followed by a quick trip to the hospital where the three were examined. Liam came out, head bandaged, looking like a war hero; Jody's ankle was taped. Otherwise, they were pronounced in good health.

Then, the hugging continued at Will's house. Ever practical, Sandy disappeared into Will's kitchen and returned with water, bread, and cheese. Back in the kitchen, he filled a kettle and set it on the stove to boil. "It seems as if all I ever do is make tea." He pretended to grumble, but gave it up because he couldn't stop smiling.

Emberlee's braids danced on her shoulders, and her eyes sparkled as she told the story of what they'd been through. "And you should have seen Liam swinging that hatchet." She made chopping motions imitating Liam hacking at the timbers. "And then all this dirt, and mud, and rocks, and, and everything all fell on top of him; and he got buried, almost. He sort of looked like a lying-down snowman, only dirty. And Jody was afraid he was dead, but then he sneezed. It was gross."

Jody elaborated when necessary. Sandy and Will listened, horrified. Liam didn't say anything. Instead, he backed away from the group and, as soon as he could, disappeared into his bedroom.

<<<<>>>>

After Will had found out where the three had been and what they had seen, he called his station, and a team of Mounties was dispatched to the mine. Even though Steve and Montford were not there at the time, the Mounties found enough fingerprints and other evidence to obtain a warrant to arrest the two.

The next day, the Mounties picked up Steve in Mayo a few hundred yards away from the high school. They arrested Montford in Diamond Tooth Gertie's men's room.

<<<<>>>>

That night, Will, Jody, Sandy, and the kids sat around the dinner table at Will's house. For a while, no one spoke, afraid to broach the subject on everyone's mind.

Finally, Will broke the silence. "I'm not going to punish you. You've already been through enough. Spending the night in the cave, being chased by drug pushers, surviving a cave-in. No, you've been punished more than enough."

"Yay, no consequences." Emberlee jumped down from her chair and pumped a fist into the air. "No consequences! No consequences!"

Will turned to Emberlee, searching his mind for kind words. "There won't be any punishment, but there will be consequences, I'm afraid."

"Uh, oh!" Emberlee grabbed Jody's hand.

"Those two men tried to kill you, and they caused a lot of harm with their drugs." Will looked at the three of them, one by one. You three will have to testify in court. By telling everything you know. And I mean everything. That's your consequence."

Emberlee looked down into her lap. "Okay, Papa."

Liam stared at his food and didn't say anything.

<<<<>>>>

'Consequence number one,' thought Jody, as she knocked on the door to Liam's room.

"What?" He opened the door looking sullen, but he gestured for Jody to come in.

"Liam, I guess it's truth time. I tried fibbing. It didn't work out so well." She sat down on his bed, stalling for time.

He looked away.

"I wanted you to like me, and when I saw that you were trying to get a girl's attention, I figured out a way to make it happen."

Liam rolled his eyes and gave Jody a disgusted look.

Jody squirmed but went on. "So, I told you that I know voodoo and that I could make a love potion." She squared her shoulders. "Well, I made that up."

"Yeah?"

"Yeah."

"You didn't do voodoo?"

"No, I didn't."

"Then how come . . ."

"How come what?"

"Then how come Jessica acted like she liked me?"

"Jessica did like you, but not because of any love potion. She liked you because you listened. Because you were considerate."

Jody could almost see wheels spinning in Liam's head. "And you could talk about hiking and fishing, the things she liked too; being with you was fun." Jody smiled. "Hey, Liam, you're a likeable guy."

So much information to process! "We didn't do any voodoo?"

"No."

"So, what am I supposed to do now?"

"Come clean. Tell her I made up the bit about voodoo. Tell her you gave her a regular muffin because you wanted to get to know her. And apologize."

"I'll look like an idiot."

"Yeah, well, sometimes that's the price you pay for love. Maybe she'll forgive you; maybe she won't. I hope she does, because you really are a good person—when you're not acting like a little snot."

Liam stared at his shoes.

Jody put an arm on his shoulder. "I'm talking to you as if you were a grown-up now, and you're fourteen years old; but this is important. You'll always want to touch boobs, and that's part of love; but there's so much more to it than that. There's caring about what your girl is feeling and trying to do what's best for her. And if you can be honest with her, if you can be genuine instead of showing off . . . that's love, the real thing.

Liam was quiet for a long time.

"Like Mom and Dad," he finally said.

Jody nodded. "When you find that, don't ever take it for granted."

<<<<>>>>

For Sandy, a dream was a call to serve.

Sandy's Dream

Sandy lies in snow, surrounded by those he loves the most. Hummingbirds hover high above and far away—behind clouds, behind mountains, behind the sun itself. He shivers and hugs Liam close to himself seeking warmth. But Liam's body is cold—not dead, but sleeping, and it provides no warmth. He reaches for Emberlee, and her body is chilled as well. Standing now, he goes to Will and to Jody, again seeking warmth and finding none. Defeated, he lies back in the snow.

Above his head, an enormous sack hangs suspended from a cloud by a single strand of human hair. At first it hangs limp, dead; then it begins to sway—slowly at first; then it gathers speed and energy. Staring up at the sack, Sandy thinks of stampeding animals. The sack is swaying faster, faster still. From inside, an unknown threat pummels the bag's skin. Hisses and shrieks fill Sandy's head.

Sandy stares, trying to still his fright with prayer.

"OPEN IT." A voice booms, and Sandy hears its echoes repeating, over and over. He must obey. With bare hands, he rips and tears. Finally, the sack bursts open, and tangles of snakes fall to the ground. Some slither, still hissing, around the heads of the children, fangs bared. Others slink towards Will and Jody. One wraps itself around Will's neck and pulses as it tightens its grip. Others loop their coils around Jody. She stirs. She opens her mouth. Instead of words, a coughing, wheezing sound emerges. It grows softer until there is no sound.

Sandy woke troubled. The dream's message was clear. Bad spirits, dark clouds, lies, and secrets hung in the air above his loved ones. Sandy was tempted to ignore the dream. His family was happy now. Will and Jody were about to be married; Liam and Emberlee were doing well in school. Why risk spoiling everything?

Because he was a healer.

<<<<>>>>

That evening, the family all gathered for a meal. "It'll be a simple wedding," Jody said, "and I want all of you to be a part of it. Per my fashion consultant, Ms. Emberlee Campbell, the colors will be pink and pink."

Sandy stood up to speak. "William, Johanna."

He spoke slowly and did not raise his voice, but the words shot through the air like bullets. "Your wedding marks the beginning of your life together." Sandy shook his head. "So many lies! So much unsaid! Do not begin your new life with guilt and secrets slinking about you."

Silence hung like smoke in the air.

"Tomorrow, we will perform a cleansing ritual. You must all be there." He looked at the four of them one at a time—Will, Jody, Emberlee, and Liam.

No one protested. You do not question a Tutchone elder—especially if that elder is a healer.

<<<<>>>>

The next day while Chioke was napping, Will, Jody and the older children assembled around Sandy's table. One at a time, Sandy smudged himself and the others.

"There are many lies and regrets among us. Secrets . . . unseen, skulking around our hearts like unquiet spirits. We must put these thoughts to rest so that Johanna and William can begin their marriage in peace."

A tiny voice broke the stillness. "Will we get in trouble if we tell?" Emberlee asked.

While Will was considering the question, Sandy shook his head. "No. No punishment. This is too important."

A two-foot-long stick painted with black lines, green circles, red zigzags, and blue dots lay in the center of the table. The stick was decorated with rabbit fur, feathers, and beads. Sandy picked it up. "We call this a talking stick," he said. "Useful for difficult discussions. While I hold the stick, I may talk, and everyone else must be silent. We pass the stick from one to another until the talking is done. I will begin."

Sandy took a deep breath and muttered a quick prayer. Then he began. "The day that Jody and Emberlee ran away to look for Liam, I heard them leave. I heard the thud of the door slamming, and I heard fear mixed with anger in Jody's voice. I chose to let Jody face her fear alone. I heard it, and I chose to believe nothing was wrong—at least, nothing that Jody could not handle by herself. I did nothing. It was cold outside, and I had a messy baby to clean up; I did not want another mess.

"And there is more.

"When our Emma died, I was heartbroken. I had

comforted many other grieving parents. I spoke to them, cleareyed and calm. This is the way my father taught me—to face my fears and troubles straight on, and I have taught others to do the same. But when Emma, my precious daughter, when she died, the sorrow was too great. It crushed me, buried me, swamped me like waves in a troubled ocean. It did not stop, and I was not strong. At least, I was not strong enough. After her funeral, I could not face my sadness. So, I escaped. I returned to Vancouver and to my work there, teaching, speaking for my people. I said they needed me in Vancouver, but my true work was here. With my family. Emma's death hurt all of us. You needed me here, not in Vancouver. You, my family, you needed me to help heal the sorrow in your hearts. And my heart would have healed as well if I had faced my grief."

While Sandy talked, Liam's foot quivered, and he turned his head away from everyone. As quietly as possible, he pushed his chair back from the table. No way was he going to spill his guts. Not about the things he knew and the things he'd done. As quietly as possible, Liam stood up.

Sandy looked down. "That is the First Nations way. We face our troubles. But I did not. I ask your forgiveness."

Always the leader, Sandy had never before shown weakness. Now, a tear rolled down his cheeks, and the stick trembled in his hand.

Quietly, Emberlee put out her hand, laid it on Sandy's arm, and stroked it. Then she took the stick. "It was my fault, too. I knew Liam was probably in Devil's Haunt Mine. We'd been there before. That time when Liam and I ran away and got our clothes all wet and dirty, that's where we were. It was really weird. I didn't know what all that stuff was at the time, but it must have been drug stuff. And I should have told Papa, but I didn't on account of I was scared that Liam's head would explode."

Liam stopped in his tracks. The brat was going to tattle! Just how much did she know? And how much was she going to spill? He sat back down because he had to find out. Because, if she told everything, he'd have to deny it all.

Emberlee didn't lay the stick down. Instead, she stroked the rabbit fur.

"I didn't tell because I was scared Liam would blow up, and besides, Liam says that no one likes a snitch. But sometimes, you have to snitch.

"I'm sorry, Papa."

Liam sighed with relief. The brat didn't know everything.

Will reached for the stick. "it's okay, Kit Kat."

He turned to Jody. "I said I'd stand by you, but I didn't. I My chief told me to convince you to leave, and as he talked, there was a second when my heart turned cold. Quick to doubt, slow to trust . . . I believed my chief, and I became fearful. A frightened Mountie—how sad is that! Instead of fighting for you, I sent you packing—back to the states, back to harm's way where you were almost killed. And I wonder . . . How can you forgive me, or love me, or marry me? But there are miracles, and you are one of them." He fiddled with the stick.

"There's not much more to say. After Emma died, I'd built walls and moats around my heart. And then you came along, and melted them away. I love you."

Jody reached for the stick. "I have something to tell all of you." Her cheeks burned bright pink as she looked around the room. "This is harder than I thought." She stared at the stick, and the silence was palpable.

"I'd always been honest," she finally said, "scrupulously honest. And no one believed me. The more I tried to tell the truth, the more everyone thought me a liar, so . . . so I decided instead to, to . . ." She sighed. "I started lying. And then I found I liked it. It made me feel strong and smart; and for a while, everything was so much easier when I told people what I wanted them to hear. So, I kept on lying. That's how I was responsible for the fiasco in the mine. I told Liam that I knew . . ." Jody sighed. "I can't believe I did this." She looked away and rubbed her forehead. She sighed again and turned back to look into Sandy's eyes. "I said I knew voodoo, and I could whip up a love potion that would make a girl fall in love with him. If I hadn't made up the voodoo story, well, we probably wouldn't have all ended up in the mine where the kids almost died."

Jody felt like a runner at the end of a marathon. She looked around, but no one reached for the stick, so, she set it down on the table.

And there was silence until Liam finally sprang up. "What? I don't have anything to say. He picked up the stick and twirled it in his hand. "This is really lame." He rolled his eyes. No one spoke, and Liam was uncomfortable with the silence. "I need to pee, and this dumb talking stick thing is stupid, stupid, stupid."

Will leaned forward to grab Liam, to stop him from leaving the table, but Sandy put his arm across Will's chest, holding him back.

"Bloody nonsense!" Liam drummed on the table with the stick, waved it about like a Jedi light saber, and threw it into the air and caught it. He cleared his throat and scratched his head. "It's no big deal. I needed some money. That's all. And I heard about this woman who'd found a bunch of gold nuggets, and I figured I'd see if I could find some so I could get a present for this girl. Like I said, no big deal. I was only going to be gone for an hour or two."

Then he made his big mistake.

He looked at his father. Will didn't make any sounds or gestures. He simply sat with his eyes focused on his son.

And then it was like a dam breaking. The words poured out of Liam's mouth, and he didn't even try to hold them back. "I used to do drugs. Not a lot, but I used to do drugs. Mostly meth."

Will gasped.

"I bought 'em from Steve. I bought 'em from Shrek a couple of times, but he scared me. I tried to stay out of his way."

Will shut his eyes and shook his head slowly.

Liam saw it but kept going. "See, after Mom died, everything was awful. It hurt, and hurt, and I couldn't make it stop. Then Jody showed up at Sandy's, and it was as if she was trying to take Mom's place. But no one can do that. So, I was hurting even worse.

"When I took the drugs, it was better. I was strong and smarter than everyone else, but I was also, well, I was kind of a shit, if you want to know the truth. I used to get crazy mad, and I'd want to break stuff. Like that time I got so furious that I punched Dad and he slapped me. The drugs gave me power. But afterwards, they wore off, and I felt worse than ever. I just wanted to hurt someone. Anyone. But I especially wanted to hurt Jody.

"And then, Jody made me that love potion guaranteed to make a girl like me, and I didn't want to be a shit anymore. I mean, I didn't want to get all weird and freaky in front of a girl. I never took any meth after that. And, well, Jessica let me feel her boobs and everything, and that was awesome."

Liam's palms were sweating. "For a while, everything was perfect; but then she got all huffy on account of she thought I'd cast a voodoo spell on her, which I hadn't. I thought I had, but it turned out that they were just regular muffins, like Jody said. Anyway, Jessica was mad at me, so I needed money to buy her something cool so she'd like me again.

"That's why I ran away and snuck into Devil's Haunt Mine. But not because I thought I could find gold. I'm not that stupid. I went in there because . . . well, because I wanted Steve and Shrek to let me sell some of their drugs."

He looked at his dad, but Will's face was inscrutable.

And the room was silent.

Liam looked down, staring at the stick in his hand. "I figured I'd just sell one or two batches so I could buy a really nice present for Jessica. Like maybe a necklace or a Game Boy or something like that. Me and Steve—I thought we were solid. Only, Steve and Shrek told me to beat it. They said I was just a kid, and since I wasn't buying their drugs anymore, they weren't going to let me sell them. And then Shrek grabbed his axe, and I ran."

Liam wiped his hands on his jeans. "So, I figured if they were going to be that way about it, I'd just swipe the meth when they weren't looking. I hitched a ride back to my house for my sleeping bag and some food and water, and then I hitched another ride and snuck back into the mine to wait for when Shrek and Steve went home. I figured that's when I'd just take a little meth, and then I'd sell it, and everything would be cool. And Jessica would like me again. Except, they didn't leave, and I had to wait until the next day to get the meth. So, I just went to sleep."

He rolled his eyes. "Only then, Jody and Emberlee showed up and wrecked my plans.

You all know the rest. The tunnel was caved in, and we couldn't get out the way we came. We took a nap, and followed the bats, and chopped our way out of the mine with the hatchet that had been stuck in a dead guy. And then we went home."

He looked at Will again. He couldn't believe it. There were tears running down Will's cheeks.

"And that's everything," Liam said.

"Except . . . except I was the one who sent the letter to the Mounties. I stole Jody's fake ID and copied it on Dad's printer, which was how come they believed me. And that's all I have to say." Liam wiped his forehead.

"I'm sorry, Jody."

<<<<>>>>

Emberlee was the one who started the hugging; and then there was more hugging, and laughing, and a sense that something almost magical had happened.

CHAPTER 24

It was a June wedding. Jody didn't want her mother dealing with a Yukon winter. "You're beautiful, darling," Martha said as they waited in the back of St. Mary's Church. Jody wore a floor-length, A-line gown with a lace bodice. Her hair fell in loose curls from a hairband entwined with fireweed blossoms. With a final kiss for luck, Martha left to take her seat in the church's front row.

First, the girls, dressed in fluffy pink, walked out into the sanctuary. Chioke giggled tossing fireweed blossoms into the air, while Emberlee walked solemnly holding the wedding rings which she handed to Liam who stood next to his father in front of the altar.

And finally, it was Jody's turn. Walking down the aisle on Sandy's arm, she couldn't take her eyes off Will in his parade uniform—the blue trousers and red serge coat that Mounties are famous for. And then she was standing next to him, as Father Michael began: "Dearly beloved, we are gathered together . . ." Jody had heard those words many times, but they'd never been spoken for her before.

"Do you, William Campbell, take this woman to be your

lawfully wedded wife?"

"I do."

"Do you, Johanna Jacobson, take this man . . ."

"I do," she said. A lingering hint of incense hung in the air as if it were surrounding her with Will's love. 'I love you, Will,' she thought. 'I'll love you forever.'

And, unexpectedly, Jody sensed something otherworldly. Something she'd known as a child. It was as if God were holding out His arms to Will and to her in welcome.

"God among us," Fr. Michael said. "We mortals, earthen vessels, sometimes catch a peek of divine love, a glimpse of a world beyond. We only get a hint of that world, a glimmer, a glimpse of that pure love. God's love is so much more than we can ever imagine—brilliant, all-consuming in its majesty. We mirror that world beyond by loving each other. Earthly love is paltry in comparison, but it is divine and splendid nevertheless."

<<<<>>>>

In Will's special meadow, blossoms bloomed brighter, and birds sang louder. Or so it seemed to Jody. As if the meadow, with its flowers, grasses and animals was welcoming her.

Surrounded by friends and family, Sandy blessed Will and Jody: "You will no longer feel rain, for you will shield each other. Nor will you know cold, for you will be warmth to one other. You will not be lonely, for you will be each other's companion. Before, you were two. Now you are one. Your lives are twined together.

May God the Creator grant you many years on this earth, and may you live in peace and love."

With her body next to Will's, Jody felt herself enveloped in love. So much joy! This day was a lifetime of goodness compressed into a few hours. But there would be more times like this—more moments to treasure, more days when her heart would dance with happiness. There would be a lifetime of moments like this.

"Now kiss the bride," Sandy said, and Will took Jody in his arms and kissed her gently. "You call that a kiss?" Liam yelled. "Smooch her like you mean it!"

Jody shrugged. "Go on. Smooch me like you mean it."

So, he did. The kiss was wild. It left Jody breathless.

"Any more of that, and you'll have to rent a motel room," Spencer yelled.

Intoxicated by the kiss, Jody laughed with all the might in her body. And Sandy watched Jody laughing as if he were seeing a young bird flying from its nest for the first time. As if he were saying "Goodbye" to a daughter leaving for college. Jody was healed. She was whole and ready to begin her life with Will. A tinge of sadness touched his heart.

Earlier that morning, Will's Mountie friends had set up tables and chairs, and they'd loaded one of the tables with the food that Will, Jody, and Sandy had brought: salmon steaks, vegetable stews, fresh berries and a four-tiered wedding cake—enough for three weddings with leftovers for the next day. The Mounties roasted beef and caribou over an open fire and served thick slices of the meat on top of toasted bread.

Emberlee ate two pieces of cake.

After the cake, a young man began drumming. His fingers and palms flew across the drumskin like galloping horses, as he improvised a rhythm. One by one, more drummers joined in. A guitar and a flute materialized, adlibbing melody.

Then, a woman in traditional Tutchone dress began dancing. She stepped and swayed, mesmerized by the haunting rhythm; and the fringes of her deerskin vest swayed along with her. More dancers joined in. 'Now, we will never be lonely,' Jody thought, dancing next to Will, 'for we have each other.'

Sandy joined the group too, but soon he tired and left the dancing. The weather was warm. With a jacket under his head for a pillow, Sandy lay down beneath a pine tree out of the way of the celebration and watched hawks and eagles circling in the sky above him. Staring into the heavens, he whispered words he'd recited since boyhood:

"Oh, Great Creator, whose voice I hear in the wind, whose breath gives life to all the world, hear me; I need your strength and wisdom.

Let me walk in beauty, and make my eyes ever behold the red and purple sunset. Make my hands respect the things you have made and my ears sharp to hear your voice.

Make me wise, so that I may understand the things you have taught my people. Help me to remain calm and strong in the face of all that comes towards me. Let me learn the lessons you have hidden in every leaf and rock.

Help me seek pure thoughts and act with the intention of helping others. Help me find compassion without empathy overwhelming me.

I seek strength, not to be greater than my brother, but to fight my greatest enemy, myself.

Make me always ready to come to you with clean hands and straight eyes, so when life fades, as the fading sunset, my spirit may come to you without shame.

Oh, Great Creator, whose voice I hear in the wind."

Sandy's Dream

Behind Sandy's closed lids, a young child sits cross-legged facing an old man. Sandy is both the child and the old one. The child is given tea and told to drink. Although the taste is bitter, he drinks it all, not wishing to displease his elder. And in the dream, the old man speaks:

> *"Two road diverged,*
> *One red, one white.*
> *I travelled both."*

The child and the elder join hands. They run through Yukon's forests, and they run through the streets of Vancouver. They run past Toronto's university, and they run through Sandy's childhood village. Always, there are two roads—one red and one white. As they head towards the sunset, the two roads come together and become one. The old man and the child become one man, and he walks cleareyed towards the setting sun.

A raven soars in the heavens above him. Winds lifts him up to the raven, and he floats on currents of air. Below him, his childhood village, bathed in twilight, lies small, cozy, comforting. Currents lift him ever higher; the village, meadows, mountains, and the whole earth below become smaller. He looks toward the setting sun, which grows brighter—becomes all-consuming.

In life, he planted seeds of kindness; now, they greet him with forests of love.

Elaine Glimme

His dream self speaks:
"I am old.
My eyes close, salty with tears.
Two roads become one.
My walk on earth is finished.
My spirit begins a new adventure."

ABOUT THE AUTHOR

Elaine Glimme began her unlikely writing career with a few unplanned explosions in the lab where she worked. In the interest of safety, she turned her hand to writing.

Elaine also wrote *Temporary Address*, the prequel to *Refuge and Warm Tea*, and *Through Unfamiliar Waters*, the final novel of the *Temporary Address* trilogy. She also wrote *The Molly Chronicles*, a novel written from a dog's eye view. Her dog, Molly, claims authorship for *The Molly Chronicles*, but Elaine says that Molly is delusional and has always had a swelled head.